ASHLORDS

BY SCOTT REINTGEN

Ashlords

Bloodsworn

Nyxia

Nyxia Unleashed

Nyxia Uprising

ASHLORDS

BOOK 1

SCOTT REINTGEN

EMBER

Text copyright © 2020 by Scott Reintgen
Cover art copyright © 2020 by Sammy Yuen

All rights reserved. Published in the United States by Ember, an imprint of Random House Children's Books, a division of Penguin Random House LLC, New York. Originally published in hardcover in the United States by Crown Books for Young Readers, an imprint of Random House Children's Books, a division of Penguin Random House LLC, New York, in 2020.

Ember and the E colophon are registered trademarks of Penguin Random House LLC.

Visit us on the Web! GetUnderlined.com

Educators and librarians, for a variety of teaching tools, visit us at RHTeachersLibrarians.com

The Library of Congress has cataloged the hardcover edition of this work as follows:
Names: Reintgen, Scott, author.
Title: Ashlords / Scott Reintgen.
Description: First edition. | New York: Crown, [2020] | Summary: Follows alchemists Imelda, Adrian, and Pippa as they reach for their dreams of glory riding phoenix horses at The Races, the modern spectacle that has replaced warfare within their empire.
Identifiers: LCCN 2019009360 | ISBN 978-0-593-11917-4 (hc) | ISBN 978-0-593-11918-1 (glb) | ISBN 978-0-593-11919-8 (ebook)
Subjects: | CYAC: Alchemy—Fiction. | Racing—Fiction. | Horses—Fiction. | Fantasy.
Classification: LCC PZ7.1.R4554 Ash 2020 | DDC [Fic]—dc23

ISBN 978-0-593-11920-4 (pbk.)

Printed in the United States of America
10 9 8 7 6 5 4 3 2 1
First Ember Edition 2021

For the Reintgen boys, who have torched me in every video game, sport, and board game in existence. I am who I am today because you taught me how to get back up and try harder the next time.

CONTENTS

PART THREE: STORM

PART ONE

LIGHTNING

Our people's history is written in great bolts
of lightning. Clear skies for a century or
two, and then a single remarkable moment
strikes. It illuminates a new way, even as it
kills the old.

—The Brightness,
An Address to Patriots

1

THE ALCHEMIST

IMELDA

Farian wakes me at some ungodly hour.

He comes in like he lives here, drags me out of bed, and gets me into a pair of boots. My corner candle's out, so I can't even see which cloak he throws around my shoulders or which hat he slaps on my head. Farian would say that's for the best. According to him, fashion and I were never properly introduced. He's always threatening to throw away my favorite dresses. It is a point of contention between us.

We stumble through the dark. Someone's asleep on the couch. An uncle, but I couldn't say which one. They all snore the same. Empty bottles spin away from my clumsy steps. Farian keeps a steady hand on my back until we're in the candlelight of the kitchen. He sets a cup of coffee in my hands, lets me take a few sips, and then pushes me out the door.

It should be black at this hour, but the sky's cloud-clear,

and the stars recognize a stage when it's there. Dueling nebulas slash over the dark, rolling mesas. I hear Doctor Vass explain, *"Each light is a sun. To each sun, planets. To each planet, moons. How endless it all is. . . ."*

Farian looks back. "You awake yet?"

"No talking until I can see what color your clothes are."

He laughs. Farian has always laughed easily. Doesn't know his way around a joke, but he always makes you feel like you do. My best friend and confidant lopes ahead, his limp barely noticeable, a satchel full of camera gear tucked under one thick arm. He's always been big. Fourth son in a family of farmers, with three older brothers that have all grown even bigger than he is. But that's because Farian's made his world more than digging irrigation pits. He skips out on his chores to enhance photographs or edit our film series. He's bound for an education if he keeps at it, as long as his parents don't disown him before he can get there.

We're not the only ones awake at this hour. The door to Amaya's bar bangs open, and three ranch hands slide out into the slick shadows, laughing and singing the wrong words to "The March of Ashes." Farian hums the tune long after we've passed them.

Down the road, a pair of postmen trot past on slender mounts. Both tip their brims, looking like any other riders but for the government-issued gloves threaded with gold and the sacks full of letters strung to their saddles. We arrive at the ranch well before sunrise. It's dead and dark, quiet-like. The stars are fading.

"Looks empty," Farian says. "Only Martial is out there."

I squint, but Farian's eyes have always been better than mine. I can't make out much beyond the nearest row of fence posts, but there's nothing surprising about the quiet. It's a holy day. "The Ashlords only bow to the gods," I remind him.

He snorts but says nothing. We've caught hell for skipping Gathering the past few years, but we both know it's the only way to get any respectable riding time. Martial owns the only Dividian-friendly ranch in the district. He won the Races about twenty years ago and used the prize money to build his own ranch and buy his own herd of phoenixes. He promised it would be a training ground to hopeful Dividian riders who couldn't afford their own horses. Like him.

It was a stunning kindness.

Until the money started running out. It always does. Gold is worth less when it's in Dividian pockets. Not to mention they tax Dividian landowners twice as much. A few years back, Martial opened the ranch to some of the lesser Ashlord nobles. Carved out just a few days of the week at first, but it wasn't long until he was booked solid. I don't blame him, either. Ruling-class gold pays too well to turn down.

"What's it going to be today?" Farian asks, glancing back again. "Something new?"

"Something old," I reply with a smile. "Something long forgotten."

We head in different directions. Farian strides out to talk with Martial. He's been working up to asking the old champ to do a biopic, but Farian's about as careful as thunder.

Won't make any noise until he's sure lightning's already struck. I leave them to it, heading for the stalls.

Martial might have sold out to the Ashlords, but there's still no ranch like his. As a Dividian, I get to ride his phoenixes free of charge. And he slashes component prices by half. He even lets us pay off all the expenses through a little side work. I'm pretty sure there's no better setup in the Empire, at least not for a Dividian like me.

His barn is a fine thing, too. All stone, with slightly sloping roofs and lamps dangling every few paces. I walk the outer courtyard, hearing horses occasionally stomp in their stalls on my left, seeing columns and arches running on my right. Martial sank most of his winnings into the place. People called it a mistake, but the quality of the facility is the only reason gold keeps moving from Ashlord pockets into his accounts. He has seven city-bred families boarding horses here, and more on the waiting list. I'm just glad he hasn't turned the whole place in that direction. He's still got about eight of his own horses, and they're the closest I'll ever come to calling one my own.

At the end of the yard, a great red door waits. I lift both latches and put my whole body into a shove. The door opens into the dark. I smile as a great smash of scents carry through the opening. I follow them inside. Practiced hands find the lamp thread and I give it a pull. The bulb takes its time, warming the room with light, brightening until I can see the endless containers with all their precious powders. All those possibilities . . .

I remove a half-ripped theater poster from the pocket of my riding jacket. Proper paper is too expensive, but street litter and old playbills are always free. I copy ingredients from the poster to one of Martial's inventory forms. I cringe, though, when I see the price he has listed for unborn ash.

"Seventy legions. Pick my pockets, why don't you, Martial."

After a second, I scribble the component down. I know today's video will make up for the cost eventually. It still stings to use *anything* that costs that much. I haven't taken on a component with a price that steep since my disaster last year with powdered gold. Burned through a hundred fifty legions in less than two clockturns. But I won't make that mistake again.

After noting each component, I take five racing containers and link them up. Martial's cubes are a cheaper version, about a fourth the size of the Race-regulation ones, but I'm only doing one rebirth anyway.

It takes a few minutes to locate each component, measure out what I've purchased, and strap the cubes to my riding belt. I lock the door behind me and find Martial rolling a cigarette outside. He keeps his thinning hair long and pulled back in a knot. His eyes are bright and blue, so shockingly Dividian that it's like looking across oceans, a few hundred years into our past. I can almost see our ancestors arriving on the shores of the Empire for the first time, eyes bright with desire.

He nods once. "Imelda Beru," he says. "The Alchemist."

"That name was Farian's choice. He says we need a brand if we want it to sell."

Martial taps the end of his cigarette. Dissatisfied, he starts rolling it again.

"Smart kid," he says. "I watched your last video. Some twelve thousand views, no?"

"Enough to pay you back, and buy Farian a new lens."

"What an age," Martial says. "Getting paid for people to click on a box."

"The modern world has its charms," I reply. "Speaking of which, sun's rising."

He glances out, nods once. "Seventh stall. Your ashes are waiting."

I thank him and head that way. He and I both know the sun won't touch the ranch for another twenty minutes, but talking with Martial makes me nervous these days. He's a man of hints. Idle comments intended to stir me up. Too often he talks about the Races with Farian. He thinks I have a chance to be chosen as this year's Qualifier. There's also a chance I'll be devoured by wolves, but I'm not betting on either one. Martial was chosen all those years ago, and a man who's been struck by lightning always thinks it's likely to happen again.

Opening the seventh stall, I find the ashes piled neatly in a metal box. I lift them up, careful with the lid, and start my search for Farian.

The land stretches north and south of the barns, and even though the estate's massive, Farian's been complaining about the shots getting stale. Like me, though, he knows we're lucky to even have this option. I find him at the south end of the property, navigating the low limbs of Martial's lonely shoestring tree. He doesn't like climbing, but by the time I reach him, he's wedged fifteen feet in the air. The mountains glow with coming gold. I frown up at him.

"You're going through all this trouble to film a Stoneside rebirth?"

Farian shoots me a furious look. "You serious? Why would you do Stoneside again?"

I grin at him. "Just snacking on you, Farian."

He flicks me off, laughs, then almost drops his camera. We both gasp, then laugh again when he catches it to his chest. He shakes his head, like I'm the one who almost dropped the thing.

"I hope you have something good for me," he says, glancing back through the branches. "I think this lighting will be flawless. It's the only time we've ever done a camera angle this high, you know? I'm thinking of doing some crosscutting for this one, if you ride well."

"Crosscutting," I say. "Glad to hear that. I was going to suggest . . . crosscutting."

He makes a face. "It's when you—"

When he sees my face, though, he goes quiet. We've played this game too many times. He talks like a textbook and I end up . . . distracted. He gets annoyed; I get mad.

"You film. I ride. It's simple."

"Gods below," he says, eyeing the light again. "Get me to a university already. I'd like to have a proper conversation about montages and backlighting with someone."

I smile up at him. "I thought you talked about all that stuff with Doctor Vass."

"For fifteen minutes." Farian shrugs. "Not his area of expertise."

"Guess you'll have to go to university."

"Guess so," he says, but his voice is full of doubt.

His family doesn't send off to school. Neither does mine. Every uncle and cousin is proof enough of that. Education is reserved for Ashlords and city-born Dividian with deep pockets. Out in the rural villages, we're more likely to inherit trades. Both Farian and I spend most of our time ignoring the trade we've been pegged for since birth. Farian knows as much about farming as a chicken. And I know even less about charming and getting married to a boy. My parents are already hinting that I can't spend my life riding other people's horses. One day they'll shrug and say that all we can do is make the best of the world the Ashlords offer us.

But on holy days—while the Ashlords worship their gods—I forget all of that. I walk out to greet the sunrise and become who I *really* am.

"Ready, Farian?"

He jams an elbow into his lap, turning the lens slightly. At his signal, I start spreading the ashes out over the ground. They're still warm, so I take quick handfuls and sweep them out in a flat, even circle. I don't flinch away from the heat, not after Farian claimed my cowardice ruined his shot a few months ago. I am as bright and fiery as the creature I will summon.

Once that's done, I unclip the cubes from my belt, flipping the individual lids so Farian has a good angle on each stored component. Sunrise isn't far off. I lift my eyes to Farian, focused on the camera. He's been walking me through the acting cues, but I always need a deep breath before we start, no matter how many videos we've made. He signals, and I begin.

"Good morning." I offer the camera an unnatural smile. "My name is Imelda Beru, also known as the Alchemist. First, I wanted to thank all of you for watching our recent videos. If you missed our Stoneside or Fearless rebirths, you'll find the link to those videos below.

"Today, we're staying with the theme of vintage rebirths. Everyone knows the standard resurrections these days. Those are tired. They're boring. All we have to do is look back at the pages of history to see just how inventive phoenix rebirths used to be. Since you don't have time to wade through codices and scrolls, I've done your homework for you. Here's a rebirth I like to call Trust Fall."

Farian leans out from behind his camera long enough to roll his eyes at my chosen title. I kneel down, hiding my laughter as I take a healthy pinch of locust dust.

"You're going to start with an outer ring of locust," I explain, letting the powder feed between my fingers and highlighting the circle's border with a deep tan color. "Keep the circle unbroken. You want your locust to burn hard and quick. You'll know you did it right if there's the faintest trace of sandstone coloring just as sunrise hits.

"Next: gypsum and limestone." I empty those containers into a central pile on my ashes, mixing them slowly with both fingers. "You'll want to lightly mix them, but don't spread them out too far. Three fingers of height will guarantee your mixture doesn't burn away."

As I hold up the last cube, I throw a wicked grin at the camera.

"Now, unborn ashes are as vintage as it gets. Our ancestors lived in a crueler world. Blood sacrifices every month and gods roaming the land. Unborn ashes aren't the cheapest component in the storeroom, but they're what you need if you want to call on the powers of old. Make another circle." I take a handful of the dead ashes. They're so cold that the hairs on that arm start to rise. "Place them inside the locust powder, but ringed outside the mixture of gypsum and limestone. Make the circle thick and add them just before sunlight hits."

I stand back, wiping my hands clean and gesturing past the camera.

"Which is about . . . right . . . now."

Sunlight spills over the plain. I take a step back and hear the obvious gasp of a creature coming to life. My piled ash stirs with movement. The wind turns the ashes in quick circles before raising them up, where they howl into a sudden dust devil. In all that chaos, I see my phoenix starting to take form, a dark, inconsistent mass. Then sunlight fractures against the growing magic, sudden and blinding.

I shield my eyes as a glorious figure staggers free of the storm. Farian keeps the film rolling, but I know the phoenix is still too bright to see. I can't even look at it without squinting and shielding my eyes with both hands. The horse itself isn't all that marvelous. As the light begins to fade, I note that it's Martial's gray pinto with the steel-tipped tail. Stand her up next to any Ashlord-bred stallion and you'd think she was a miniature horse, but Farian's filming will make her look twenty feet tall, and my alchemy will add what his filming can't.

"Our ancestors used the Trust Fall rebirth to leap off

cliffs," I say, raising my voice above the phoenix's un-settled stamping and snorting. "I suggest starting with ten- or fifteen-foot drops, and keep in mind this is a dangerous rebirth. Even if you're an experienced rider, use caution."

Farian hates disclaimers, thinks they're boring. But I'm not going to have some rookie breaking their neck and blaming me for it.

As quietly as possible, I approach the horse's left shoulder. I keep my voice soft and patient. Most riders would just use constants. They're with their horse through every death, every life. Feed them a certain apple, whisper a certain word. That's all it takes for the Ashlords who can afford to own their own horses. It's a little more difficult when you're trying to convince a creature you haven't seen in months to trust you again.

She trembles beneath my fingertips, but she's quiet when I stand at her side. Still whispering, I start sliding a saddle over her back, fumbling at the buckles that attach the girth on both sides. As I slide forward to work on the bridle, Farian's moving, too, adjusting his angle. We've got instructional videos up for saddles and harnesses, so he never films this part. Our viewers subscribe for the new rebirths, and for Farian's brilliant production values.

"Trust Fall?" he says, starting to climb down from the tree. "We need to have a conversation about your creative decision making."

I ignore the dig, knowing the horse will feed off any anger or nerves this early in the connection. She huffs once and settles back into calm.

"What does the mix even do?" Farian asks. "I don't see anything different about this one."

"Just keep filming."

He's right, though. She looks plain as sand. But that's the beauty of alchemy and phoenixes: They're like an ace hidden up a sleeve, magical if you know how to make the trick work. I finish with the saddle and move up to look the sweet thing in the eye. She's not nervous now. She likes my hands and the sound of my voice.

"Let's do this," I say, eyes back on Farian. "What do you say, Catcher?"

Farian stands over his tripod and signals for me to say the name again. Not my most creative work. He looks annoyed that I didn't consult with him first, but names matter with phoenixes. If Farian knew what kind of stunt I'm about to try to pull off, he'd understand why it's the perfect name for the horse.

"All right." I raise my voice. "You won't see much difference in Catcher until I leap from her back. I'm going to ride along that upper ridge there. Keep your eyes on the screen once I'm in the air. And say a little prayer for me that this actually works."

I can tell Farian's eyes are wide behind the camera. He's adjusting his lens and prepping the tripod for a perfect shot of the ridge off to our right. I wait for his signal before turning Catcher around and making sure my face is visible before our first gallop. A normal horse might need the warmup, but phoenix horses run hot, always ready for that first sprint.

"Get, get! Let's ride, girl!"

I dig in my heels, and she shoots forward. She opens up quick, trying to take control from me, so I rein her in and make sure she knows that where I'm heading is where she's heading. Both of us taste the wind for a few seconds, galloping in a dead straight line away from Farian. When she's got the swing of me, I loop us back around. Martial's property has a handful of little ridges and hollows. Good spots for practicing elevation changes or learning how to bail. The ridge I'm aimed at isn't much higher than Catcher, but it's high enough for what I'm planning.

Farian has us locked in his sights as we nose toward the first rise. I start to stand up in the saddle, freeing my feet from the stirrups and tightening my grip. Catcher's a little unnerved by the change, but the ridge is smack up against a second rise, so there's nowhere for her to scare to. She holds the path I've chosen as I push onto my knees, then onto my feet. I crouch on her back like a statue, waiting for the right moment. When we reach the crest, Catcher's in full frame for Farian.

Fear slips away. I become something more.

I release the reins and leap to my left.

There's nothing but air and ground. The sudden drop steals my breath. I can feel my stomach twisting as I turn in the air, widening my stance, falling to the ground below. The earth rushes up to devour me. Only it doesn't, because Catcher *appears* beneath me.

From ridge to ground level in an impossible blink. I land hard against her back, nearly slip off the saddle, and scramble for the reins. She snorts with delight when I manage to hang on. Farian's already got one fist raised in triumph. I'm lost in the glory of it, that the rebirth actually worked, as I yank her to a stop right in front of him, grinning my wildness down at the camera.

"Trust Fall," I say breathlessly. "That one's called Trust Fall."

2

THE LONGHAND

ADRIAN

Sixteen hats on the table, set down in front of their own-ers, each as meaningful as words on a page. There's Maggie and Maggie, snipers both, with their black and white brims. Trick is knowing which Maggie's which. The one with the black hat's sweet as pie. One in white has the devil parad-ing around her twisted little heart. Knowing is living. Daddy has taught me that much.

Beside them, Antonio Rowan. Looks like he spent all morning kicking his hat through the sticks to get it properly dusted. The man is a legend, as good at talking as he is at keeping the right people quiet. He's even going at it now. Telling a story about a time and a place.

The hat across from his is as pristine as its owner. Gale Gusto doesn't have a speck of dirt on her. I wonder how she got here, which street she asked them to shake the dust out of before she agreed to sidesaddle her way into town for a meeting. She doesn't smile, but when you're as rich as she is, there are only so many folks you have to play nice with.

I know all their names, their favorite drinks, too. These are our people, every rotten one of them. And, of course, there's Daddy. The only one in the room who sits taller than me.

His hat is a brown brim with a leather braid snaking quietly around the crown. There's a little tear right of center, noticeable, but no one knows the story. The brim edges up on one side because of how often he lifts that eyebrow in curiosity. That's how he's always been. A man of questions. He sat me on his lap when I was five and said the man who asks the most questions gets the most answers. Knowing is living. I stopped being so quiet after that.

"Well," he says, and that one word gives Antonio Rowan's story a new ending. The man falls quiet. Everyone else follows suit. Daddy sets a hand on his hat. "Shall we get started?"

"About time," Gale Gusto replies. "I've business to attend to."

Daddy smiles a trademark at her. "That you do, Gale. We all do. Welcome, friends." That word is a stretch, but he makes it sound fitting enough. "I imagine you're awfully curious about such a gathering. Deposed generals, oil magnates, sharpshooters. What a crew we make."

"We're breaking a few laws, aren't we?" Old Trent asks.

"Two very specific ones," Daddy answers. "But it's not much off our noses if word doesn't make its way to the wrong ears. I'm sure what's spoken here won't leave the room."

Hearing that settles the group. Daddy's word is the steadiest currency in the Reach. And even if they're afraid of what he might say today, they've spent most of their lives waiting for someone to say it. I look around the table again and know these are the Rebellion's children. Each of them grew up hearing stories about Gold Man Jones or the Running Rabbits. But their parents told those stories like they were tragedies. That's what you do after losing a war. You tell your histories at the fire and you make them as quiet as you can.

Daddy's never liked quiet. "It's time for the Reach to rise," he says. "Our war debt has been absolved. The population has more than recovered from the Purge. Between Gale, the Foresters, and myself, we have enough money to mobilize at least half the troops we'll need. The state treasury is ticking its way to heaven in spite of Ashlord sanctions. We're far more formidable than we were at the start of the first Rebellion."

"A rebellion? To what end?" Grayson asks from my left. "You're right. The Reach has flourished, but it has done so in peacetime. What happens if we go to war? How many of our boys will we lose to battle? I've read Paxon's latest book on the matter. . . ."

A few snorts sound. Gale Gusto rolls her eyes. Only Daddy doesn't react to the name. Paxon is too liberal by half, but Daddy makes me read all of his books. It's always harder to defeat an enemy you don't know. I've even read the book that Grayson's mentioned.

The Grave Illusion.

In it, Paxon examined the idea of a second Rebellion, and the inevitable war that would follow between the Reach and our current rulers: the Ashlord Empire. His analysis of the economics was surgical. There wasn't much to argue with, honestly. His conclusion was that a second war would be bad for everyone.

"I'm just saying," Grayson goes on. "There are consequences to war."

Daddy nods at that. "You're not wrong. I imagine we all lived through the consequences of war for a time. Felt like I ate nothing but potatoes one year. Our parents reached for glory and couldn't quite get a hold of it. This time will be different. You know I've read Paxon's book, too. The economics in it are staggering, aren't they? Can't say I like the man, but he's got an entertaining perspective on things. There's one word he doesn't mention even once in the text, though, Grayson. Do you know which one it is?"

Grayson frowns, quiet now. The others are leaning forward, licking their chops. It's a dysfunctional family that likes seeing its members laid low, but none of them know that Daddy talked with Grayson months before the meeting. Asked the man to stick his boots in the mud and brace himself for a good drag through it. He's played his part well. Now it's time to play mine.

"Freedom," I say, letting them hear the deep certainty in my voice. Daddy wanted me to be visible today, memorable. "He doesn't talk about freedom."

Daddy nods. "Not once."

"You can't evaluate the cost of freedom," Grayson complains.

"Agreed." Daddy's moving quick now, everything rehearsed. "Freedom is invaluable. Paxon ignored the idea because it weighs too much. We all know how much a drum of oil costs, Grayson. We can sell you a horse for the right price, too. But freedom? Too dangerous to set that on the scales. Paxon knew the men and women of the Reach would set every oil field on fire if it removed the chains the Ashlords still have around our wrists. It's been centuries. Our ancestors came up here after the Dividian War and asked for one thing: freedom. And it's the one thing that we still don't have."

Antonio Rowan raps his knuckles on the table in agreement. The Maggies are grinning like murderers, and even Gale Gusto's wearing her little crease of a smile. Old Trask has war in his eyes, and the rest of the generals look like they can hear the sound of soldiers marching. Daddy has the room in thrall. They wanted to rise; he just needed to remind them they could.

"If you want war so you can line your pockets," he says, "go on home. The war we start will cost us everything. The world will burn. We have to be brave enough to put the torch to it."

Gale Gusto nods. "I know where you can get some oil."

The room shakes with laughter, but it's plain as day they're still on the fence. Most of them have whispered rebellion into their cups, at their dinner tables, in their beds. Daddy knew they needed more than words. It's easier to trust a man who stands to lose as much as you do.

"Adrian," he says. "Stand up."

I rise. Most of them remember the boy I was, but Daddy wants them to leave in awe of the man I've become. Standing is a good place to start. I'm a hand or two taller than any of them. I inherited broad shoulders, but the arms and chest are my own. I've spent the past few years making power into an art form. They all see it now. I am everything the Reach could be.

I am endless possibility.

"Adrian's heading south," he says. "He will be the first Longhand in twelve years to compete in the Races. When he wins, our people will remember. They will rise to war. My son will remind the Ashlords who we are, what we can do. Their world will tremble."

They look from me to him, more convinced than ever. No one objects to the plan, or to the war, but there's still a fear that they'll leave today and have their throats slit within a week. The Ashlords have faced insurrections before, and they always put them down in fire and blood.

Luckily, we've got one more show for them.

I unsheathe a blade from my hip, take two steps, and let it swing. The metal shines a silver arc before stopping an inch shy of Sweet Maggie's throat. The room takes in a breath. The other Maggie stands, pistol rising to my temple, her eyes a storm.

"You've got that aimed at the wrong person," Daddy tells her. "Sweet Maggie's been sliding secrets back to the Empire. Informing for the Ashlords since the incident in Vivinia. I always did wonder how you slipped your charges on that nightmarish expedition."

Bad Maggie's still got her gun to my temple, close enough that I can smell the loaded powder. But I was taught to show no weakness. Give them nothing. So my blade hangs steady over Sweet Maggie's blotchy throat. After a second, Daddy stands, angry at this show of distrust.

"Unless you are her accomplice in this betrayal," he says, "set the gun down."

Bad Maggie's reply is mostly spit. "Like hell. She wouldn't."

"She would. She did," Daddy says. "Set it down."

"He's right." Sweet Maggie can pick someone off from a hundred paces, but she's too honest to carry a lie. "Ashlords snagged me. I should have told you, Mags, but I thought it'd be easier this way. All I sent them was a few notes. The information wasn't even that good."

There's a few seconds where the tension holds. Bad Maggie makes a noise, no doubt feeling fouled by it all, then lowers her gun. My eyes flicker to her for a second, and that's as long as Sweet Maggie needs to go for her knife. It's off her hip and driving toward my stomach, but I'm quicker. I slam the grip of my sword down and crush her at the wrist.

She fumbles the knife and I bring my elbow up and across. The blow sends her staggering to the ground. Before she can even think to reach for her fallen weapon, I have the sword at her neck again. She goes still, her chest heaving, eyes wide and defeated.

"It was confusing enough having two of you," Daddy says. "Get her out."

Antonio Rowan sweeps up from his chair. Bad Maggie's still fuming, like she's angry at the whole world, but her pistol's back on her hip and she's punishing the back of her chair instead of me. I sheathe my sword as the traitor is escorted out. Daddy nods approvingly at the decision before turning back to a room full of rebels and warlords.

He sets his hat on his head and smiles recklessly.

"Well," he says. "Who wants to go to war?"

3

THE FAVORITE

PIPPA

You hit the replay button again. Stylists are arranging your curls and fussing over your makeup, but you're too fixated on the screen to care. The Chats lit up this afternoon. Everyone and their mother's sharing the Alchemist's video. It's not hard to understand the obsession. You watch the girl leap from the horse's back. She vaults through the air like a dancer. The horse vanishes from the ridge and appears beneath her. She sticks the landing, and gods does she look *shocked* when she does, then grins at the camera like a fool.

It's not half bad for a Dividian, you think. A glance shows the video's been watched two million times. A clip of you dancing on the beach last week had double that number, but still, not bad for a Dividian.

"Stage in twenty seconds," Zeta announces.

You nod, shedding stylists to glide through the backstage labyrinth. You like the quiet darkness, but you like the bright chaos even more. A thousand cameras flash as you take the stage. You brush a dark lock behind your ear because you know Bravos is watching, and he'll love that little display of calm control. When you flash your commercial smile, the media attendants swoon. Automated applause echoes out from each of the metallic chair mannequins.

Life has readied you for the stage. You know to keep your eyes level, your back straight, and your legs crossed. The designer's auction only finished an hour before the interview. Seven thousand legions pile into your personal account from some off-brand company just so you'll wear their jacket during the live feed. It has the most absurd silver loops you've ever seen for buttons and a vintage collar. Not really your style, but the video will feed through the Chats and before long you'll see it featured in storefronts on Promenade Avenue. A little sacrifice for a little pocket change never hurt.

House lights come up and you get your first look at the audience. People are still bidding for seats, so the faces and clothes keep changing inside the vacant, crystal mannequins. Bidding on the front row's even fiercer than usual. You watch the faces change. Bearded men replaced by bald women, diva stylists outbidding political dignitaries. Everyone wants a taste of *you*.

Overhead, a clock ticks down bright-red numbers. When it hits zero, the auctions will end and the interview will begin. Only the back row's not subject to the grappling of public hands. You promised yourself you wouldn't look there before the interview, that it's the grown-up thing to do this all on your own, but you can't help it. You've always needed them.

Father and Mother sit in their customary seats, back left. Father's hair is swept into a traditional topknot. So old-fashioned, but he makes it look classic somehow. You know most men who've won the Races put on weight as the years pass. Fifteen years of endless training lead to fifteen years of banquets and parades. But not for your father. In the same way his haircut and uniform are timeless, so is he. A mark of something better, something the years can't wash away.

Beside him, your mother. That famously pointed chin, those famously watchful eyes. After her victory in the Races, women actually purchased illegal surgeries, hoping to look a little more like the famous Prama. The government agencies had so much trouble regulating the industry that they just changed the law instead. For three years in a row, your mother was *Going Girl* magazine's "Most Desirable Bachelorette in Furia"!

Until she married your father.

The perfect couple.

Which left you with only one choice: to follow in their perfect footsteps.

The red numbers vanish. You lift your chin and turn as the crystal mannequin in the opposite seat animates, filling with color. A blue suit and pink buttons. The famous showman, Maxim, sweeps a robotic hand through his perfectly combed hair and smiles for the cameras.

"We're *back* and *live* with our coverage of this year's Races. But there are some people who would argue that our coverage is *only* beginning as we arrive at the interview that *everyone* in Furia has been waiting for. Gods be good, Pippa, you look astonishing."

Smile once at the audience, once at Maxim, prepared answer.

"All thanks to the designers at Press Emporium and the unbelievable makeup artists that Flight Forever sends over before *every* interview. Where would I be without those girls? They're the ones who inspired my catchphrase, after all. You remember it, Maxim?"

The showman smiles. "I'm really not sure I've heard *anything* about a catchphrase."

Incredulous look, wink at the audience, wide smile.

"Really? And I thought you were the kind of guy who knew things." *Second wide smile.* "Let's see if my real fans know it: I *totally* believe in luck. In fact, the harder I work . . ."

Raise an eyebrow to cue the audience.

Everyone shouts, "The more I have of it!"

Maxim claps his hands and smiles. Your publicist found that quote in some gods-awful library up north. The team ran through catchphrases for hours before settling on that one. You know they'll be filling back orders on the glittering T-shirts you designed for weeks to come. Your father said you should be more focused on training than sales, but you've always been a best-of-both-worlds kind of girl.

"Pippa," Maxim says, leaning conspiratorially close. "If we're being honest, last year's event was overshadowed by the knowledge that you would be eligible for the Races this year. It doesn't mean we weren't entertained, but we were simply *ecstatic* to get to this year's ride. Everyone was very pleased when you decided to submit your name in your first qualifying year. Was there any pushback on that?"

Amusement, a shake of the head, firm voice.

"Not at all, Maxim. My father preached caution in the past, but after seeing me in training sessions and on the amateur circuit, he withdrew those concerns. It's pretty clear now that I'm ready. As the daughter of two former champions, this is in my blood. I'm not here to put on a good show or smile for the cameras, Maxim. I'm here to win."

"As sharp as your mother and as fiery as your father!" He looks back to the audience. "I'm glad you're up to the challenge. We've been looking forward to this, so much so that we just set the record for audience calls! Ready to field your fans' biggest questions, Pippa?"

Soft smile, playful wink. "Of course, Maxim."

"All right, let's get to it!"

The interviewing mannequin shimmers. Maxim's tie disappears and a woman with a bright-red scarf and square-framed glasses replaces him. You smile as your first caller lets out a rather hideous squeal and wiggles with delight in her seat.

"It's actually you! You! Here! In front of me!"

You smile wider. "Pippa, at your service."

"Well, I just *had* to ask you about what happened with Bravos."

Show a flash of anger. Follow with a playful front. Respond with a question.

"I thought he'd come up tonight. What did you want to know about Bravos?"

You keep your smile steady as a knife. Only two days ago, you and Bravos put on quite a performance for your dinner guests. He contradicted you on something. You pointed out how boring his tie was. It wasn't long before the Chats were *full* of rumors about Furia's favorite couple. Were they *really* breaking up?

"Well," the fan says. "I've followed your romance since day one on the Chats! So hot and steamy and just, I don't know, *fun*. But the reports claim it's over. Say it isn't so."

"It is so." Every audience member punches their gasp buttons. The room fills with robotic sadness and you're careful to let it die down before continuing. "Bravos and I had our time. But in a few weeks, he becomes my enemy. Anyone standing between me and the finish line can only ever be that: an enemy."

You know the words are lifted directly from your father's first interview. The publicity team concluded you looked soft in the eyes of other contestants and that you needed to adopt some of your father's intensity. Loom larger and look wilder. It was easier to take Father's words and carve your own threats out of them.

The fan nods sympathetically before the interviewing mannequin goes blank again. There's a lottery shuffle of faces and clothes before a thin man with dark eyebrows and a severely angled face appears. You smile as his eyes widen in surprise.

"Oh dear gods."

You laugh. "A mere mortal most days. What's your question?"

He blinks before speaking. "I was wondering about your training. The Chats say you were in Baybou last week and the Sunsickle Islands before that. Some of the other contestants post training videos every day. Are you really as prepared as Etzli or Revel?"

Bite the lip, exasperated sigh, firm eyes.

"I saw a few of those videos. Impressive, but nothing I saw in any of them has me worried. I'm one of three contestants riding a pureborn phoenix. I went to Baybou to get him accustomed to the thinner air. Then I visited the Sunsickle Islands so I could practice quick water and land transitions. People only ever see the pictures of me sunbathing on the beach or attending Crossing matches, but every hour in between the stolen photos is spent training. I'm ready, sir, and any competitor who thinks I'm not is just giving me one more way to beat them."

Applause buttons flood the room with noise. The next fan doesn't look a day over twelve. But she doesn't stutter through a question or shake with nerves. She's focused, a young Ashlord girl who looks like she's trying to learn a valuable lesson from a worthy teacher.

"Pippa," she enunciates clearly. "How are you going to handle the Longhand?"

Nod seriously, keep chin raised, show no fear.

"So you saw that announcement yesterday?" *Proud smile, little wink.* "I suppose the entire Empire's heard about Adrian Ford by now. Looks big, doesn't he?"

The girl gives a nod, grinning. "I wouldn't want to wrestle him."

You laugh. "Me neither. Fortunately, this isn't a wrestling match. It's the Races. Adrian made a lot of noise yesterday, but remember, that's all thunder ever is. Noise. It's the lightning you have to worry about. Ever seen a good storm out on the plains?" The girl nods. "You always see the strikes before you hear the boom. That's how I'll handle the

Longhand. I'll ride hard and I won't look back. I'll be in the distance, and he'll just be the noise that follows."

The girl nods like she's the lightning, too.

"Besides, we know the Longhands aren't accustomed to winning."

That draws a laugh from the crowd. You watch the mannequin spin through an endless sea of faces. It stops on a fourth fan. Pretty eyes, round face, hair styled short like most middle-aged women in Furia. She doesn't smile and she isn't nervous.

"Pippa, I wanted to know something." The voice isn't familiar, but you hear something in her tone that's like a second language. Your fame has negative consequences, too. It comes with denouncers and haters. You know the kind of words that always dance with a tone like this one. "How many Beholder shots did you pose for? How many marriages are you planning on ruining as you put yourself out there for money? Do you have any idea how it makes *us* feel?"

It's the only question you're not ready to answer. The natural cues don't come. You stare at her, wondering how to lie to her and to the cameras and to everyone, but she doesn't let you get that far. The mannequin lunges out of its chair. You duck back instinctively, but the chair you're sitting in is high-backed, and your escape routes are all cut off. Your eyes widen as the metallic hands reach for your throat.

And fall short. The machine's fail-safe system hums to life and the hands hang lifelessly in the air, just a few inches from your neck. The audience stares in horror until Maxim's blue tie appears and the mannequin takes its seat again. He sweeps a hand through that perfect hair and starts to apologize.

"We're so sorry about that, Pippa. Always a few people out there trying to ruin the fun."

He's smiling, but you see his head tilt slightly to one side, and you know his producers are feeding him some fresh bit of news. You remember he's got a show to put on. To him, that's all that matters tonight. Not you and not your feelings and not your privacy.

"We *are* receiving reports," he says, "of several sources claiming these Beholder shots do exist. My producers would kill me if I didn't take the time and at least ask—"

"This is done," you say, because if it's not done now, you're going to get burned to ashes in front of a live audience. "Thank you for your time, Maxim. Goodbye."

You're backstage in seconds, crew swarming around you, studio door opening. One photo shoot. That's all it was. You did *one* Beholder session. It wasn't even anything scandalous. A few pictures of you in a bathing suit. A little skin, but nothing you don't see on the streets of Furia every day. Your publicist was all warnings, but the cash was too good to pass up.

Beholder shots of a girl like you sell *very* well. Only twenty-seven were produced. For each picture, only the first person to open the portrait can see the contents. That's the two-way beauty of Beholder shots. It gives the buyer something private and unique, something only they can see. And it promises anonymity. You agreed to do it because you thought no one could prove the picture was of you, because no one but the first Beholder can see it.

"What are they saying?" you hiss.

Zeta just shakes her head. "He says it's a completely revealing shot. The descriptions are crass and crude, but the account's been seconded already. It's a nightmare."

"But they're lying. You can't see *anything* in those photos."

She frowns back. "It doesn't matter now."

And she's right. It doesn't matter. Beholder shots work both ways. No one can *disprove* what they're saying because no one else can see the shots. All that matters is what they've said, and the doubt they've already planted in the mind of every fan, every critic.

"We release a statement," you say. "Dismiss the rumors."

"Not yet," Zeta replies. "Go home. Be with your family. I'll have to come up with a whole new branding strategy. Give me a few hours. I'll come by tonight."

"Great," you say. "Just *great*."

But your mind's skipping ahead. You're trying to imagine what your parents will say, what they'll think. And then Bravos. You never told him, either. Dreading all of it, you change into your sponsored evening wear, wrap yourself up in a summer scarf, and storm out of the room. Reporters catch you at the back exit, flash bulbs bursting, but you don't answer questions as you mount your phoenix.

Instead, you smile wide, look unconcerned, and show them no fear.

4

BIRTHDAY DANCE

IMELDA

The next day there are seven million views.

Farian's page on the Chats has two thousand new subscribers. Our older videos are getting clicks, too. We skip the second half of the school day, apologizing to Doctor Vass, so the two of us can monitor our pages and make money on all the advertising. We knock on the back door of Amaya's bar just after lunch hour and she grins us inside.

"Imelda Beru," she says. "I didn't know Alchemists could fly. Lucky you didn't break your neck, girl. Take any hub you want. I'm not expecting anyone else this afternoon."

Every house in Furia has dual connections to the Chats, but our village is a far cry from Furia, or any city with decent tech. Most homes have incoming feeds, because watching Crossing matches or the Races is a national expectation, regardless of creed or homeland. Outgoing feeds are costlier and a lot less common. I know the town hall has a few hubs.

Our village's overseeing Ashlord, Oxanos, likes to complain about how slow the feeds are in our scab of a town. Amaya's place is the only business that's taken a swing at the modern world.

"Thanks, Amaya," Farian says. "Normal rates?"

She shakes her head. "Free of charge."

Farian frowns at her. "We finally have money to pay you, and you don't want it?"

"On the house," she repeats. "For Imelda's birthday."

Farian snorts a laugh. I thank her, but both she and Farian *know* I hate birthdays. Farian's played nice for once, not mentioning it all morning, but that just makes me think he's got some stupid gift wrapped somewhere for me. Every year I dance away from the ridiculousness of the celebration, and every year it still finds me. There's nothing worse than being celebrated for an event in which I was basically a nonparticipant.

Farian's still laughing as we set up Amaya's equipment. He hooks me into the first hub before hooking himself into the second. Farian knows how to work a camera, but he's even better on the business side of things. He diverts incoming messages about our old videos to my screen. Little companies have sent us a few offers, gambling on the hope that views continue to come.

But the real cash will come from the auction he's running for our next big advertising spot on the Trust Fall video. I watch his fingers dance over the keys. He pulls up financials on one page and starts reading through our numbers for the last twenty hours.

"We've almost peaked," he says. "They'll move on to a new video tomorrow, but we've already pulled more money for this than *all* of our other videos combined."

It's hard to believe. "What's the take?"

"Three thousand legions?"

"No way," I say, eyeing the screen over his shoulder. "There's no way it's that much."

"On top of whatever we get from this final auction."

"Music to my ears," I say, grinning. "Where'd the views come from?"

"Riders," he replies. "Bravos and Eztli both shared the video. Actual *riders,* Imelda."

"Hey, I *am* an actual rider."

He ignores me. "Most of the views are from Furia, obviously, but we've got people from every corner of the Empire watching. Someone even interviewed Martial this morning."

Farian pulls the video onto his screen. The old Dividian victor stands with some self-styled Ashlord princess of a reporter. She's got the dark eyes and those impossible collarbones, skin as rusty as a sunset. I was born knowing my place in the world was beneath people like her. It's easier to convince myself that's the truth when all of them look like timeless beauties.

"So tell us about the Alchemist. Is she the *real* deal, or was this video a fluke?"

Martial grins, and for a second it's like he's looking directly through the camera at me.

"Fluke? Only fluke is how long it took the world to notice her," he says. "There's no one with her arsenal of rebirths. She knows more mixes than I ever did when I won the

Races. And that video shows she can ride. If she'd grown up with her own phoenix, she'd be the favorite to win this year. But now she's gotta hope she gets picked out of thousands just to get a shot? You want to talk about flukes, that's the fluke."

The reporter signs off, smiling one of those classic Ashlord smiles, and I'm left shifting uncomfortably in my chair. Farian glances over, but he knows better than to say what's on his mind. He and Martial want to build me up, tell me I've got a chance. The views are a good thing, the money even better. But I'm not going to jump off a cliff just because they say I can fly.

"Let's take another look at the auction," I suggest quietly.

For the next few hours, it's all business. I read through comments and articles, trying to ignore the growing dread I have over being so centered in the spotlight. Farian's wrong. This video isn't going away. Our auction adds another three thousand legions to our account, and now we're looking at enough money to cover a year at a tech university for Farian, not to mention new saddles for me. It's more money than we've seen in our entire lives.

The sky is almost dark as we pack up to leave. Farian stops me at the back door.

"Amaya wanted us to lock it," he says. "Go out the front."

I nod absently. "She did?"

He bolts the back door, shoulders his bag, and leads me past the hubs. I'm still caught up in thoughts of fame, in the words of Martial's interview, when Farian shoulders our way into the bar area. The lights are all on and overly bright, but it's the explosion of sound that ends me.

Farian's quick to move aside, and quick to laugh obnox-
iously, as my *entire* family shouts "Surprise!" at me. Uncles
are crowding the back walls and cousins are darting between legs. My mother's smiling at the center of the group
like she's done something wonderful. I consider running,
but Farian's planted himself across my escape route, and he
laughs again when he realizes my first instinct was to bolt.

"They planned this for you," he says, nudging me forward.

"You're a dead man," I whisper back.

But I turn a blushing smile on my family so they know
their surprise worked. The chaos spins back to life as half
the uncles take my entrance as a sign the drinking can com-
mence. I watch them race across the room to Amaya, el-
bowing each other out of the way, ordering their favorite
whiskies. Dividian music dances from the far end of the
room. I grin wildly at the sight of my cousin Luca, strumming his guitar and nodding along with the notes. His family
lives all the way out in the Gravitas Mountains. It probably
took them a few days to get here.

The first person to come vaulting in my direction is my
little brother, Prosper. He barrels into my legs, wrapping his
arms around me and smiling up. We've got the same round
face, the same slight brows, but Prosper's eyes are a deeper,
darker shade of green. He's only eight, but it seems like he
shoots up an inch or two every few weeks. I sweep the hair
from his forehead and lean down, planting a little kiss there.

"Prosper, did you get *another* haircut?"

He's glad I noticed. "It's the new style, Imelda! I used *my*
money for it."

"Such a fashion icon," I reply. "Come on, let's thank Mother for this lovely surprise."

He grins even wider. "You're totally mad, aren't you? I told her you would be. You hate surprises, and birthdays, and parties. But wait until you see the three-fires cake she made for you. And someone from the mountains brought *actual* dreamnots, Imelda! Oh, and you'll get presents, too, you know? So it can't be that bad!"

"I know, I know," I say, messing with his hair. "Come on."

Mother and Father are waiting for us. He sits, wearing the day on his shoulders, both elbows planted on the table like they've been hammered down for good. She stands un- bent at his side. As we cross the room, and as I kiss their cheeks, I realize this is the only image I've ever known of them. My mother like the moon, bright and beautiful. My father like the stars, scattered in the dark backdrop of her radiance. Always so different, always inseparable.

"I know," my mother starts in. "You hate birthdays, but not having a party wasn't an option, Imelda. Look how happy everyone is. Look how loved you are. Why not try some cake?"

Smiling, my father offers me a plate. I wink at him be- fore taking a bite. My mother has her faults, but cooking isn't one of them. Her rendition of the traditional three-fires cake has my feet lifting off the ground. The smoked cara- mel, the roasted chocolate, the burned creams. She powders her version with enough fire dust to have me sweating.

"Why is it so good?" I say, taking an even bigger bite.

"Glad you like it," she says. "And I'm glad you're alive to *taste* it. I'm still having nightmares about that horrendous video. I'm not sure how many more birthdays I'll get to celebrate with you. Makes me glad we've thrown a proper party to celebrate you before you go off and try another stunt like that."

Father sees an opening. "Can't believe you stuck the landing."

We share a grin before Mother can swat away the fun.

"Don't encourage her." She uses her glass to gesture at the swirl of bodies all around. "Say hello to everyone, please. Especially the mountain Berus. Their crew traveled through the night to get here. Poor Ismay. And don't forget to give your great-aunt a kiss."

Father glances in my aunt's direction. "Just remember to check a mirror if she decides to kiss back. What shade of lipstick is that anyway? Turquoise?"

"Just thank her," Mother repeats. "Go on. And do make sure you say hello to the gentlemen at that last table, in the corner. We saw them on our way over and couldn't resist inviting them. You know them from school, don't you?"

My eyes skip that way. I let out a groan. The Shor brothers are sitting at the corner table. Farian's made his way over to them, but the conversation looks like it's going nowhere fast.

"Very subtle, Mother."

"What?" she asks, all innocence. "They're nice boys."

I give her a scathing look, take a final bite of cake, and start making my way around the room. Like most Dividian birthdays, it's a great smash of bodies and sound. I'm toasted by some and trapped by others. At one point my little cousin Elna finds her way into my arms. I set her against a hip, spinning her with me to each new conversation. She's a warm little thing, and she keeps asking me when the dreamnots will be released. Uncle Briel toasts my video, and his two gangly sons launch a hundred questions in my direction. I'm thankful when Aunt Ismay pulls me to a new conversation.

By the time everyone's seated and eating, I'm starving. One of the Shor brothers tries to say hello, but I answer him with a mouthful of roasted quail. He smiles his way politely back to the corner table, which has Mother fuming. Father sits back, though, sipping his drink and laughing at me. Some of the girls my age already have matches lined up. They'll be married in a few years, making babies in a few more. I'm not them. At least Father understands that truth.

When most of the plates have been picked clean, my uncles start clearing out tables in the main room of Amaya's bar. They leave behind a great sprawling space for the dreamnots.

Prosper rushes over to join a handful of my younger cousins. All the girls wait in colorful dresses. The boys adjust their little neck scarves. Catching dreamnots is an old Dividian tradition. They're one of the few creatures our ancestors brought to this land on that first voyage, and the only breed that didn't die out in the brutal wilds of the Empire. So much of our culture—our dances and our songs— died the same way.

The Ashlords even took our names from us. The joke goes that—after the war—the Ashlord census takers were too lazy to write down our full names. Our braver history teachers whisper the truth, though. Reducing all of our surnames to four letters—Beru and Rahm and Shor—was a reminder of who was in power and of how much we still had to lose.

So I smile wide as my father stands to begin one of the few traditions they couldn't destroy. The whole room falls quiet. He's not particularly big, but he's still the kind of man everyone notices. He walks across the room, and all the children take up eager stances. It's not hard to remember when I was that little, how much I looked forward to trying to catch the dreamnot with my friends and cousins.

The children see the twinkle in Father's eye as he stops before the door to Amaya's supply closet. He smiles back at them and sets his hand on the knob. The door rattles loudly and I laugh, knowing Father's just making noise to rile them up. The children in the front row take a cautious step back, eyes wild and excited. He opens the door and a herd of gray-blue creatures comes stampeding forward, each of them about the size of a teacup.

Farian always called them baby wolves with wings, and it's not a bad description. The children scream with delight. One of the creatures takes flight, scrambling to get clear of swatting hands. Another set sprint off to the right, the fur along their backs bristling. Prosper's the first to catch one and the first to draw out the true nature of dreamnots.

When he snatches it by the leg, the creature vanishes instantly into mist.

Laughing, he chases after the next.

One by one, the little creatures start to disappear. But this is the fun. Only one of the dreamnots in the room is ac-

tually the *real* one. Tradition says that the child who catches
it gets to make a wish. I laugh as little Elna pins one, tickling
its belly until it laughs into nonexistence. The other cousins
start teaming up, eliminating the illusions until there are
only a handful of dreamnots left in the room. It's my favorite kind of chaos.

Prosper ends the game with a lunging grab. He rolls onto
his back, clutching the creature to his chest, and lets out a
scream when it doesn't disappear. The dreamnot squirms at
first before resigning itself to being captured. After all, the
creature knows what Prosper does: His wish will not come
true unless he sets it free again. The uncles begin chanting
for him to make his wish and the other children shout out
their own ideas.

The scene is so loud and bright and perfect, that it takes
a long minute for anyone to notice the figure standing at
the door. A portion of the room quiets, until silence has dug
its cold claws through all of us. The laughing children back
away uncertainly.

I'm one of the last to see the Ashlord standing at Amaya's
front entrance.

Oxanos is a tall man, absurdly slender. His skin is char-
acteristically polished, his eyes lightless pools. Like most of
our overlords, he seems genetically predisposed to pride.
It's in his chin, his shoulders, his hands. This is a man who
is certain he is superior to everyone else in the room. Unlike
most of his kind, Oxanos has little reason to be proud.

The Ashlords assigned him as an overseer of our village. They wrapped the whole thing with a neat bow, but

it wasn't hard to figure out that sending Oxanos here was meant to be a punishment. He knows that and we know that. It makes him a cruel man, and even if some of our cousins don't know him personally, none are foolish enough to think he's welcome here.

Nor are any foolish enough to stop him from entering.

"A birthday?" he asks in his rich, city-born accent. "That's the cause of all this noise?"

Amaya steps forward. "We'll keep it quiet."

"Too late for that," Oxanos replies. "I've already been woken up twice by it."

Amaya's mouth opens again, but Oxanos cuts her off with a raised hand.

"Don't bother arguing. You've broken rules here tonight. Noise ordinances. Crowd ordinances. I see alcoholic beverages in the hands of underage drinkers." He pretends to scan the crowd, but his eyes inevitably fix on me. We are not strangers, nor are we friends. Like most of the girls in our town, I've had to suffer the leering attention that Oxanos considers a part of his charm. "Exotic creatures, too? Do we have permits for the use of these?"

No one answers, because no one in the room's ever needed a permit for dreamnots, or to throw a party, or to make noise in a bar. I realize the idea of us waking up Oxanos is just as laughable. Amaya's bar is on the west end of town, almost a mile away from his cozy quarters above town hall. I'd bet ten legions he was passing by and was bored enough to try feeling important.

The rule of the Ashlords is unquestioned. We know better than to complain about our lives to them. They've never looked on us with mercy, but to see Oxanos trying to take these small joys builds fury in me like fire. I'm not alone. Half the room looks ready to breathe smoke.

"No permits," he says, shaking his head. "Illegal activities. Arrests will have to be made."

My mother stands. "Ashlord, please, it's my daughter's birthday."

He ignores her. His eyes find me like Mother's pronouncement has given him a right to stare. The entire room holds its breath. There's not a man or woman in the bar who wouldn't enjoy taking a swing at him, but striking an Ashlord isn't an option. Defiance leads to death.

"Imelda Beru." He tastes the name. "You're to blame for all this, then?"

Father rises. The sight makes Oxanos smile, like he's finally struck a chord of music he enjoys. Oxanos has probably heard stories of Ashlords inciting riots among the Dividian and getting killed for acting like fools. Those stories are rare, but every now and again it happens. Rare because rebellion has a cost. Battalions come, villages burn. The Ashlords always offer retribution, even for the lives of their most unlikeable exiles.

"A special occasion, but no excuse for illegalities." Oxanos smiles. "I'll pardon them, however, in exchange for a dance. Consider it a gift to you, Imelda."

Murder is written on my father's face. Uncles are sobering toward dark possibilities. Oxanos knows what he asks. A woman's first dance belongs to her father, or her intended.

I am old enough now to have a man who could ask that of my father, but it should never be someone like him. Oxanos is greedy and petty and undeserving.

I will not risk my father's life on a man like him.

"I agree. One dance."

Oxanos stares. "Of my choosing?"

"Of mine."

He's surprised by that little defiance, but it just brings out a nastier smirk. My eyes drift back to my father. He knows what I'm doing and why, but it doesn't make the burden of his anger any lighter. It's unfair that he has to shoulder this shame just to keep us alive. He looks away. It's the closest I'll get to approval. The room is silent as I cross to the center. The Ashlord's eyes flick around the room before settling on me. He looks delighted by it all.

My cousin Luca watches with clenched fists. His guitar's been abandoned to a corner. I call over to him and smile. "The Contested, Luca. Play the Contested."

Oxanos looks surprised again, but he crosses over and takes his position diagonal from me. It's a dance he should know, if he's had any formal training at all. The Ashlords have their traditional dances, but the Contested is something they created just for us.

Our people sailed to their land centuries ago, intending to conquer. Only, we failed. With the help of their gods, the Ashlords defeated our ancestors. We were stranded on foreign soil, and the Ashlords forced us to bow to them. Most Ashlord dances tell a story. The Contested is a dance that's meant to show our role in the Empire, not as rulers, but as subjects. The longer strides and gliding turns are intended to favor them. Each year the dance is performed to remind every Dividian that our ancestors came and failed. It is a reminder that we live at their mercy.

But I will dance a new dance.

The music begins fast, but it's the Contested, which means it will only get faster. When Oxanos reaches for my hand, I give it to him freely. His skin is nearly burning, each palm furious with heat as he turns me twice. The steps of the dance have us circling, darting forward only to dart back again. Oxanos is a fine dancer, a graceful thing. He matches my rhythm easily as we reach the first chorus. Then I spin away, and clap twice.

The signal surprises Oxanos. The Contested is a competition, a battle of wills. Traditionally, the Ashlord will clap to the players, asking for a feverish pace the Dividian dancer struggles to match. My cousin sees the signal and the speed of his strumming doubles. I spin back into the Ashlord's arms as the rhythm of our steps and hips races to match the music.

Oxanos is nearing the edge of his comfort now. He doesn't sweat, because his kind never sweat, but he's gritting his teeth in concentration. As we reach the second chorus, I spin away, and clap twice more. Oxanos's eyes go wide. I hear the gasping echo around the room. My cousin answers. The pace doubles again. I spin back to the Ashlord, but he's far from ready.

I move my hips faster than he can match. My steps are lightning, his a flawed and broken thunder. He loses me on a turn and I dance a cruel circle around him, eyes fixed with fury. This is not how the Contested goes. When they televise their galas, it's always the Ashlord leaving the Dividian dizzy by the end. But Oxanos is not my king. I am not his slave.

He loses me, again and again, and suffers red-faced through the embarrassment of trying to catch back up with my steps. I answer without mercy. I punish him through perfection. I stomp my feet and swing my hips and toss my hair until he knows, at least tonight, he is nothing but a side-show. When the music ends, I'm sweating and breathless.

It's traditional for the loser to bow, but the Ashlords are fond of telling us they only bow to the gods. Oxanos glares around the room, then at me, before setting his jaw and walking out the front door of the bar. It's quiet. The only sounds we hear are the door banging shut, his boots crunching in the desert dark. No one's foolish enough to cheer or shout or celebrate, but Amaya slips a cold drink into my hand. She taps the neck of her bottle against mine and smiles.

"Look sharp, girl. I don't think that's the last Ashlord you'll have to outdance."

5

TRUE FREEDOM

ADRIAN

Daddy's got us set up well before the Crossing match begins.

His private box in Lady's Stadium is normally the opposite of private. He's always believed with the right drink and the right view, any man will be willing to make a deal. I've watched him cozy up to oil tycoons and ship builders, tobacco farmers and war veterans. I didn't know the scope of what he was planning, but every conversation was a brick in the road to a second Rebellion. He's been crafting his war quietly, patiently.

Which means his final pitch is for me.

He's got his money, his troops, and his rebels. All he needs now is a face to put on the posters. The other seats sit empty. It's just Antonio Rowan and Daddy, sipping their drinks and talking up the two teams below us like a game could possibly matter right now.

"I like the kid from Panhandle," Antonio is saying. "Fastest quickling I've ever seen."

Daddy makes a thoughtful noise. "Never seen him before."

"He'll keep it interesting," Antonio replies. "But Sanctuary's defense is one of the best in the league this year. I've got a little side action on them."

I sip my own drink, watching the players stretch in the arena below, my mind leagues away. We spent all night watching the broadcasts. How would Furia react to our announcement? Only natural that the gossip wove its way through every newscast. We saw Pippa's interview. An Ashlord noble; this year's favorite. Daddy pulled videos of her amateur races months ago and had me studying them. She's fast and smart, a hell of a rider. But most of the amateur races are contact free. The *actual* Races require knowing how to fight, how to defend your ashes, and how to strike someone down without killing them.

One broadcast called my entry a revolution that could change the stagnant scene in phoenix racing. Others described it as a doomed sideshow. I'm too big, or too blunt, or too slow to matter. Some channels were crude enough to link footage of the last Longhand who entered the Races. He was beaten to death just before the second leg began. A team of Ashlords took their time killing him. Murder's not legal, even in the Races, but only one of them ever got put on trial for it. According to reporters, that rider spent the last twelve years in prison. The newscaster was kind enough to predict I'd make it out alive, but whether or not I'd be in one piece at the end was another question altogether. Daddy says they're blowing enough smoke to call it a fire.

His war depends on the attention, on me. I try not to think about how much it all weighs as I take another sip and the two teams line up below us. Crossing is a simple and brutal sport. Two teams of seven. The court is fifty paces wide and three hundred paces in length. When the gun fires, both teams release. The first team to get one of their players across the opposite line wins that round. Teams are made up of quicklings and bruisers, sometimes a few hybrids. It's easy to tell the big boys from the fast ones.

My eyes settle on the Panhandle runner Antonio mentioned. He's short and lighter-skinned, with legs as wide as doors. Daddy raises his glass and toasts with Antonio as both of the teams settle into racing positions. The arena is narrow, but the starting block's even tighter. All seven members hunch shoulder to shoulder, waiting for the burst, their minds racing through practiced formations and counterformations. Their only weapons are their bodies and how fast they move them.

A gunshot thunders out. The crowd erupts as both teams launch into motion.

Panhandle's team swings five right, two left, an overloaded formation. Sanctuary's formation is a reaction to theirs. A classic balanced set. Two on the right, two down the middle, and three to the left. At least one bruiser runs in each pack.

It takes two seconds for both teams to get up to a full sprint, and two more seconds to collide in a crunch of bone and body at center court. Panhandle's quickling darts out from behind a veil of bruisers, cutting center and bursting through the gap in Sanctuary's defense. Antonio's right.

He's the fastest person I've ever seen. He highsteps the first lunging tackle, avoids a second swipe, and looks like he's going to break free.

But a desperate shoestring tackle catches him by the ankle, staggering his strides. On the opposite side, two of Sanctuary's sprinters have broken free, and they race to cross the finish line, chased by Panhandle's too-slow bruisers. The horn blows and the first point goes to Sanctuary. Match attendants pull the weak and wounded away as substitutes step in to replace them. "Didn't I tell you?" Antonio asks. "Sanctuary is brutal."

The remaining rounds play out the same way. Panhandle steals a few points, but they can't keep up with Sanctuary's athleticism. I find myself half watching the collisions and the sprints and half watching the crowd around us. A few rows beneath our booth, a couple's enjoying the game. They're about my age, and it looks like a first date. He's nodding a lot, talking too fast, laughing too loud. She's nervous, too, though. Every now and again something he says has her blushing like a desert rose.

Down a few rows, a father sits with his three boys. He orders them a bag of salted hardpans and shows them how to crack the outer shells with their teeth. They laugh at a face he makes, and watching them, it's like they'll live forever. The crowd's full of similar moments.

Something about the whole scene has my stomach turning.

The match ends. Antonio heads off to collect his winnings. Daddy tells him to come by around dinnertime. We walk together, matching each other's quiet. He leads us away from the stadium, but doesn't take us home. I follow him—the way I always have—and figure out where we're heading as we reach the outskirts of town.

I frown. "This is your pitch?"

"It's more of a plea than a pitch, Adrian."

We wind through the dusty streets until they widen out, dumping us into a red-dusted desert that's empty of houses but full of ghosts. The graveyard waits at the edge of the city.

"You saw that couple?" he asks. "Right in front of us?"

I nod to him. "Looked like a first date."

He laughs. "I suspected as much. You know, the two of them are old enough to fight in our revolution. More than old enough. What else did you see?"

My stomach turns again, but Daddy is waiting for an answer. I take my time with the details. I talk about the father and his three sons. Daddy points out that they're too young, but the father wasn't too old. I describe a few of the vendors moving through the grandstands. The crowd of university students who were off to our right, laughing and drinking loudly enough to annoy everyone but each other. He nods and listens. I know he saw those details, too.

"We start this war," he says, "and they march with you. I wanted you to see the cost, Adrian. Sons will lose fathers. Husbands will lose wives. Friends will watch their comrades take their final breaths. I took you to that game so that you never forget the cost of what we're about to do. But you needed to see this, too. There's another side to every coin."

There's no fence to mark the area. Just stones rising up unnaturally from the sand. Some are wreathed in flowers,

others long cracked and faded. An attendant patrols the opposite side, hunting rifle settled against his shoulder. Daddy
lifts a hand in greeting and the man nods back.

"Our ancestors came north after the Dividian were defeated. That was the first division. Our people didn't like
the sudden reliance on the gods. We valued freedom too
much. And while the Ashlord gods offer many things, freedom is not one of them. It is a relationship of bondage. It always has been. That's why we separated from the Ashlords.
That's how the Reach was born."

It's not hard to see where he's heading. The truth of this
story is in my bones. I keep walking at his side, thinking
about our history. I've heard him tell the story he's about
to tell hundreds of times, but I've always felt like there was
more. Truths he kept quiet because I was only a child. I
have a feeling this time will be different.

"Early treaties failed. The Ashlords—and their gods—
didn't like the idea of a group of people unwilling to bow.
They tried to take all that from us. The Rebellion happened.
It's been forty-eight years since our war with them ended."
Daddy starts down the familiar graveyard rows. "As you
know, we failed. We lost. Most of the Purge happened in the
years that followed. Every first son and first daughter from
the Reach was rounded up and executed. Some escaped.
Sailed north and never came back. Others took new names
and went back to new villages. But the Ashlords had our inscription lists. They knew who fought. How many children
they had. Where they lived.

"It took thirty years of hunting, but eventually they found
every single name. Your mother told me her real name after

you were born. It was the first time she was ever really afraid. The Ashlords hadn't executed an escapee in nearly a decade, but now we both had something to lose. We thought the trails had gone cold. . . . I killed the first Ashlord they sent for her. It was easy, once I figured out why he was there."

The graves whisper at our passing feet. I never knew he killed anyone. The sun shines down overhead. We keep walking.

"She was smarter than me. Always was. Said they'd keep coming. They'd send more and more of them. She took the blame when they came back since they were going to take her anyway. Told them she'd killed the man. They took her and she made me promise not to do anything. She wanted me to raise you. Make you a man."

He doesn't cry, but his voice buries itself in grief. We stop in front of Mother's headstone. This stretch of land was set aside for them: the firstborns. Sons and daughters who paid the price for the Reach's rebellion with their lives. She was the last one they buried here. I was only two years old. I don't remember any of it. I can barely remember her face.

"You saw what we might lose if we go to war. But this?" He gestures to Mother's grave. "This is what's already been taken from us, Adrian. We dared ask them for freedom, and they put our loved ones in the ground for it. My older brother was killed, too. I'm alive because I was the second. Your mother's dead because she was the first. It was just a number game to them."

I can feel a tightness in my chest. Until now it's all been practice. Training sequences. Riding phoenixes. Studying alchemy. For the first time, it feels like there's an actual weight on my shoulders. I am walking into the unknown. Real blood will spill.

"I know you're unsettled," Daddy says. "I'm sending you down there to start a war. I've been around you long enough to know that you're not afraid for yourself. I know full well you can survive anything. You're afraid for everyone else. What happens if you win? What happens if we actually go to war?

"But hear me say this, Adrian. Everything you saw today, that first date, that man and his three boys? That's all an illusion. A false peace the Ashlords allow us to have. The truth of this world is buried all around you. They did all this to send a message. You are not free. You are at their mercy. And if you rise again, this is what they will try to take from you."

He kneels, and he's old enough that it costs him something. I watch him wipe dust from my mother's grave. "I ask this of you, Adrian. Rise. Stand up. Show our people true freedom."

6

DREAMS AND NIGHTMARES

PIPPA

You spend the whole morning surrounded by publicists. Statements are drafted and dismissed. The critics are still flocking and frenzied. Your most suggestive photos are being paraded on every news channel, half screened with the blurred faces of your accusers. There's nothing shocking about what they say. It is how men have always seen you, and dreamed of you, and wanted you. The accusations are welcomed by other men who will never get to dance with you, or taste your lips, or know your bed. The rumors work because they're feeding the desperate what they've always wanted and could never have.

Your publicists turn away thirty-seven interview offers. Money slips back into the pockets of certain sponsors who are pulling out amidst the storm. They forget that dark clouds and strong winds only mean lightning's about to strike. You know they'll want back in when you're illuminating the whole damn sky, but you will not forget and you will not forgive.

You're far more worried about Bravos. He sends you a single text from his public phone:

> if it wasn't true, you would have denied it, right? finding
> out this way? c'mon.

That's the text the hackers will pull and parade around the Chats. The two of you have given them little tastes just like it ever since the fake breakup. That was always the plan.

Feed the public, let the other racers think you'd split, and then win the Races together. Bravos can't hold a candle to you when it comes to riding or alchemy, but he's one of the top duelers in Furia. Together, you'd have taken first and second place easily, but now you're not sure if his recent message is part of the plan or a sign of *actual* anger, because you know he's right. You didn't tell him about the beholder shots and you feel so guilty about it.

As the publicists flap around like caged birds, you keep checking your burner phone. But Bravos hasn't texted and you know he's been awake for hours now. It has you half worried and half furious, because you actually love him. Bravos is the one man you want to dance with you, to taste your lips. The idea of losing him to Furia's hungry circuit of false rumors is enough to make your teeth grind.

Evening arrives and your head publicist, Zeta, has two action plans for you.

"First thing: you win the Races. You're the daughter of two former champions. Fulfill their prophecies for you, and almost all of this will go away. Just ask the Longhands or the

Dividian. The only thing that matters in the Empire is who wins. Do that and this all goes away."

You nod. "Consider it done."

Zeta says, "You won't like the next one."

"Why not?"

"You need to throw the spotlight somewhere else. Even if it's just for a few hours."

She's right. You don't like it. "Fine, who?"

"Have you ever heard of the Alchemist?"

Zeta pulls the video you saw the other day. You watch the girl leap through the air and land on the reappearing horse. You're nodding, but not understanding what Zeta wants.

"And?"

"We did some research," Zeta says. "In the last fifteen years, fourteen of the Qualifiers have been boys. The Empire Racing Board always talks about how equitable the Races are."

"And they are," you reply. "Girls always outnumber the boys in the Races. They win more often, too."

"Which is true," Zeta counters. "But in the one instance that the Empire Racing Board gets to *select* a participant, they're completely biased against Dividian girls. So all you have to do is talk up the girl's video. Say it shows the kind of brilliant riders the Empire Board's been unfairly keeping out of the Races. Make it about the advancement of women. I'll write up something about how this is their chance to put the most competent scholarship rider in the Races, regardless of gender."

You're nodding now, seeing the genius of Zeta's plan.

"So the spotlight is on the Dividian girl and the Empire

Racing Board. What will that get us? An hour of newscasts without those blurred creeps claiming me as their mistress?"

"An hour or two," Zeta says. "We just need to stop the bleeding long enough to get us to the Races. Once we're there, the talk won't be about the way you look. It'll be about how you ride."

You know that's not entirely true, but no point correcting Zeta now. She's done her job. It's time for you to do yours. "Set up the interview," you say. "Let's get it over with."

The interview's arranged, and brief. You recite the memorized script, and Zeta's plan sets everything into flawless motion. As you sit in your room, alone for the first time all day, the talking heads hound representatives of the Empire Board about sexism. Ten minutes pass without your name on anyone's lips, and that's the freest you've felt all day.

Until your burner phone vibrates. It's from the phone you gave Bravos a few weeks ago.

> finally, they've stopped spitting out these lies about you.
> so sorry, love. i've been stuck in interviews all day. left
> my burner phone at home. But I love you. The plan's still
> the plan, right? Call me later.

You're so thankful to read his words, to know that he's not mad, that you start typing a response. But halfway through the first sentence you remember the rules. Always ten minutes between texts. Hackers will catch quick signal bursts if the two of you aren't careful. If other competitors know you're teaming up, strategies will change. You want to keep the damage control to a minimum. Dinner and your parents are waiting downstairs, but you sit there in bed, the burner phone clutched to your chest, until the ten minutes pass.

you ARE my plan. I'll call in a few hours.

You descend the marble steps. The hall is silent, except for the occasional clatter of silverware. Dividian butlers move in and out of the dining room. One holds the door open as you approach and offers a wide smile. Mother and Father are already seated at the crystalline dining table. You're expecting to be scolded, but they both look up with smiles of their own. The table is big enough to seat thirty, but it's just the three of you tonight. You take your seat across from Mother, who sparkles in her eveningwear. Father's looking fine, too, in his charcoal suit.

You remember they're attending a play tonight.

"A little late, Pippa."

"Sorry, Father. I had an interview arranged. I wanted to watch the responses."

He nods. "I'm certain Zeta has everything sorted out."

"She has. All I have to do now is win."

"That's the easy part," he replies with a smile.

Mother's more sympathetic. "It's not the easy part. It's the hardest part, but you think like me and you ride like him. If it wasn't illegal, I'd throw a few thousand legions down on you."

Father offers a roguish smile. "Who says I haven't already done just that?"

You can't help but smile. You love it when they joke. A

butler sets a plate in front of you. Flamed merepeck, encircled by roasted greens and dappled in a boiled rose sauce. It's the first thing you've eaten since breakfast, and gods is it better than the rest of your day. You catch your mother winking at your father. You'll never get tired of seeing how in love they are.

"Tell me the story of how you met again."

It's always been your favorite, because it never gets old. Besides, you're still fighting the butterflies Bravos gave you just by sending a text. In a way, you've always held your romances up to theirs. For the first time, it feels like you have something that can stand its ground, because for once you're actually in love with someone who feels worthy.

Father laughs. "Well, I was in my room, going through my morning routine."

"Late for class," Mother corrects. "He was in a dorm that should have been empty. I volunteered that year to help with the gardens around the property. One of them was just outside the men's dormitory. Some of the windows . . . looked into the baths."

You love how Mother always blushes at this part and how loud Father always laughs.

"A fact that's always made me curious," he says.

Mother raises a single, perfect eyebrow. "It helped clarify the claims of hopeful suitors."

You groan at that confession. "Mother."

She laughs, which makes you laugh. You don't ask what needed clarification.

"So there I was," Father says. "Wearing only my long underwear and my riding cap. Shirtless and shaving in front of a mirror. I'd gone to the sink nearest the window, because it was just so stuffy that day. I opened it a tick and started. Wanted to look fresh for class."

"To make up for how late you were?" Mother asks.

"Exactly," he replies. "And then I heard this noise. I swear, the blade almost slipped across my neck and ended me, then and there. I turned, though, and there was this beautiful woman at the window. It was so unexpected. I couldn't think of anything to say. So instead, I turned to her, tipped my cap in that old-fashioned way, and went back to shaving.

"And though this next part is unproven, I believe your mother stood there and stared a little longer, because she liked what she was seeing. Certainly, accounts of the event differ."

Mother shakes her head. "I ran, Marcos. You know I ran."

"But you couldn't run forever," he adds, smiling. "When I submitted my name for the Races, she was the clerk working the Empire Board's front office. I handed her my papers and when I realized who she was, I just sort of went speechless in front of her."

"You should have seen his reaction." Mother laughs. "It was adorable."

"I asked her on a date. You know what she said, Pippa?"

Of course you know, because this is your favorite story.

"She said she didn't date riders."

Father nods. "And I asked, 'Not even if you've seen them half naked?' She reconsidered after that. We went for drinks at the Beguiler. She told me she was glad I was entering the Races that year, because she planned on winning them the next. I remember laughing, but gods, you should have seen just how serious she was. I knew then and there I'd marry her."

They smile at each other again. You and Bravos met at a bar, so you won't have some classy shaving story to tell your children, but you think it's more than enough that they'll see the two of you smile at one another like your parents are smiling at one another now. You're so hopeful for that future that you ask the one question you've always been too afraid to ask.

"What would have happened if you had raced the same year?"

They both smile at the question. Mother's the first to answer.

"I would have won, obviously."

It's such a quick, direct response that you all laugh, but Father can't hide his first reaction to it. There's a flash of something on his face and you recognize it instantly. He wants to object, to beat his chest, to call himself a champion again. That burning and competitive part of him snaps back to life at your mother's words. He takes a long swallow of wine before answering.

"I would have raced like hell," he says eventually, with false humility. "And she still would have waltzed across the finish line before me."

You smile at him, but you're startled by the lie, the pride he's still breathing out like smoke. For years, you've been watching the old Races on vintage chat-casts. And you've always favored your mother's chances in an imaginary race between the two of them.

Watching Father was like watching a storm. Fast and reckless and vengeful.

But watching Mother? That was like watching whatever person, whatever god, had summoned the storm into being. She moved every competitor like a piece on a game board. Her phoenix rebirths were masterpieces, her chosen route flawless. No one in the history of the Races has ever won by such a wide margin.

As they head to the theater and as you return to your room, it takes a long time to figure out the real question you wanted to ask, the one hiding beneath the words you spoke aloud:

Would you have ever married if one of you had lost to the other? Would I even exist?

You didn't ask the question because you think you know the answer. Your father's pride would have never borne such a burden. He couldn't have ever faced the prospect of a life with someone who bested him. Fate favored him enough to let him ride in his own year, leaving the question of who was the best a permanent mystery.

Lying down, you let your eyes trail the dark walls. You think about Bravos. How often has he said second place would suit him just fine? How long has he been hiding his own pride? He's not quite as competitive as your father, not really, but you know that when the Races begin and eternal glory is on the line, people change. Could Bravos really live with second place? Or would it eat him alive over the years?

You hate the answer to that question. Deep down, you know Bravos would not suffer second place. Not for long. Champions wear their crowns for life. It would always be

you stepping into the spotlight, always you giving interviews, and always you smiling at the crowd.

All while Bravos withered in your shadow.

It would break him, and eventually break the two of
you. As you trace the inevitable steps, it's not hard to see
where that road would lead.

He's not strong enough to be second, but you are.

You already know that you're the best. You've already
pulled all the necessary strings to arrange a victory, so now
all you have to do is hand him the crown and live happily
ever after. Your parents will think it a grand disappoint-
ment. Zeta—and maybe the rest of the world—will call it a
disaster, but stubbornly you remind yourself that this is *your*
life, it's *your* future.

And you want that future to be with the man you love
at your side.

7

THE QUALIFIER

IMELDA

The knock at our front door comes early in the morning.

I stare at the ceiling, listening to house sounds. Someone is on the couch, stirring sleepily. Someone else is at the table. I'd guess Father, sipping coffee. The door creaks open and I can imagine my mother smiling out at whoever's waiting there.

Farian wouldn't knock. Anyone who really knows us wouldn't. I'm scared it's Oxanos. Last night was his fault. He asked for the dance, and we all know how he intended it to go. He wanted to press his hips to mine for a few minutes. He wanted to make my father's skin crawl, to bury my family's honor with a smile. All I did was beat him at his own game.

The dread doubles when I hear the voices. Several people introduce themselves to my mother. City-bred voices. None of them are Oxanos, but all of them are Ashlords. I'm terrified; then I hear my mother's voice calling my name through the paper-thin walls.

"Imelda."

I don't bother putting on proper clothes. It's not our clothes the Ashlords look down on. It's our skin, our height, our everything. I fix the strap of my overalls and walk out to face them.

Father's at the kitchen table. He looks up, worried and helpless, as I walk past. I don't know how to tell him it's all going to be okay. Mother holds out a protective arm and wraps it around my shoulders. The three Ashlords stand just outside the door. They're all tall and graceful, skin so polished they're almost shining in the sunless dawn.

"Imelda Beru?" One is a woman. She steps forward and eyes me. "The Alchemist?"

I nod, a little surprised she's using that nickname. "That's me."

"My name is Ayala," the woman says. "You're to come with us. You've been chosen as a possible candidate for the scholarship position this year. We'll escort you to the capital to be interviewed. There's a chance you'll be competing in the Races as the Qualifier."

Mother's staring at me. Back in the kitchen, Father chokes on his coffee. I hear Prosper's voice and my uncle quieting him from the couch. Ayala's words have woken everyone up but me. I still feel like I'm walking through a dream world, grasping at impossibilities. I stare at her and say the only thing in my head that sounds rational.

"How many will be interviewed?"

One of the male Ashlords stiffens, like a Dividian asking a question offends him. Ayala doesn't mind at all, though. She just smiles a little wider. "Seven others."

Seven others? If Farian heard that, he'd freak. My odds of being the Qualifier have just increased dramatically. Thousands of applicants and hopefuls spread out across the Empire. Now there are only eight people left? I want to ask about the kinds of tests they'll use, what kind of etiquette I'm expected to show. Instead, I let those questions drift away on the wind. I'm not going to start off by looking ignorant in front of the Racing Board's hired officials.

"When do we leave?" I ask.

"Once you've packed your things," Ayala replies. She turns to my mother now. "We'll arrive before nightfall. Your daughter will stay in one of the finest hotels in Furia. An attendant will accompany her and keep her safe at all times. Tomorrow, she'll be interviewed. After the interviews, there will be a dinner for all the candidates. She'll be sent home if she isn't chosen."

"And if she is?" Mother asks.

"Training. Publicity telecasts. Then the Races await."

Mother nods absently. She's imagining Maxim or Gavriel or Cassiopia sitting down with me to ask interview questions. All the shows she pretends not to watch every morning.

I speak softly, not trusting my voice. "Thank you. I'll get ready."

Mother closes the door. She hooks her arm in mine, kisses me on the forehead, and leads me back inside. The room's almost spinning. Father stands. Coffee's spilled all over the table behind him, but he ignores it. Only Prosper has a voice.

"Is this serious? Are they serious? This can't be serious!"

They sit me down on the couch because my legs are

starting to shake violently. Mother rushes into my room, pulling clothes out of corners, stuffing whatever's clean into a travel sack. Uncle Manu stands in the corner, reciting names of racers with Prosper and laughing like he's a kid again. Father comes back with a glass of water and makes me drink it.

"You're going to be okay."

I try to give some sign that I hear him, but everything's still spinning.

"Imelda," he says. "You are Imelda Beru. Last night, you proved you've got as much fire as any of them. Be respectful, be careful, be yourself. You can do this."

I nod.

Mother calls, "Where are your socks? Why don't you have clean socks?"

I don't answer. The room's stopped spinning, but my mind's racing ahead to Furia. I have to beat out the other scholarship kids first. I wonder who they are and what they've done to make the final cut. Even if I do manage to get myself chosen, it won't matter if I'm not ready for the *actual* Races. Every year there's a Qualifier, a Dividian rider like me. We always cheer for them to do the unthinkable. They rarely do. Only two have ever won.

I can be the third.

Fear and dread rise up in my chest, threatening to choke me.

"Hey." Father's voice cuts through the noise. "You can do this."

He offers a hand and pulls me to my feet. Prosper nudges up against my side. I push back his hair and smile down.

Mother's there, too, pressing the travel bag into my hands. I kiss them all before shouldering the bag and heading for the door.

"Tell Farian what happened," I call over one shoulder. "If I'm chosen, the exclusive is his!"

They call out their love and I force myself to turn, to walk, to not look back. Ayala's up in the saddle, one hand on the reins of the *gorgeous* horse she's leading toward me. It's more finely groomed than most of the phoenixes in Martial's barns. She hands him off to me and waits until I'm up in the saddle to start trotting back to the road. Ayala wears her hair short for an Ashlord, but she rides a horse the way they always do, like a straight-backed statue.

"Why was I chosen?" I ask.

A few faces sneak glances from behind curtains. The other two Ashlords lead us north, through the last section of village and into the waiting desert.

Ayala turns back to me. "You didn't see the video?"

I frown at her. "I made the video."

"Not that video." Ayala smiles. "That one was impressive, but I meant Pippa's interview. This year's favorite. She stood up for you. Accused the Empire Racing Board of favoring men. She said if they let someone in who had less skill than you, it'd prove how sexist the board members are. Don't tell anyone I told you this, but you're pretty much a lock."

I'm stunned. Pippa. If there's a name everyone knows in this year's Race, it would be hers. The daughter of Prama and Marcos, both former champions in their own right. It has me thinking of all those famous Ashlords and their catchy, singular names. Which echoes into a second thought about all the Dividian with their reduced four-letter surnames, entire histories erased by the very people who are inviting me to their glorious Races.

The newscasters have been treating this year like it's Pippa's inheritance, like she's destined to win. I'm surprised someone of her status has even heard of me.

"Why would she stand up for me?"

"She likes you?" Ayala suggests. "Or she wanted the spotlight off her own scandal?"

The road twists, rising up and around. The sun's diving down at us out of the clouds. I slip my riding hood overhead and tug at the chin until it fits comfortably. Ayala and the other Ashlords don't do the same until a few hours later, when they finally feel the heat of the day. We ride hard as we make our way to the city.

Not a racing standard pace, but fast enough to have us tearing across the terrain, passing towns and villages. It doesn't feel like a normal, twelve-hour day. Time speeds up, slows down. The six hours become six seconds or six eternities, I can't decide which. The sun sets and mountains loom to our right, cutting through clouds to break the sky into great, smoky sections. Ayala talks freely with me, but the other two Ashlords don't say a word the entire trip.

I learn that she works for the Empire Racing Board. In fact, she turned down a bunch of other jobs so she could help with the scholarship program. She's passionate—almost too much—about the Dividian people. When she asks me personal questions, my other escorts glance back their disapproval, but she outranks them and doesn't seem to care what they think, either.

"There it is," she says as night falls around us. "Furia."

A distant brilliance lights the valley. The glow dances between the bordering mountains like a lake of gold. Ayala leads us down and it's hard not to stare at everything. Even the buildings along the outskirts tower above us. The nearest city to us—Avass—has a few high-rises and temples, but nothing like this.

It's like the Ashlords are bridging their way to heaven.

We pass the first of several pyramids. Surrounded by glass-and-steel buildings, the temples look more like god-sized fists punched up through the earth. Great tiers of mortared stone slabs, all rising and narrowing to the flat-roofed prayer rooms in the upper temples. Stairs run up each side like rib cages. Each god's servants flock in the shadowed interiors.

Somehow the world stops moving at an impossible speed. As we dismount, stable boys come forward to collect our horses. We stand before a dark-bricked building. It sits squarely between much larger buildings, but Ayala assures me it's the finest and most historic hotel in the city. She says this like I might somehow be disappointed by it. And only as we stand there, waiting for a bellhop to answer the door, do I notice the people. We're on a main drag and it looks like everyone's gathered for a parade. Except there's no parade. Just thousands of folks living their lives.

There are plenty of Dividian. The women wear fine business dresses. The men too-tight suits. They weave in and out of everything like this is *their* city, but every time an Ashlord strolls down a sidewalk, or prowls into a bar, they fade to background noise. I listen as the owner of a nearby restaurant tries to lure a passing couple in with the promise of the finest food in Furia. They smile their no to him with divine elegance.

"Come on," Ayala says. "Your room's ready."

The entire interior is carpeted. Not even our town hall has carpet. Just some fancy rugs here and there. I glance down at my dirty shoes and dusty ankles, but Ayala smiles again, leading me off to one side. A trio of Dividian men stand there in neat bow ties. The other Ashlords sit first, letting the men slip off their shoes one at a time. The trio works fast. One scrubs away mud and polishes each riding boot. Another takes a wet rag and wipes the dust from Ashlord ankles. The third sizes up their feet and provides them with a pair of the hotel's complimentary slippers.

Ayala gives me a shove forward when the other two Ashlords are finished.

"Do her next," she orders.

Her fellow escorts lift an eyebrow at the decision, but the Dividian rush to obey Ayala's request. I'm helped into a high-backed chair. They remove my tattered riding boots and get them as clean as they've been since I first found them. Something snakes through my gut as the second man starts rubbing away at toes and ankles. There's something wrong about being made clean, made like the Ashlords. He sees my frown when he's done and whispers up to me.

"The dirt's gone, but don't worry, I couldn't get rid of the calluses."

We share a grin. The third Dividian steps forward, sliding slippers over both of my feet. I thank them all so pro-
fusely that Ayala has to pull me away.

My heart beats in triples. Then skips beats. It's the first
time I've seen it all so clearly. There are two worlds, and I
know *exactly* which one I belong in. Even if Ayala's offering
me a temporary glimpse of their world. The men bow as she
leads me off through the hotel.

The other Ashlords abandon us. She nods them off before
escorting me to the third floor. "You have a corner room,"
she says. "It's quite a view."

She swipes something by the handle and the door whisks
open without a touch. I follow her in, feeling as disoriented
as I felt that morning, like the world's started spinning just
a little too fast. Ayala shuts the door behind us. As she does,
the casual calm leaves her face and she steps closer. I can
smell some kind of cherry tobacco on her breath.

"I need to know," she says. "Do you want to be in the
Races or not?"

I stare at her. "I thought—Isn't that why I'm here?"

"But do you *want* it? Qualifiers get hurt, you know? It
will be hard riding, hard fighting. You'll have to be smarter
than all of them. I need to know if this is what you *really*
want."

It is what I want, what I've wanted since I was little.
Martial always terrified me. Not because he's scary or anything ridiculous like that. Looking at him is like looking at
the impossible. Farian and I could play as riders on holy
days, but I never let myself believe it'd be anything more
than a game. "Yes," I finally answer. "This is what I want."

Ayala smiles. "Good, because you're the one, Imelda. There have been discussions all day. The Empire Racing Board wants you to be the scholarship rider in the Races. The others will interview tomorrow, but you've already been chosen. You're going to ride in the most prestigious event the Empire's ever known. We start training tomorrow. And with my help?"

She sets a firm hand on my shoulder.

"I think you could actually win it."

8

TEN FACES

ADRIAN

Furia.

The whole place is a clogged artery. Bodies, people, noise. Antonio's standing out on the balcony of our hotel. Daddy's tasked him with getting me to the start of the Races in one piece.

We arrived a few hours earlier by carriage, which felt every kind of wrong. Sitting and bouncing around in a box? Antonio's just being smart about it. We don't need every news outlet outside the hotel before I can settle in. Half the waitstaff is already casting sideways glances at us.

Besides, the carriage was practice for the city. The whole place is just one big box. Our room's tight as a noose. The hotel's in a confusing borough of claustrophobic streets and shops. We're on the top floor, but you look out and all you can see are more buildings. It's like a million people forgot the beauty of open space. Antonio saw I was restless and offered to take me out for a stroll, but I told him I'd rather sit in bed than knock knees with half the world.

When night comes, the noise is still there. Voices echo up from the alley below. People shouting and laughing, flirting and yelling. The Reach settles its bones before dark. If there's something that needs doing, it can be done at dawn. I lie there, turning from side to side, until Antonio knocks on my door. I glance out. It's still the middle of the night.

He looks in. "It's time. Come with me."

We walk through empty hallways. The front desk attendant has vanished. The lights in all the common rooms are low. Only our boots make any noise. Antonio leads me to the kitchen. It's empty, too. Great rows of plates and piles of spoons are set out to dry. He kneels in front of a brick-fire oven and lifts the latch. It leads down into the dark.

Antonio doesn't say a word as we descend. Every foul scent imaginable turns beneath our feet. Our movement stirs it all up, and before long I'm hacking coughs. Antonio just keeps moving through the labyrinth like he's walked this path a hundred times. I'm still coughing when the darkness ends. Antonio climbs a ladder and I follow.

Another hatch opens into a wine cellar. The place is bright with light. Ten men and women stand there waiting for us. They're bunched together, whispering, but at the sight of Antonio, everyone straightens. They line up, set their jaws, and wait for him to speak.

"Take a good long look, kid."

I do. There's a little bit of everything. Six are Dividian. Four are women. One's an Ashlord, which sits uncomfortably in my gut. He styles his hair in a faux-hawk, but he's a little old for the look. Next to him, a pair of Longhands grin out from among the rows of shining, corked bottles. I take time to look at each face, to memorize each detail. Freckles on noses, hats on heads, and all the little nooks every face has.

These are Daddy's people, which makes them my people.

"This is your extraction team." Antonio gestures at the standing group. "If something goes wrong or if something happens, you are to trust only these ten faces. You might have some smooth talker come up to you at the pre-event galas. Or after your victory. Whatever. If their face isn't in this room right now, you do not trust them. The *only* people worthy of your trust over the next few weeks are these ten faces."

Antonio points to the Dividian on the far right.

"Quay," the man says.

And the next.

"Elizabeth."

"Darby."

"Atl."

He works down the row, then asks me to repeat each name. When I can't, he has each person say their names a second time. This time I pay attention and when he asks, I can repeat them easily. But Antonio's careful, because Daddy's taught him how to be. He has the group say their names a third time, then shuffles the order.

I go down the new row and nail every single one. Then Antonio turns me around. He has them all say the word *freedom*. Without looking, I'm supposed to identify them by their voices. I get a handful right, but Antonio turns me back around, has them say their names *and* listen to their voices before running me back through it again.

The whole thing takes an hour, but by the end of it, I know their names, their voices, their faces, and their favorite foods. Antonio doesn't explain why the last one's necessary; he just wants to make sure this is a dossier I'll have in my head forever, because there isn't a scrap of paper he'd dare write any of this information down on. These are the Reach's spies. When we're set, he tips his dirty hat to them and we watch as they ascend a stone staircase.

"Those are your people," Antonio repeats to me. "I'll leave the city when the Races begin, but they know the extraction plan. Each of them has come over to our side— for one reason or another—and your daddy's set each piece spinning into motion just to make sure he gets you home safe. Arranging all this has cost money and lives. Do not forget those names. Do not forget those faces. And when you cross that finish line, don't you dare trust anyone whose favorite food you don't damn well know."

PART TWO

THUNDER

A storm wouldn't be all that fun without a
little noise.

> —Gold Man Jones, spoken
> three minutes before his
> death at the Battle of Oranges

9

IN THE MORNING QUIET

IMELDA

A polite knock wakes me up. It really is polite, too. It's not paired with a raised voice or drunken laughter or anything. Silence follows. I roll over, squint through the half-opened window, and realize the light funneling into the room is *not* from the sun. I grumble out from under the covers and throw a shirt on before opening the door.

Ayala is there. "Good morning!"

She smiles and I like her a little less. I actually raise a hand to shield my eyes from the glow of the hallway behind her. How is she dressed already? Is she wearing makeup?

"Huh," I say.

It's not a real response. It's not even a word, just a half-formed grunt. She continues smiling, maybe waiting for something more eloquent, but it's so very clear I have nothing else to offer her. It takes me a few seconds to figure out that I'm blocking the doorway.

"You're coming in?" I nod to myself. "You're coming in."

She laughs as I step aside. In the time it takes me to close the door, she already has both lamps on in the room. *I guess I'm waking up now.* Stumbling over to the table, I plunk down in the seat opposite her. She's busily setting out packages and bags that I didn't even notice she was carrying. I'm staring at them helplessly and trying to figure out how she carried them all with just two hands when my eyes find the most important thing she's brought me.

"Coffee!"

She slides the cup across and starts to scold me about the heat. Too late. I've already disappeared behind the mug's alabaster rim. It tastes rich, smooth. A little weaker than what Father makes, but that doesn't stop it from feeling like a step in the right direction.

Ayala waits for me to resurface. "I've brought a few training gifts."

From one of the bags, she removes a set of clothes. I see three pairs of riding pants and matching tops to go with them. At the bottom of the pile, an *official* Empire Racing Board jacket.

"Looks fancy," I manage to say.

"Expensive," she counters. "All the very *best* gear. The undergarments are a new flame-resistant line from Dominus. It might take you a few days to get used to reading your phoenix's temp with them on, but it saves you from the wear and tear of a full day's ride. Each of the shirts has breathable hoods to shade the sun. I'd guess you recognize the riding jacket."

Of course I do. It's the same one that's been worn for the last two decades. A simple black piece with the Empire Racing Board's echoing horse emblem on the right breast. The joints and shoulders are made of a stretching, smoke-gray material. Protection without sacrificing flexibility. It's the kind of outfit I've seen in all the pre-race advertisements. Only the models have always been Ashlord racers: Pippa, Bravos, Revel, Etzli.

This set belongs to *me*.

"Do they fit?"

Ayala looks offended. "No, you'll have to roll up the sleeves a few times."

I almost snort my coffee. Standing, I unfold one of the shirts. Ayala did her homework. The sleeves ride out perfectly. Even accounted for my shorter torso.

"It's a reactive fabric," she says. "It will wick your sweat during the day and keep in the warmth at night. On the house. But the last gift is something to borrow. I'll need it back."

She slides a wooden box across the table. The coffee is starting to kick in. I suppose if I *have* to wake up before dawn, I'd rather do it by opening very expensive and thoughtful presents. I'll have to let Farian know that a new bar has been set for our morning adventures.

My fingers find the edges of the wooden lid. It slides down along carved grooves and reveals something I've been waiting to get my hands on since arriving in Furia.

"A switch."

My fingers heft the weapon into the air. I marvel at the weight and balance of it. There's no question of the weapon's authenticity. It is a Race-standard switch. Not the knockoffs I played with as a little girl. The baton runs about the length of elbow to fingertip. It's polished brightly, and the wood is that clearly *burned* color that looks on the edge of flame. Only trees from the Burning Forest look that way. Cheaper vendors will use birch or oak and do their best to dye the material the same color. I've owned enough of them to know the paint peels after a few weeks. My fingers settle on the leather grip. I tilt it to get a look at the stamped *V* at the base of the handle. Versa's patented sweat-resistant leather. It's a thing of beauty.

"Give it a try," Ayala encourages.

I double-squeeze the grip. Ashlord magic snakes through the material and the wooden frame retracts. A leather whip shakes out to the floor. Light catches on the little glass claws dangling dangerously from each strand. I let them dance along the floor before squeezing the grip again. There's a *zip* noise as the whip returns to baton form.

"It's heavy. . . ."

It is beautiful, majestic, pristine.

Ayala nods. "You'll get used to the weight in training. That one belongs to my family. I wanted you to use it, though. It's exactly what you'll be using in the Races. I wondered if you had a style of fighting that you prefer? It will help us make the best use of our time."

Holding the switch makes everything feel *real*. I sit back down on unsteady legs and stare across at my mentor. I feel guilty for the first time. She's here to help me, what? Win the Races?

I might be closer than ever, but it sounds impossible all of a sudden.

"I'm not—I don't have a style. I'm one of the best alchemists you'll ever meet. I've always had a hand for it. I'm a strong rider, but I haven't had access to a horse for longer than an afternoon in a few years. As for fighting . . ." I have a hard time meeting her eye. "I don't know. We fought as kids, I guess? We were brawlers, though. Schoolyard fights. There's no style to it."

"I can work with that," Ayala assures me. "Sometimes a blank slate is better than a broken one. We'll run you through the basics. Stop looking so worried."

I nod, but the embarrassment still colors my cheeks. I set the switch down and it doesn't look dangerous on its own. It only becomes deadly when the hand that holds it can make it a deadly thing. My mind flashes back to previous Races. I've spent my whole life watching them, dreaming of being one of the riders. In all the excitement of the past few days, I somehow forgot the basic truth. There are three measures for every racer.

Alchemy. Riding. Fighting.

I was born for the first two, but I've never spent much time on the third. I trace back through all the Races I've seen and I can't remember too many champions who won *without* winning at least one fight. Some riders get out to big leads, sure. Others are clever enough to trail the group and make their move at the end. I can try to avoid duels, but what happens when I'm on the back of a horse coming down a tight stretch? Or in the dark of night with my back to my ashes, staring down an opponent? I'll have to fight.

I nod to Ayala. "When do we start?"

"Now."

I'm not tired anymore. The adrenaline running through

me tastes a lot like fear. Ayala waits while I slide into uniform. We gather the equipment and leave. The hallways are empty. The lobby boasts a lone Dividian bellhop at the front desk. He bows as Ayala breezes by him. The second she's past, he glances up and winks at me. I smile back.

The streets are alive still. Not bursting with the same life and noise they were when we arrived, but far from abandoned. We pass a pair of swaying girls. Both have their dancing shoes in hand, and dust coats their ankles. It is the end of the evening for them, but the beginning of a new day for others. Delivery carts take advantage of the empty streets. A pair of Dividian boys—no older than Prosper— hustle back and forth, setting little crates on the doorsteps of towering tenement buildings before leaping back onto the still-moving vehicles. Cats scurry down alleyways. An elderly woman taps out a cigarette on the balcony above us.

We earn a few looks. At first, I think people recognize me. Maybe they saw the video Farian posted. But then I realize that Ayala is the only Ashlord making her way through the quiet morning traffic. "Come on," she says, leading me off the main drag.

Streets intersect ahead. She guides us to the western edge of the city. I've only been through the city once, but I recognize the direction we're heading.

"The temples are this way."

She nods back but stays silent. I take my cue from her. It's not long before the sleeker buildings give way to the more bone-thick temples. There's a cruelty to them, almost as if they were summoned from the ground rather than built. No one in my family ever converted to the Ashlord religion. There are Dividian who have taken up worshipping their foreign gods, and I've never understood the decision. The gods are the reason we became their servants in the first place. They're the power behind every Ashlord threat, the reason we keep our heads low and our dreams even lower.

I might not worship their gods, but only a fool doesn't know the names.

On our right, the Fury's temple looms. The Ashlord god of strength and bravery. Great bonfires burn in every corner of the ziggurat. Each one surrounded by waiting priests. Firelight glints off the horns of their bull masks. The men are shirtless. The women in plain shifts. There's a healthy mix of Ashlord and Dividian in their number. No surprise that every tier is crowded with servants. The Fury has long been the most popular god in an Empire that worships war.

We round the building—close enough to catch warmth from the nearest fire—and head in the direction of a second temple. This one is less adorned. None of the rib cage–like tiers the others boast. In fact, it looks much more like a tower than a temple. Steep walls reach unbroken to the circular crown of the building. It's high—at least four stories—but I can still see the murder holes that look out in every direction over the city. I don't need to see priests in falcon masks to know this is the home of the Curiosity. The god who wakes, watches, and whispers.

Other temples flank the main road, each the domain of a different deity. The Butcher and the Hoarder and the

Dread. There's one temple at the end of the lane that's back-lit with electric blue light. It's the only one I can't figure out. "Which one is that?"

Ayala nods. "The god of next, the creator of progress. We call him the Striving."

Of course. The Striving. I eye the flickering, alien lights before our path takes it out of view. The same god who created switches in the first place. The one who hands the Ashlords their next technological fad every few years. We slip between worship cathedrals before arriving at our destination. An undecorated temple. There are no priests, no fires, nothing at all.

My skin starts to crawl. What is this place?

"This temple once belonged to the Veil," Ayala whispers.

Proximity breathes cold air over us. The closer we get, the more *surrounded* I feel by that empty feeling. Ayala glances left and right before leading me into the shadows.

The dark interior is massive and drafty. I'm wondering how we'll possibly train in here without any light when I spy the gaping holes in the back of the temple. Through them I can see the western gates framed by the first rays of sunrise. My eyes start to adjust to the light.

At the center of the room, there's a pile of waiting ashes. "Your horse," she says.

There's movement deeper in the temple. I watch the shadows resolve into the form of a young man. He can't be any older than twelve, and yet he's taller than I am, his arms roped with muscle. An Ashlord. It isn't until he grins that I recognize what's so familiar about him.

I've seen his face. The smile too.

"My cousin," Ayala announces. "Zion will spar with you."

I nod a greeting to him. He smirks back with that annoying Ashlord confidence. I try to remind myself that I have wiped smiles off Ashlord faces before. If I can outdance Oxanos, why not this boy? Why not the other racers? I have a fury that they'll never understand.

"Let's get started." I fix my eyes on him. "Try to keep up."

10

BRIGHT AND LOUD

ADRIAN

I take a seat across from the crystal mannequin. Squinting, I can see other identical machines filling the endless theater with a roulette of faces. It's like taking a step into the future.

The Reach has plenty of high-end tech, but nothing quite like this. The failed revolution set us back ten years, and for the first time it's glaringly obvious. Furia's advancements show no sign of slowing down, either, if the Striving keeps giving them new ideas to chase.

The woman interviewing me *appears* in the seated mannequin. Her skin glows golden, her hair's spiked and dark, and her eyes flicker with flame. I straighten my shoulders as she gives me the head-to-toe. The sight of me has her smiling, delighted.

"Ten seconds," someone calls from offstage.

Most of the competitors have completed their mandatory interviews. Pippa's already had three of them. I'm one of the last to go because hosts kept backing out at the last minute. Maxim and Tessadora and Gavriel. Antonio calls them cowards. I call them wise.

Interviewing me is a dangerous proposition.

Everyone talks about the Longhand rider who was killed in the Races, but only a handful of folks remember the showman who interviewed him. He was murdered, too.

The Empire thought he showed too much sympathy for the Reach. That's the mistake Cassiopia will be hoping to avoid today. Make me look good, and she's the host who gave the Longhands a national stage. Make me look too weak, however, and she's the host who drove down interest in the all-important Races. It's a fine line to walk.

I sit up a little straighter as Cassiopia's eyes find the camera. Her voice echoes out over scattered applause and cheering. Everything in the room dances with too-bright light.

"Welcome back to our coverage of the Races! The one hundred forty-first year is poised to be the most entertaining one in recent memory. There's a clear favorite everyone's chasing."

Behind her, an image of Pippa appears. She's leaning over her horse, jaw clenched and hair in a dark braid that drapes over one shoulder. She looks terrifying and beautiful. The graphics frame her like she's a descended goddess. It's such blatant favoritism, I almost laugh.

"Who's hot on Pippa's heels? There's the Alchemist, and the Spurned Lover, and Ever-Steady Etzli. . . ." Cassiopia casts a curious look in my direction like she's just noticed me. "But the casinos and bookies of Furia have pegged someone else as her most likely and looming threat. Ladies and gentlemen of the Empire, meet Adrian Ford."

A chorus of boos echo out. There's a little clapping, but the people most willing to drop thousands on a live seat are those who hate me. The thought has me smiling.

"Hear that, Adrian?" Cassiopia asks. "Not exactly a warm welcome to Furia."

She gestures, cueing my response. I keep the lazy grin and look right into the cameras as I say, "Guess I'll count myself lucky that fans aren't what gets any of us to the finish line."

"That's true, but are you at least worried the other riders will feel the same way the fans do? Let's be honest, the Longhands don't have a great history when it comes to the Races."

Before I can answer, visuals color the wall behind us. Cassiopia glances back at them.

"The last Longhand winner was nearly eighty-three years ago. Prior to that, no Longhand had successfully placed in the top three. Since the Reach's failed revolution, there have been three entrants. The first withdrew. The second, as you know, was killed. You are the third."

They flash the boy's portrait, then segue to footage of the brutal attack. It's hard to watch as the three Ashlord riders circle, as he falls to his knees, as they don't stop swinging their wooden switches. It is the fate the Empire predicts for me. They want me backing away and afraid before the Races begin. Even though genuine fear rushes through me, I decide to take a different road. Respect. I bow my head for a thoughtful second. I hope the family of the lost Longhand understands I am *with* them. Now and always.

Then I turn on Cassiopia. "I trust the rules of the competition. Murder's illegal in the Races. If someone tries to kill me, they risk throwing away the rest of their lives. Everyone who signs up for the Races knows this is a dangerous event. People die. Correct me if I'm wrong, but thirty-seven contestants have died since the Races began, and I'm pretty sure only three of them were from the Reach."

Cassiopia smiles. "So you're not afraid of the other riders?"

"It's hard to feel fear when you're bigger, stronger, and faster than everyone else."

"Bold words," Cassiopia cuts back. "Maybe you can help us understand this misplaced confidence. Can you give us a good reason to think you're anything more than a glorified sideshow in this year's event?"

I smile, thinking about that, and the answer that comes almost makes me laugh. Daddy told me to rise. So I rise. Standing up, I offer a little wink to the audience and start unbuttoning the front of my shirt. I'm halfway down before Cassiopia tries to wave me off.

"Adrian, I'm not sure this is entirely appropriate."

But the audience stirs excitedly. The stagehands all look unsure about whether or not they should intervene. Seconds later, my shirt is open and I'm grinning at the camera.

"*This* isn't a sideshow. *This* is years of hard work. *This* is how we're built in the Reach. I can ride, I can fight, and if you do both of those things, you can damn well win the Races."

I sit down and start buttoning the shirt back up. Across from me, Cassiopia is fanning herself, letting her eyes roam, and half smiling at my boldness. She's trying to treat my answer like it's cute. Maybe something a child would say, but it's hard to make me look small now.

"Bold move," she says after a moment. "But all they'll see is a bigger target."

"Yeah? Well, they better not miss."

I realize how far I'm straying from Antonio's plan. He wanted soft answers. A bare-bones pride. Too late for that. Cassiopia's smugness and the audience's distaste have every single one of my veins pulsing. These people have no clue what they're waking up. They've grown complacent, full of themselves. They've forgotten the people of the Reach were always destined to rise. They've forgotten that we almost did once.

Cassiopia wisely directs the interview to talk about my phoenix and my alchemical abilities. Both of them are safer topics by far. Conversations that will keep her head on her shoulders. She eventually veers into one topic that actually troubles me.

"What about the Madness?" she asks. "It's been some time since the god of passage intervened in the Races, but it happens. What will you do if that occurs this year?"

The Madness. One of the Ashlords' deities. Daddy had me watching footage from each of the years that he supposedly involved himself. Riders pulled off impossible stunts. People fell almost at random from their horses. All the research pointed to the same phenomenon that shook the foundations of both major wars: the Ashlord gods and their otherworldly armies. Secretly, I know that if the Madness involves himself this year, my chances drop down to almost nothing.

"I guess it could happen, but I'm far more likely to face

a wild creature. People have been attacked by wolves and wraiths and sunbursts more often in the Races than by the Madness."

"Still, the threat looms," Cassiopia replies. "Hasn't that really always been the separating factor in competition between Longhands and Ashlords? Our connection to the gods? Can you really say that you don't fear their meddling?"

The question is as big a trap as she can lay for me. Say yes and I make my people look weak. Say no and I'm taunting their gods. Daddy taught me to be brave, not stupid.

"Everything's a threat in the Races," I reply neutrally. "Everything."

Cassiopia nods like she's regained a foothold against me. Sensing a new theme working in her favor, she decides to keep pressing. But this time, she turns the conversation to Pippa.

"I want to end with a quote," Cassiopia says, glancing at her cards. "Pippa had this to say about you: 'It's the lightning you have to worry about. You always see the strikes before you hear the boom. . . . I'll ride hard and I won't look back. I'll be in the distance, and he'll just be the noise that follows.' Any response to that, Adrian?"

"She knows jack-nothing about storms."

Cassiopia frowns. "It sounded like an accurate description to me."

"If you're an observer."

"I'm not sure I follow."

"An observer," I repeat the word. "That's how a fan sees the Races. You and everyone else will be watching it from a distance. But that's not how storms work when you're in the middle of them. Storms are chaos. Rain pouring down, lightning striking, wind blowing, the thunder shaking everything. If you're right in the middle of it, there's no telling if the lightning or the thunder came first. Most times, you're too busy trying to stay alive to notice anything else."

"An interesting perspective." Cassiopia smiles. "Well, any last words before we close?"

I turn my eyes to the dark circle of the camera. It's not hard to imagine every boy and girl in the Reach leaning forward to listen. I can see Daddy in his chair, a drink in hand.

I want to wake them up.

I want revolution.

"Enjoy the storm."

The screen cuts away from me instantly. Cassiopia is quick to take my words and make them her own, describing this year as the most exciting storm they've had in decades. She lists a schedule of appearances and pre-race events before signing off with some catchy tagline.

House lights go up. The crystal mannequins in the audience start winding down. I watch the faces disappear before glancing back at Cassiopia. She looks unsmiling and cold as her image flickers out. She's afraid of how that went, the possible consequences. Maybe she should be. Stagehands flock forward to prepare for the next interview.

As I move into the shadows backstage, I turn a corner and almost walk right into Pippa. Her dark eyes flick briefly up. She doesn't look surprised. Her kind never do. But a pulse of heat fills the air as she takes a step forward and unexpectedly sets one burning hand on my shoulder. Her voice is lower than a whisper.

"An awfully pretty package. It's a shame they're going to break it."

I can only watch as she glides past. The heat goes with her, leaving the room feeling ice-cold. A shiver runs down my spine. She's just trying to intimidate me, get in my head. Let them try to break me. I press on to my dressing room and find Antonio waiting there for me.

"Not exactly what we planned," he notes.

"I'm just glad my hands weren't shaking as I undid the buttons."

"What made you unbutton your shirt? What angle were you playing?"

I offer him a grin. "Give them something to remember?"

He nods slowly. "Well, at least we know which night they'll come for you now."

"Which one?"

"The first night," he answers. "And the second. And the third. And the fourth."

A cold truth. His guess echoes Pippa's.

"Sounds about right. I'll be ready when they do."

Antonio nods. "You're more like your daddy than you know."

11

THE GREAT DISPLAY

PIPPA

Eleven riders and eleven horses. Decorators from the Empire Racing Board flutter back and forth, making sure riding shirts are tucked in and flowers are positioned just so. Naturally, you're standing front and center in the arranged display. A glance shows the other riders staggered in artful formation on your left and right. Morning light brightens the surrounding desert landscape. Hip-high barriers have been erected around each rider and their phoenix.

Interviews have been running all week. Revel promised victory. Etzli reminded the Empire she never makes mistakes. Imelda Beru's interview was almost painful, full of mumbled answers and hesitant smiles. Adrian was quite the opposite. The Longhand went bold and called you out, but you know champions aren't crowned for giving a good interview.

Words are wind.

Father would tell you that a champion has to be as

wicked as they are quick. Mother would say that every detail matters. The difference between glory and ruin can be
measured in a single stride. You take both of their lessons
into account today, because the Races don't start with a gunshot. They start now, your boots coated in red-desert dust,
at the Great Display.

A crowd of five hundred gathers. Each of them purchased an absurdly expensive ticket in order to attend. You
scan the ranks and recognize a good number of the waiting faces. It's a crowd of royal cousins, influential gamblers,
renowned journalists. These are the tastemakers who will
curate the Races for public consumption. They'll take back
the information they learn today and spread it like a flame
across the Empire.

An announcer begins. You half listen to his rendition of
the story of the Great Display. Every part of the Races is a
reminder. Each ceremony is a nod to the gods and the wars
your people won with them at your side. The Great Display
honors one of their very first gifts: the phoenix horses.

You have heard this story thousands of times. In past
years you have stood where the gathered crowd stands
now, proud of your lineage. But this year the presence of
the Longhand and the Dividian serve as a reminder. It is
not a story about one group of people, but three. It begins
with the Dividian ancestors arriving at *your* shores. Invad-
ers. Their great ships numbering in the thousands and their
soldiers pouring into the coastal cities with every intent of
conquering your ancestors. Until the gods answered.

The Madness opened the gates of the underworld.
The Fury honored your people's blood sacrifices and sent

thousands of flaming horses stampeding into battle. Those horses were the ancestors of the same phoenixes your people ride today. Their arrival marked a turning point for all three cultures. The Ashlords became rulers. The Dividian were defeated, abandoned on foreign soil, and eventually subjugated. Lastly, a group of disgruntled Ashlords headed north after the war, disliking their people's sudden taste for the gods. Proud men and women who refused to be dependent on something bigger than themselves. The town they founded grew into a city, which grew into a state, which blossomed into a country: the Reach.

It's a story you will never forget, and so as this year's announcer retells it, your eyes drift instead to your competition. Etzli stands on your right. She's shorter than you by a breath. Everything about her is reserved. She wears the Race-standard jacket, little makeup, her hair up in a tidy ponytail. She doesn't smile. Her hands do not shake. Like you, she was born for this.

On your other side, Adrian Ford. You try not to notice the way he looms over everything like a second sun. You note the sharp line of his jaw, the sprawl of his shoulders, the veined backs of his hands. He looks like he was carved by the gods themselves. Instead of fear, you feel adrenaline pulsing in your chest. You were born to ride, but you were also born to fight. Looking at Adrian Ford makes one thing clear: a worthy challenger has arrived.

"And we honor that day," the announcer is saying, "with a Great Display of our own. Behold your riders. Behold their horses. There are placards along each barrier that describe the chosen components for each summoning. As a reminder, these will be the first combinations that each rider has locked in for the opening of the Races. It's the first hint of what might unfold after the gunshot sounds. Come forward, witnesses! Let's see how this changes the gambling lines!"

You raise your chin and smile. Money and power have bought each person in the crowd access. It is their chance to ask questions and inspect the horses. The first patrons make a line straight for you. A well-dressed Dividian nods in greeting, pen and notepad in hand. Clearly a journalist. He kneels and inspects the waiting placard. You watch as he scribbles down components and reads the inscription. Others are circling curiously.

"Vibrancy," he notes with surprise. "That was your father's opening rebirth, no?"

Your smile widens. He's done his research. After a long deliberation, you decided to open the Races with the combination your father made famous. It was the one that helped him storm to an opening lead on the first day. You've trained with it for months. Vibrancy horses are known for two things: long strides and building speed. The longer they ride uninterrupted, the higher their top speed climbs. It is a summoning that has risks, too, though.

"So you're hoping to jump out into first?" the reporter guesses.

It's always better to let them wonder. You've learned that much from previous Races.

"Starting first is fine, but it's finishing first I care about."

He grins at that. "A summoning like Vibrancy depends on not bumping shoulders with other riders, right? Pretty risky considering the presence of Adrian Ford. Not to mention the recent breakup with Bravos. Tight quarters will slow you down."

"Nothing slows me down."

He scribbles that line on his pad before tipping his cap and heading on. The rest of the crowd presses forward. One of your father's friends waves to get your attention. You shake his hand before answering more questions. You know that the crowd has only a short time to inspect the horses and make their interrogations. Some are just here for fun, but others will report back to newspapers and spread the word for gambling dens to make more informed bets.

You smile, answer questions, and do your best to shine as bright as the sun.

Finally, the announcer calls the crowd back. Some of the royal princes start chants for their favorite riders. You smile a little when your name begins to drown out the rest. The whole crowd weaves back toward the city gates as the announcer turns to address the contestants.

"Riders," he says. "You now have exactly ten clockturns to inspect rival horses. As is the custom, no writing materials are allowed. Anyone caught with eye-cameras or recording devices forfeits their right to participate in the Races. You may begin."

And so the Races begin.

You move with methodical precision. You do not spare glances for the other riders, because you only have so much time to take in all the details. Naturally, you head straight for Adrian's horse first. You're more sure than ever that he is your greatest threat. And gods, the thing is massive. You ignore the placard and circle the horse yourself. You want to drink it in with your own eyes. It's a lovely creature. No surprise there. You've always wondered if Adrian's size might work against him. Bravos has always had similar troubles. Both of them are too big. You are the right size and make for a proper rider. Adding thirty more pounds really tests a horse down the final stretches. But on a horse like this one . . .

"It's perfect for him."

Across the clearing, Adrian has made his way to *your* horse. There's an intensity to the way he circles and studies, digging for the answers that might help him succeed on the first stretch. Clearly he's more than a finely carved statue. The thought has you smiling.

You refocus, circling back to the front of his horse. The creature shuffles inside of the barrier and you take note of the almost-hidden claws. There are telling bulges along the backs of the legs, too. Your eyes flick down to the placard, and the written description confirms your guess. He's chosen to start the Races with a Ravenous rebirth.

Pretty damn clever. It's the kind of rebirth that's built for riding tight. His horse will thrive in a more predatory role. It will welcome contact and interlopers, and after his interview, Adrian Ford is sure to have plenty of both. You watch for a few seconds. The unsettled horse pulls back its lips long enough to flash dagger-sharp teeth to match the razor-like claws. Anyone who presses Adrian on the first day is in for a nasty surprise. You know the only weakness to this particular rebirth is that they can be a little rebellious. Weaker riders can't hold them on a steady course, but you saw Adrian without a shirt on. He's not going to have a problem reining a horse in.

You nod once before moving on to the others. Etzli is next. You can't help shaking your eyes when you see it. It's a protective rebirth. Armored shoulders and neck. It's such a conservative choice. You thought the girl might break loose in time for the *real* Races. Make a bold move for once, but clearly you were wrong about that. She's after second place, again.

Revel's got a true burner of a horse. Built for sprinting and little else. He's tested you on a few of the shorter courses. No one gets off the line quite like him, but the Races are almost always four or five legs. You'll never fear a man who doesn't know how to finish.

Imelda Beru doesn't disappoint. Her first rebirth is one you've never heard of before. The placard calls it "Changing Skies." The description is just as enigmatic: "Allows the horse to defy gravity." It sounds cool, but you're also thinking it just means the horse can jump high? You look around long enough to find Imelda roaming through the other horses. Most of the group cycles quickly past, memorizing details, but Imelda almost looks like she's touring a museum. You shake your head again. Poor girl doesn't stand a chance.

Bravos's horse draws your eye next. Its coat has darkened to a midnight purple that verges on black. Razor-sharp spikes rise from each shoulder. You can't help smiling. Bravos is such a brawler. His first instinct has always been to lower a shoulder, hit someone hard, and trust that he'll be the one standing when the dust settles. You're pleased to see that he's taken your advice, though. This horse combination isn't *just* a bruiser. It's a hunting horse. Designed to follow a trail—even *your* trail. It's actually perfect.

Beyond his phoenix, you find the horses that belong to the only two relatives in the Races—Thyma and Capri. The siblings have disappointed on the amateur circuit. Capri was heralded for years as a riding prodigy. He snuck into an amateur event when he was seven years old and was leading the first two legs until his mother figured out where he was. The officials pulled him from that race, but not before his face was made famous on the Chats. Like you, he entered the amateur circuit with a crown already half on his head. The only difference is that you've worked hard to make sure yours still fits.

Thyma is his violent half sister. She just finished serving a one-year suspension after breaking the contact laws on the amateur circuit. You remember the race well. It was one of your fastest times, overshadowed by the fact that she'd shoved some unfortunate soul off a cliff.

Unsurprisingly, the two of them have elected to go with the exact same stamina rebirth. You've assumed they would team up ever since they announced their eligibility. An identical summoning just acts as confirmation. They'll work together. Pairings are common enough.

You lift an eyebrow, though, when you inspect Darvin's horse. He's from out on the coast. The son of a famous general in the Helio Wars. Too bad his father didn't teach him the basics of the Races. His combination is the *exact* same as the siblings. Teams of two? Normal. But three riders all working together? That borders on embarrassment.

The final two riders are barely worth the effort, but Mother would insist on thoroughness. *Everything a rider doesn't know is a potential weakness waiting to be exploited.* So you circle around to get a look at Ashtaki's horse. He's finished last in every single amateur race to date. The favorite cousin of the Brightness himself. Entering the Races is more a fashion statement for him, and sure enough he's gone with a flashy rebirth that will make him invisible on the horse's back. It's about the most useless idea you've ever heard.

Last is Nelli. Her paper-brown horse looks the same way it *always* does. It's a thin thing built for a much slower burn because Nelli is the only slow-rider in the field. Really, she's the only slow-rider in decades. She's beloved by some of the alternative newspapers as the only rider who does not sprint. Instead, she'll marathon her way through each night. A slow pace. No deaths. No rebirths. No switches. She treats the phoenix like it's a lesser breed, carefully observing the limitations that their magic allows the rest of us to break. Too bad her method has been disproven. Her own record proves that. You know she's never finished higher than fourth.

You circle back to your own horse and smile. It's nice of Nelli, you suppose, to donate one hundred thousand to the winner. Bravos is already back by his horse. Same for Adrian and Etzli. Some of the others are still memorizing details when the announcer steps forward.

"The time has ended," he says. "Teams are standing by to collect your horses and return them to the proper stables. You are free until this evening. Tonight you will join us in the Hall of Maps for the Unveiling. Rest well until then!"

The adrenaline in your chest pulses. Eleven riders. Eleven horses.

You briefly lock eyes with Bravos.

Only one winner.

12

SOUNDS LIKE THE TRUTH

IMELDA

I slide to the right, arms tired. Zion senses weakness. I've been sparring with Ayala's cousin for six days now. I've learned to set my feet before parrying a blow. I've learned to ignore the ringing sensation in my hands after a particularly sharp contact. The hardest lesson has been in humility. I thought this would be a matter of will. I thought I could just clap my hands and outdance other Ashlords the way I outdanced Oxanos. But for six days I've been completely outclassed in our makeshift dueling arena.

Zion is just twelve years old.

Compared to the riders I will face, he is a *child*.

He jabs the tip of his switch forward. I bat the weapon to one side, but he turns the reflected blow smoothly into a second swing. Instinct has me backpedaling. My own raised arm barely deflects his attack. Reverberation shakes me from elbow to hip.

He cuts forward again, resets his footing, and brings in a

blow from overhead. This time my weapon spirals from my grip. I stand there helplessly, and the only thing that stops Zion from cracking my skull in is Ayala's voice. "Stop."

Zion steps back. He glances to her and then back to me.

"You did better that time," he says.

Like Ayala, he's kind enough to lie.

"Let's take a break," Ayala says. "Come back in an hour, Z."

He nods and ducks out. My chest is heaving. It takes effort to pick myself back up as Ayala fetches the fallen switch. She sets the thing back in my hand and shrugs it off.

"Dueling isn't your thing. Let's try the whip again. You're more natural with it."

Dueling isn't my thing. What an understatement. I can feel the bitterness building. Each new day adds to the foundation of my doubt. I am *not* ready for what awaits me in the arena. Still, I force myself to follow her across the sunlit room. She paces off the appropriate distance and I loosen my switch into whip form.

"Remember your stance," she coaches. "Steady body. Firm arm. Flicks first."

I fix my eyes on the half-rusted railing that fronts the distant wall. It takes effort and concentration—especially after getting run around by Zion—but I bring the whip overhead. The motion is smooth. I hear a satisfying snap. The glass tips graze the edge of the pipe.

"A step closer," Ayala suggests.

I slide forward and bring the whip up again. My wrist gives a delicate flip and I marvel at how fast the leather snakes out. This time it coils twice around the pipe, glass shards digging, and I almost drop the weapon in shock. "It worked," I say. "It actually worked."

"Not bad," Ayala says. "Let's try some overheads. Get the whip snapping for closer combat. Honestly, if you can just *look* like you know what you're doing, that might be enough to keep a curious rider away from your ashes at night. Remember the motion?"

I nod back to her. For the next fifteen minutes, I run through the three most standard motions. Ayala admits there are twelve other stylings that are just too complex, that we don't have enough time. It's an effort to bite back my response to that. Of course there isn't enough time. I came to Furia with genuine hope. I was excited. The whole city was so bright I thought it was made of gold. This was the opportunity of a lifetime. I had been chosen.

I thought I was destined to win. Just like Martial did all those years ago.

Training has illuminated the reality *behind* their gold curtains. More and more, I'm learning that my invitation here is a show of Ashlord mercy. My entry—and my performance—are both of little consequence to them. I am the representative Dividian they'll march out for show. I am not supposed to win. This morning was just another reminder of that.

The Great Display.

All of those horses standing in one place. Ayala prepped me beforehand. She taught me a few strategies for memorizing the rebirths that other riders would start their first leg with. That part was easy. Alchemy has always been my strong suit. Besides, most of the riders went with pretty standard combinations. Not a ton of surprises in the group.

The real surprise was the horses themselves. The Ashlords have gifted me a gorgeous blood bay for the Races. She's a finer horse than any I've ridden on Martial's ranch, but one circle around the horses my contestants will ride revealed the truth. All of their horses are superior. Magnificent creatures with long ancestral breeding lines. Each one the offspring of former champions. It took me a few clockturns to understand the truth. The Ashlords have given me a finer gift than I could ever afford, and it's still far less than all the grandeur they enjoy. They have trimmed off their excess for me, offered a splash of leftover gold.

And I am expected to bow in thanks for it.

I am only here to play my part in their brilliant performance.

"Imelda?"

Ayala is staring at me. I look up and realize my whip is firmly tangled around the distant pipe. My grip is secure and my feet are set. I realize I've been pulling on it with all of my strength. The pipe has dented inward and the fixed mountings groan on both ends.

"Planning on bringing down the roof?" she asks with a smile.

I take a deep breath and shake the whip loose. A quick squeeze draws the material back into baton form. "Sorry. I'm just tired. And you're right. Dueling is off the table. If I get cornered by any of the other riders, I won't stand a chance. No one is going to team up with me, either. So it's all flight and hiding. I have to steer clear of everyone else."

She nods again. "It all depends on the course. You'll see the map tonight. Let's talk through your strategies for that. How good is your memory?"

We start back toward the hotel. Ayala runs me through breakdowns of old courses. A few days ago, I'd be thrilled to chat about it. We could talk about the year an entire pack of sunwolves dug under the course walls and terrorized the riders each night. Or the year that half the course forced riders down the River of Poems. It was such a spectacle. Horses that could run on water and riders who'd sink straight to the bottom if they got knocked off their mounts.

But I don't bring up any of my favorite Races.

I'm too deep inside my own head. I'm brooding about all of it. The bright lights and pageantry have faded away. My vision is clear now. I'm finally noticing the details that broadcasted Races have always carefully hidden from our people. Announcers never talk about the fact that Dividian riders don't own their own horses. They'll never think to remind the audience that I met my mount less than a week ago, that establishing a proper relationship with a phoenix takes *years*. I doubt they'll bring up the lack of military training on my résumé or the fact that I haven't logged combat classes with famous Ashlord generals.

When we line up in the starting gates, they'll point out that everyone has a chance. Everyone is dead-even with everyone else. And that's the illusion.

The audience doesn't know that I'm starting the Races a

hundred paces behind the others. I am not here to win. I am here to be grateful. I am here to give false hope to all those Dividian viewers huddled in their downtrodden villages.

Ultimately, I am here to lose.

". . . you'll definitely want to figure out how many re-births it will take. And you're clever as hell with your al-chemy. So it might be worth looking at points on the map where you can do something the other riders won't think to do. You'll want to map out the routes, so . . ."

Ayala keeps talking. I nod along until we're back inside the hotel. It's a relief when she leaves me in my room and tells me she'll be back to collect me that night. I close the shutters. In the dark, my mind is drawn back to my family. Father hard at work. How every grinding hour adds up to a grinding day, how days become months, become years, be-come decades. I think about my fierce mother and the small kingdom she reigns over. No Ashlord will ever recognize that she is a *queen*. When they look at her, they don't see anything at all.

And finally I think of Prosper. My little brother will turn on the Races and *actually* believe I can win. It breaks my heart to imagine Father spending extra money so he can tune into the channel that will feature *my* riding, not just the general broadcast. Tonight I'll be led through the ancient and famous Hall of Maps. It's meant as an honor, but now I can't help wondering on which day I'll disappoint my loved ones.

At the start of the Races? On day three? At the very end?

It takes an hour for despair to burn into anger.

And anger breathes life into a new mentality.

I stand up and find the dress Ayala set out for me. I can't help noticing it's an Ashlord style and cut. Sliding into their clothes just gives my anger more momentum. Something about it feels righteous. For the next few days, I will smile. I will play their game. I will be their polite model of Dividian inclusion. Right up until the moment the gunshot goes off.

And then I'll break the whole damn thing.

13

CLATTER

ADRIAN

More of the circus.

I stand in a sea of Ashlord nobles. How they glitter and shine. There's a high-rise table in front of me. I rest my forearms on it, thankful for the distance it puts between me and the rest of them. Not that they're here to talk with me. Mirrors run down the full length of one wall. An endless number of chandeliers cast swirling light over everything. I'm sweaty and bored.

My mind is fixed on what comes next. We're about to walk into the Hall of Maps. All this talk and chatter? None of it matters. But the Unveiling? That *does* matter.

I am more than muscle. Daddy made sure of that much. Every hour spent on the training floor was matched by an hour doing memory exercises or logic training. He reprinted the last fifteen courses used in the Races and had me break them down and memorize every detail. After, he had them reprinted with slight changes and he made me find the flaws. Hopefully, the Ashlords will look at me and see only muscle. If they make the mistake of underestimating me, it might mean the difference between winning and losing.

The other riders move in and out of sight. Revel stands the closest. A pair of much older Ashlord women swirl their drinks, eyes glittering, as they hang on every word he says. Ashtaki stumbles past their table, already slurring his words. The siblings share a table in the corner. Capri's posing for pictures with a few young fans. His half sister— Thyma, I think—catches me glancing their way and actually bares her teeth. How charming.

My gaze finally settles on Pippa.

As always, she's surrounded. The flattering nobles drift apart long enough for me to get a full glimpse of her. I've been searching for weaknesses, but I haven't found one. Her opening rebirth flashes confidence, and looking at her now, why shouldn't she be confident?

The daughter of champions. It would be one thing if she were just a pretty face. The rider in me sees the truth. She has the perfect build for long distances. The slender frame, the coiled muscles, all of it. Nothing about the girl is wasted. I was half hoping I'd come to Furia and discover that all the rumors were nothing more than myth. She lets out a bright laugh, and it's clear that she's very, very real. The thought has me gritting my teeth. Our revolution starts with beating her at a game she was born to win. I force myself to look away.

The bright evening continues mercilessly on.

My eyes keep trailing back to the main entrance. I just want to get on with things. I know we're waiting on the pleasure of the Brightness, the Ashlord king, a direct link to the gods. He'll reveal the map himself. What an honor. I lift a forearm to wipe sweat away as someone finally slides free of the crowd. The man makes his way straight for my table, two drinks in hand, like both of us came here together or something.

A Longhand. Most Dividian think we look just like our Ashlord cousins, but if someone grows up in the Reach, they can spot the differences a league away. He sports a fashionable cowboy hat that no Ashlord would be caught dead wearing. His skin is slightly paler, his fingertips slightly rounder, and his eyes a few shades lighter. It's only as he stops a few feet away that I confirm my guess with the final detail. Ashlords are *warm*. There's a heat on their breath, along their skin. They claim it's a sign of their link to the gods. And this man doesn't have it.

"Adrian Ford," he says with a smile. "In the flesh."

I raise an eyebrow as he sets both drinks down on the table. He slides one across to me. It's a familiar muddy color that brings a smile to my face. I lift the glass to inspect it in the light.

"You ordered me a Revolver? In this place?"

The stranger lifts his own glass. "Well. It's their excuse for a Revolver. I highly doubt they got the ratios right, but I figured you deserved a proper drink. Something from the Reach. I know you're heading for the Hall of Maps. So it's just a taste. Don't want your head spinning."

I nod my thanks. Revolvers are a classic drink. Daddy doesn't like them, but Antonio has something of a thirst for them. It takes true craft to get right. Each sip should revolve. A taste of ale, a taste of firespice, a taste of ale. On and on until it's time for the second round. I'm barely old enough to drink, but knowing which drinks are which is a rite of passage in the Reach.

I might recognize the drink, but I don't recognize the man. "Who are you?"

He sets his glass down again. "Didn't think you'd remember me. I'm an old friend of your father's. Ben sent me to this city twenty-three years ago."

I take in his features again and try to match them with the story he's telling. An image of an old painting appears. I've seen it every time I've been inside the capital courthouse. It takes some mental digging but I finally pull the name that appears at the bottom of that placard.

"Emerson."

That easy smile returns. "You're Ben's boy, after all. That man never forgot a name."

"None worth knowing at least."

It takes a second to settle all the pieces mentally into place. Lefty Emerson. I've heard Daddy talk about him before. Emerson went to Furia on his orders. He's been the unofficial emissary between the Empire and the Reach for a long time now. It's not hard to hear it in his half-faded accent. He's even adopted some of the quickness and fire of Ashlord speech. Daddy's never spoken ill of the man, but there's one other detail that stands out above all else.

He is *not* one of the ten faces Antonio showed me in that wine cellar.

I do not know his favorite food.

Which means he is not to be trusted.

"Well, I pulled a few strings to be in this crowd," Emerson says. "The first time in twelve years that a Longhand rides in the Races? I was thrilled. I'm sure everyone at home . . . I couldn't resist coming over to buy you a drink. The Ashlords will hate me for it, naturally. . . ."

As he talks, my eyes drift briefly over his left shoulder. People are laughing loudly, crossing the room, offering toasts. The woman's stillness sets her apart. She's a waitress. Her back is set against the wall right near the kitchen entrance. Her eyes are on us.

And unlike Emerson, she's one of Antonio's trusted ten.

Elizabeth. Her favorite food is smoked granola. When she's dead certain that she's caught my eye, she gives the slightest shake of her head, picks up her tray, and moves away.

My eyes lock back on Emerson. He's still talking.

". . . and that's the way it always is with their kind, isn't it?"

His half-heard question hangs in the air. I'm saved from answering by a tray that crashes to the floor. Elizabeth stands over the mess, looking properly embarrassed. It's the kind of clatter that briefly draws every eye in the room. Emerson turns long enough to inspect things, and I move faster than a slickback snake. It's a trade. My drink for his. She gave me just enough time to pull it off. I hide the movement by raising *his* glass into the air and by the time he turns back around, the sight of the drink in my hand brings out a smile.

"I do love when anything they touch falls short of perfection," he whispers. "Anyway. A Longhand in the Races!

Some things are worth celebrating, no? What should we toast to?"

He lifts the glass intended for me. It's nothing more than a suspicion. Daddy would like my instincts. Antonio would approve, too. This is not one of the faces I was told to trust. Emerson might be the Reach through and through. We might both sip our drinks, talk quietly for a few minutes, and move on without anything happening. All I know is the unsettled feeling in my chest and the disapproval of someone I was told to trust.

Lifting my stolen glass, I offer a toast. "To standing tall."

He echoes the phrase and clinks his glass to mine. We both drink. It's actually not poorly made. The taste dances a little too quickly back and forth—but there's the trademark revolving nature that the drink derives its name from. I keep both eyes carefully locked on his.

"So," he says. "How are you liking this pisshole?"

I can't help laughing. "It doesn't suit me. I feel like I've bumped shoulders with every single person who lives here in the past two days. Who could stand being this trapped?"

Emerson nods. "No farms. No ranges. No manors set on hilltops. It takes getting used to."

I tilt back my drink again and take a healthy measure. He does the same.

"I'll pass on getting used to it," I reply. "I'm here for the ceremonies. Nothing else. Get me back in the open. Give me a bright sky. Give me enough desert to ride all day."

"Spoken like a true son of the Reach."

It doesn't seem like he's showing any signs of being

poisoned at first. His hands look steady. His eyes look focused. But I finally note the glaze of sweat coating his upper lip. It is warm in here. I'm sweating enough for the both of us, but he came over without a speck on him. This time when I take a sip, he doesn't match me. The veins along his neck have started to rise.

His eyes flick briefly down to my glass.

"What was it?" I ask.

He clears his throat. A rattling noise. "Pardon?"

"In the drink," I reply. "What kind of poison did you use?"

I watch as the substance digs its claws into him. He's feeling it now. Suspicion bleeds into outright panic. His eyes dart to the left—I follow his gaze but can't find the confidant he's looking for—and then he pinches both eyes shut in pain. It's a pathetic sight.

"A life of service and you'll end it like this?" I ask quietly. "What a shame. Only the Ashlords use poison. So you'll die serving *them*, using *their* methods, drinking *their* poison. I can only imagine how much money they offered. Thanks for the drink."

I finish off the untainted Revolver and set the glass back down. I can hear his labored breathing. His eyes are almost rolling back. Through sheer will, he keeps his feet for a few more seconds. Whatever he laced my intended drink with was cruel. I leave him in its grip.

I walk away and try not to let anyone see that my hands are shaking. Reality is hammering through me. This man came here to kill me tonight. I have to take a deep breath. As I reach the entrance, I hear the sound of a body hitting the floor behind me.

It's followed by gasps. Attendants rush forward. I glance back long enough to confirm that Emerson is down. His mouth twitches. His eyes are slammed shut. He might die.

I take another deep breath and remember that could have been me.

A single thought follows: *They're afraid of me.* And I smile. *They should be.*

14

MAKING NOISE

PIPPA

It takes a few minutes for the *mess* to get cleared away. A little more intrigue will work its way back through the Chats tonight. You're not sure what happened, but the Longhand emissary went down about five minutes ago, and you're close enough to see he's not exactly *moving* now.

The man was talking with Adrian. It has you shaking your head. Furia's elite do love to plot and plan and play with their food. And you're more than certain that Adrian Ford didn't come here tonight with poison in hand. It's not the way Longhands normally do business. So clearly he was supposed to be the victim. Plots upon plots upon plots. You just hope that none of their scheming gets in the way of *your* plans.

Attendants carry the fallen Longhand through a back door. The second it swings shut, the great entrance into the Hall of Maps groans open. All the gossip dies away.

An escort appears. "Riders step forward."

You wink at a few of the surrounding royals before glid-ing forward. The rest of the contestants cut through the crowd. Ashtaki has to be redirected after stumbling into the kitchen. You roll your eyes. The board's escort takes pains-taking care to line up all of you. Cameras frame the waiting hallway. You take a deep, steadying breath. It's important to put on a good show, of course, but tonight is the second step toward winning the Races.

Once more, you feel the weight of your competition as the escort leads you and the other ten riders forward. On into the Hall of Maps. Polished hardwood floors echo back each rider's footsteps. Mirrors fill the spaces between the hanging tapestries and you catch glimpses of yourself in the glass. Naturally, you look more stunning than ever.

Annoyingly, you've been relegated to the *back* of the line of contestants. The camera crews flanking each side can barely get a good shot of you in this position. It's an Ashlord habit to cling to outdated traditions like alphabetical order. The rules are upheld, even if it would make so much more sense to feature you at the front, the bright jewel of this year's event.

The gambling lines have fluctuated all day. You're still the favorite, but yesterday some footage of the Longhand leaked. He's an absolute monster. Bigger than Bravos and more than competent in a duel. He rides like storms are chasing him. Maybe they are. A quick glance shows he's walking two spots ahead of you. Ashlords are naturally tall, but Adrian Ford's got a few inches on everyone in the room, and it's hard not to notice he's even more muscular than Bravos.

It's actually very *easy* to notice that fact.

You smile. A rider like him doesn't bring fear out in you. That's not the way you're built. Instead, adrenaline kicks to life. You want a worthy challenge. You want to beat the best.

Quietly, you run back through the math again. Eleven competitors have entered the Races. The Qualifier, who you practically chose, won't pay the entry fee. Everyone else will have deposited their hundred-thousand-dollar minimums by now. The Empire Racing Board matches all entries, which leaves the total purse somewhere north of two million legions. If you and Bravos take the top spots, 75 percent of that will funnel into your accounts. Added to your sponsorships, that's enough to start a real life together. You haven't given much thought to what you'll do after the Races, but that's because you can't afford to think about anything beyond these next few weeks.

Mother's advice was straightforward: Actually *winning* the Races is the hardest part.

You're first in the gambling lines. Adrian is second. Etzli comes in third. You know there's nothing exciting or special about the girl because you've raced her several times in the amateur circuit. Most of the time, she came in second and you came in first. She makes no mistakes, takes no risks. If the leaders screw up, she's the rider who wins. If they don't, she'll coast to a silver or bronze finish like always.

Surprisingly, Bravos isn't listed fourth.

Imelda Beru is.

You look for the girl, but she's hidden somewhere near the front of the line. Too short and too small to be seen in this herd of giants. You want to laugh at the odds for her, but something about the girl is a little unsettling. She reminds you of Mother. Clever contestants usually flash some cool alchemy, then get outraced by the real riders after a few rebirths. Sometimes, though, they're smart enough to destroy a field, spinning all the other riders in a web of chaos. Sometimes they're even known to target the favorites. You have your doubts about that. You're the reason the girl is here. If anything, she should be thankful.

Bravos fronts the line. You can't see him, but you know he's grinning and acting cocky. You've asked him to do one thing in the pre-race festivities: make noise. Be the loud one in the room. Boast and brag. When you told him you wanted *him* to win, he laughed it off as a joke. It took some convincing, but he's finally figuring out how much you love him. You don't just want him to win. You want every picture and video to look like he called his victory before it even happened. He's always been cocky, but you need him to burn bright the rest of the week.

The group pauses for a series of portrait pictures. It takes several attempts because Thyma refuses to smile. Eventually the photographer gives up and our group continues down the hall. On either side, maps mark each of the previous courses designed for the Races. One hundred forty maps in total, seventy sets lining each side. Every year, the Empire Racing Board chooses a new canyon for the Races. There's no need to design or build dangers into the settings they choose. The Empire's deserts are brutal enough on their own. The designers just decide how long the course will be and which canyons will be within the boundaries they arrange.

No one has seen this year's map until this very moment. You reach the end of the hall and the contestants are finally permitted to break rank. The one hundred forty-first map waits there, hidden behind a ragged, gray veil. You wrinkle your nose at the scent of mildew pouring out from the ancient cloth. More unnecessary traditions.

It's important to position yourself apart, especially free of Bravos and the Longhand. Aside from *you*, they're the main story lines entering the Races. Most of the other Ashlord contestants come from royal houses and rich families, but in terms of riding?

They are names that history will soon forget.

You look around and know they're not like you. Your parents raised you to understand blood and fire. Most of the other Ashlords in the room are only here because their parents could afford the massive entry fees. A few of them can ride, but you are the wind compared to them.

It's a surprise when the Qualifier appears at your elbow.

"Thanks," she says, and all you can do is stare. "For what you said in the interview."

Lips pressed tightly together, you nod once to her. She understands you're not in the mood to talk, but she doesn't retreat. She just stands in *your* space like she's been invited there. As the delegates file in to witness the revealing of the map, you calmly assess the girl you've made famous. Her dress is borrowed. You know this because it hugs her Dividian hips too tightly and runs a little too far down her calves. A nice design, but a Dividian in Ashlord packaging is still a Dividian. She looks focused enough. It shows on the measured creases of her forehead.

Almost every year it happens the same way. The scholarship for poor Dividian riders was established almost a century ago. The racing boards claim it's an attempt at equality, but Mother explained that it has a lot more to do with revenue. The Dividian population is almost four times larger than the Ashlord population. Not a well-publicized statistic, but still very much the truth. Having a Dividian scholarship reels in millions of viewers, and even gives them someone to cheer for. Father admitted the board prefers to choose someone who will be competitive enough to keep up interest, but not so competitive that they give the Dividian people too much hope.

You glance at Imelda Beru and wonder where she lands on that scale. She's short and compact, naturally quiet. You're most afraid of her eyes. They're light green, and as you watch, they never stop taking in the details of the room.

Your attention is drawn back to the fore as the Brightness enters. Furia's patron leader, figurehead of the entire Empire, and your people's direct link to the gods themselves. You know that he is an old man, but it doesn't show. There's not a wrinkle on his bright, burnished face. His skin is so *bright* that it almost glows. And his voice thunders. Every rider and witness lowers their heads instinctually, even you.

"This marks the thirtieth year I've personally unveiled the course for the Races. I'm proud to continue this meaningful tradition and I'm proud to invite each of these riders to take part in it." He gestures to two servants, who step forward and flank the still-hidden map. "As is our custom, each rider will have exactly ten clockturns to assess this year's map and memorize what they see. Anyone caught with eye-cameras or recording devices will forfeit their right to participate in the Races and lose their entry fee."

The Brightness gestures again and the servants begin folding the veil down. Hills and valleys and canyons are revealed in quiet stages. You and the other riders take a hungry step forward as the Brightness makes his final announcement. "Contestants, I give you the one hundred and forty-first course in the history of the Races. Your ten clock-turns begin now."

The other riders fade to background. Your eyes narrow. You've known how to analyze courses since you were five years old. Father was the famous rider, but Mother is the smartest person to ever claim the crown. She passed on all of her strategies to you.

First, you determine how many deaths the course will require. Your eyes take in the map's scale before you begin measuring the length and width of the course. Even in the best possible circumstances, your phoenix horse will have to die four times to get to the finish line. That's not an overly long course, but still a challenge. So, a five-leg race. It means you'll have to plan out the locations of four deaths and the components you need for four rebirths.

Second, you focus on the width of the course. Compared to the other maps, it looks surprisingly slender. You use the scale again and see your instinct's right. It's a *very* narrow course. By your measure, two of the necessary passes will have all the riders within a few hundred paces of one another. The first phoenix death will be an especially crucial one.

It's illegal to kill someone in the Races, but it's never been illegal to taint the rebirthing process of your competitor's horse. In recent years, tainting's evolved into one of the main strategies of the Races. Your training focused on protection, rather than sabotage, but you know where you let your horse die and how you defend it is going to really matter in this race.

Next, you run through every possible route the course offers. There are twenty-three different combinations through the various canyons. Mother's method has you searching for the safest route, the fastest route, and the most predictable route. You cycle through them patiently.

Safest is down the right side of the valley. Safest and slowest. It's not hard to see that the other routes will get you to the finish line more directly. The fastest route stands out as well.

Gods, that is treacherous.

It splits from the main valley after the first day of riding. A canyon route through riverways that eventually lead underground. Cave riding. You've never enjoyed it. Your phoenix can handle the dark, but you've personally never taken to it. You suppose a dollop of Sunscape could give your phoenix's coat a solid glow? That'd make the caves more navigable, but no less dangerous. You file the route away in a back pocket. It's not your first choice, and you can only hope the other riders don't take advantage of your hesitation. Anyone who actually makes it through the cave will have a sizable advantage on the field. It cuts through a plateau everyone else will be forced to ride around.

The most predictable route is harder to find. You retrace your steps a dozen times and finally determine the way your competitors are likely to go. The path cuts west after the first few river crossings. Forests drape that edge of the map and you like what you're seeing there. A winding route, but faster than the eastern passes and your horse's favorite style of riding.

A glance shows five clockturns have already passed.

You retrace each of the three routes, memorizing them. When you're certain you have every obstacle firmly in mind, you begin Mother's final, suggested task:

The designers will always hide one thing in plain sight. Every map is meant to draw your eye to something so that their clever trick stays well hidden from the casual observer. Find it and you'll have an advantage that no one else has.

You're combing back through the details when movement on your right pulls your attention. Adrian Ford is bowing before the officials. They look down on him with hooded eyes.

"Thank you," the Longhand says, louder than necessary. "I've seen all I need to see."

He gives another bow and starts walking back through the Hall of Maps. As he passes you, he glances over and winks. The act has you gritting your teeth. How could someone be so arrogant? You know it's probably just a power move. He wants you to think he's figured out something important, and far faster than the rest. The display digs under your skin.

Taking a breath, you return your attention to the map.

Four clockturns remain.

All right, you think, *to what did the designers hope to draw our eye?*

You don't have your mother's skill, but the answer to that question is obvious. Every rider will reach the second pass at the end of the first day. It's incredibly narrow and you know the designers are hoping for tight racing, even a few falls. The well-bred phoenixes, like yours, will be able to ride for another five minutes if they get through the clustered valley cleanly. Even then, it'll be a nightmare trying to secure a good position on the plain to let a phoenix die. The answer's clear: The designers want havoc at the end of the first day.

So if that's what they're drawing our attention to, what are they trying to hide?

"Contestants," an official announces. "You've one more clockturn. Use it wisely."

You shake yourself. What is it? What secret does the map hide? Your eyes trace hills and valleys, creeks and dead ends. As the seconds tick away the final clockturn, you finally see it.

There, at the very beginning of the first leg, is an almost invisible trail. It hooks left and up the plateaus, into a separate section that feeds into a completely different canyon. While everyone else is hunting for a place to protect their phoenix, you and Bravos will be taking a path none of them ever noticed. It will give you an advantage most people wildly underestimate in the Races, the advantage of sleep.

Satisfied, you smile as the officials begin covering the map and the other contestants take their positions once more. Bravos glances back at you once and you give him a tight, imperceptible nod. An advantage doesn't guarantee victory, but it will separate you slightly from the rest. It will give you and Bravos exactly what you need to win the Races, together.

15

DISHARMONY

IMELDA

I'm pacing the hotel room like the world's coming to an end.

"What else?" Ayala asks. "Come on, while it's still fresh in your mind."

"It's not fresh. It was never fresh. I don't remember any of the map. There were . . . creeks? Three of them, maybe? And another one running down the right side. I don't know. It—it was hard to take all of it in. I told you I got distracted. The land around the highlighted course looked so familiar. So I sat there staring and forgetting and staring and forgetting."

Ayala takes a measured breath. "How many rebirths?"

I shake my head. "Four? I don't even know that. I forgot *everything* you told me to do."

"That's okay," she says calmly. "But you need a plan. You have to use what you have and at least make a plan, Imelda. The other riders walked out of that room knowing what they were going to do, where they would ride."

"Good for them. I don't have a plan. I just don't."

Ayala heaves a sigh but doesn't say anything. The tension between us has been growing. I'm thankful to her, and I know she means well. She's taken me under her wing since the moment I was named Qualifier. She might not speak it aloud, but I know she sees the same thing that I do. I'm not ready for the Races. My bond with my horse isn't where it needs to be. I can't defend myself or my ashes if push comes to shove. And now this?

The whole week has been a long string of flashing lights and loud noises. I've learned more about the Ashlords this week than I have in the past sixteen years. Their greatest strength isn't their physical prowess or their height. It's not the way their bodies have adapted perfectly to the desert landscape of the Empire. It's their exposure to noise, their poise under pressure.

I saw it in Pippa tonight.

Everyone calls her name. Hands reach toward her. Lights flash to capture that perfect stride as she walks the carpeted world for which she was born. All the pressure just makes her shine like a diamond. Her whole life has been a preparation for this event, while I've been given one week to pull it all together. And she's not the only one. Etzli and Adrian are the same way. All of them are ready to dance circles around me.

Unless I change the steps. I have to figure out a different way to win.

There's a knock at the door.

Ayala smiles at me and rises to answer it.

"Let's talk more tomorrow. You've got a surprise tonight."

There's a little click as the door opens, and a series of loud *booms* as someone comes barreling into the room. Ayala laughs as Farian trips into my line of sight. He's wearing his favorite cardigan and his best pants, with his hair styled like he's hoping to visit a few clubs. He's even got his handheld camera pressed to one eye, and it's pointed at me.

"And here she is. The Alchemist, Imelda Beru, a rising star from the corner of the Empire. Clearly, the fame hasn't gone to her head yet. Not if she's still wearing *those* boots."

And for the first time in days, I laugh. Down deep in my gut.

"You're here for two seconds and already snacking on me, Farian?"

Ayala heads for the door and waves her goodbye.

"We'll talk in the morning. Good night, you two."

Farian puts the camera away long enough to give me a hug. I can feel the burdens of the week falling off my shoulders as he sits down and gestures to his feet.

"Can you believe these slippers? They're so comfortable."

I laugh again. "Slippers I can believe. But you? Here? Impossible."

"I got in this afternoon," he says. "Ayala said you were resting before the Hall of Maps. Not that I minded. Spent all day filming. The light here is unbelievable. And the people. I love this place."

"A new documentary: *Farian in the City.*"

"Doesn't sound half bad," he says. "But you're deflecting from the fact that *you're about to ride in the Races.* Is this serious? Is this really happening? When you end up winning

this thing, just promise to *take me with you*. And then promise me you'll buy some new boots."

I throw a stray slipper at his head. He ducks it, laughing.

"I like these boots. They're comfortable."

"I can see one of your toes."

"Shut it. These are the boots that got us here."

"Fair enough." He sits up, looking around. "So they're
clearly hooking you up?"

I nod. "With everything. They actually offered new boots.
Gave me a riding jacket. A handful of companies sponsor
the Qualifier every year. All the money goes into a fund to
help search for Qualifiers the next year. More scholarships,
too. Ayala's been training me."

And with that thought, all the bitterness returns.

"Not that it's helped."

He doesn't hear the last sentence. "It's a dream come
true."

"Yeah, I guess."

"You guess? Enthusiasm's not your strong suit, but this
is the Races, Imelda."

"Exactly, this is the Races. I'm going to ride against the
best competition in the Empire, Farian. They've trained
their entire lives for this. They've been with their phoenixes
since they were little kids. Don't you ever wonder why the
Qualifiers always lose? Martial won his year because he was
the best Dividian duelist in history. I can't beat my way out
of a sack. All I've gotten in training so far is bruises."

"You're not that bad."

I raise an eyebrow.

"Okay, you're pretty bad, but some past winners never fought, you know?"

"I know that, but all it takes is one mistake and I'm done. None of the Ashlords are foolish enough to kill me, but a few broken bones?" The anxiety creeps in. Farian shifts in his seat and I can tell he's surprised to hear me say that I'm afraid of anything. "Have you seen the Longhand? Everyone says he's got a target on his back. Good luck with that! He's a monster. Most of them are that way. I'm pretty sure that girl named Thyma growled at me tonight."

"Wow," he says. "Thyma actually growled at you? It's kind of an honor—"

My glare cuts off his sentence.

"Right. Let's talk through it all."

He crosses over to Ayala's abandoned desk. The map she was drawing from my descriptions is there, but it's incomplete to the point of uselessness. Incomplete because my eyes were drawn to the other parts of the map. I knew I recognized them, but couldn't confirm it until I got back to look at the Empire's official atlases, the ones Ayala borrowed for me.

They're not as exact as the course drawing, but more than detailed enough to find the strip of mountains I knew I recognized. The course is near the village my cousin Luca lives in. One I know of only because we went in secret to his wedding. His father was a rebel soldier in the war. He acted as a double agent for the Longhands, and the only safe place for people who stood up to the Ashlords in the war is the mountains. If the scales are right, we're racing half a day's ride from the Gravitas Mountains. I just wish I'd been

as focused on the map as I was on placing the familiar surroundings. Now I'm left with next to nothing.

"Check out these components," Farian says, whistling
from the desk.

He holds up one of the random papers I was handed at
tonight's ceremony. I glanced at it once, but realized not
knowing the course's layout means I don't even know what
alchemy will help me win. I'm riding into the fire of the
Races with a few blindfolds on.

"Wow," Farian says. "They have Ivory of Earl."

I raise an eyebrow. "I didn't even think that still existed."

"Welcome to the Races," he says. "Some of this stuff is
high-end. I bet Martial would kill to get a few of these powders in his stockroom. You have any mixtures in mind?"

Before I can reply, his eyes go even wider.

"They've got Kisspowder! No wonder the entry fees
are so steep. Five containers of Kisspowder would sell for,
what, seventy-five thousand legions? If the entry fee was
any lower, you could just sign up and cash out on the components for a profit. I could start my own videography business with that kind of money."

The idea has my attention, but after a second I shake my
head.

"They don't let you keep components."

"No?" he asks, still scanning the sheet. "I've never seen
the officials confiscate them."

"Rules are on the back," I reply. "Only the winner keeps
what's left in their belt."

He makes a thoughtful noise. "Well, you'll just have
to win."

"Is that all?" I ask. "Would you like me to travel to the underworld afterward?"

He laughs. "Come on, Imelda. This is your chance to make history. And if you don't, so what? You're racing in an event that most Dividian will never even come close to seeing."

I give him a nod, but none of it feels right. It's more clear than ever that I'm a carefully constructed sideshow. An example of their kindness to my people. The Ashlords know exactly how good I'd have to be to beat their bright and shining stars. And their money is on the fact that I can't rise to that challenge. Never could.

Ideas are churning now. There has to be a way to change the game.

Farian sees the look on my face and switches tunes. "Forget the Races," he says. "We're in the biggest city in the Empire. Let's celebrate."

The word *celebrate* almost snaps me out of my funk. I watch as he walks over and throws open the food cupboards. Little delicacies line each shelf. There's even a fresh bucket of ice with two glistening glass bottles on the floor of the closet. Farian's eyes go wide, because it's more packaged food than either of us has ever seen. He looks back my way.

"Tell me this is yours."

"It's free," I reply, smiling. "It's all free."

"And you haven't touched any of it?"

He reaches down and pulls out both bottles.

"It didn't feel right. Everything about this place is so . . . them."

Farian plucks up the bottle opener, flicks the cap off

with a practiced motion, then grabs the other and repeats the motion. He hands it to me before holding up his own to make a toast.

"To the Dividian. To Imelda. To doing things our way!"

I grin and tap the neck of my bottle against his.

"To doing things our way."

Farian slowly resurrects me. We snack and drink and laugh. He throws open the balcony windows, and we call down to people who pass the hotel front. Everything's so bright. The city never sleeps. At the end of a long night, he heads back to his room. He mentions that Martial's in the city and wants to help with strategizing. I'm surprised the former victor has traveled all this way, but it makes sense—after all, someone had to escort Farian.

I eventually sleep, but the dreams start out dark and haunting. I'm playing a board game against the other riders, and they won't explain the rules. They move each piece flawlessly. When I try to mimic their motions, they laugh, slap my hand away, and say that's not how the game works. All of them laugh and laugh and laugh until I flip the table.

And the pieces scatter everywhere.

I wake up in the middle of the night and know *exactly* what I'm going to do.

16

A QUIET CORNER

ADRIAN

I spend the rest of the evening alone. Antonio is gone. I have no doubt that he's preparing some other vital cog in our engines of war. Readying his troops in case all goes to plan. It's nice to sit in silence. I wait in the hotel's restaurant area. Other guests see me and decide to make themselves scarce. The waiter finally takes a hint and stops asking if I'd like a refill.

It allows me a moment to trace back over the map. Rehearse the right rebirths. I'm closer now than ever to starting a war. I'm full of fear and hunger and foreboding. After a few hours of staring through the window and out into the busy Furian streets, I decide to call it a night. I'll want as much sleep as I can get. It will be scarce during the Races, even scarcer during the war that will follow. The upstairs hallway is empty. I open my door.

A shiver runs down my spine. Something strange is in the air, but as I stare around the room, the details all look the same. I search the shadows and corners. Nothing. I close the door behind me and I'm halfway into the light of the room when I see the man sitting in the corner.

He was not there a second before.

And fear trembles through me, because he is no man.

"Take a seat," the creature hisses.

He is shirtless. Dirt stains the vessel's upper body. I try to cling to the truth that this is just a man. He's flesh and blood. But my eyes trace the disturbing scars that start at the base of the priest's neck. A scaled mask threads directly into the skin. Those protective scales enclose the human head completely. I note slit nostrils, a single gleaming eye, the reptilian profile. Each feature resembles the iron turtles that live along the coast. Creatures known for their caution and their unbreakable shells. It takes a second to remember the name of this particular god.

"They call you the Dread."

The priest spreads both hands. "So they do. Go ahead. Sit."

My heart thunders. It was easy to dismiss the gods—and the role they'd play in the war—from a distance. But seeing one in person has my heart beating faster. I take a steadying breath and it's like his finger is set on the pulse of all my fears. He smirks. The animalistic features look so *alive.* Is this priest following his god's command? Or has the Dread actually entered our world for this rendezvous?

I move to obey his command—taking a seat—but I slide a hand to the knife at my belt as I do. I position myself so that his view of the blade is cut off. I wouldn't dare face one of their gods without a weapon. Better if it were a sword.

My people have never worshipped the pantheon. Blood

sacrifices disgusted my ancestors. So did the idea of depending on anyone or anything. We've paid the price for our rebellion over the centuries. Always the Ashlords have had an edge against us. Their gods turn the tides of war with impossible magic. I take a moment to recall all I know of the Dread.

He's the patient one. The safest of their kind. The one who hides and warns and waits.

"What does the god of caution want from me?" I ask.

The answer comes in a slithering voice. "I wanted to take a long look at my potential warrior. The very symbol of the war to come. We get glimpses, of course. We have eyes and ears in this world, but I have always tended to trust my *own* eyes above all others."

I stare back at him. "Your warrior? I never agreed to that."

The slit eyes narrow. "Not yet. I offered my services to your grandfather long ago. He rejected me. I came to your father before he decided to send you here. I offered my protection. He was hesitant. I thought the son might be wiser than the fathers. Did tonight teach you nothing? You are exposed, Longhand. Do you know why you were sent here?"

My jaw tightens. "I was sent here to win."

"Ideally," the god replies. "Win the Races and the Reach will march with a boldness this generation has forgotten. But surely you see what your father sees. Losing will accomplish the same that winning would. They're going to kill you, Adrian Ford. And when they kill the favorite son of the Reach, it will start a revolution. Victor or martyr, your father gets his war."

His words wash over me in waves. Briefly, I imagine

Daddy sitting at his desk, swirling his drink, accepting my death like the first piece in his great game. It hits so hard and so deep that I realize it's the only thing I have no defense against. I've built walls for every other threat. Everything but him. Then I remember who I'm speaking with.

"A clever lie," I reply. "Like I'd ever believe one of *their* gods."

The Dread smiles. "Am I? The Ashlords grow bold. They reach for the future. The Striving gives them whatever they please. They adore things that *move* or *flash* or *buzz*. The other deities are well attended, but my people neglect caution. Walk by my temple. Note the empty ramparts. My priests in this realm are few. But I assure you that it is not my intention to simply go away. I am not like the Veil. I will not lie down and die. I will not accept defeat."

My mind races again.

The Dread continues. "I seek new worshippers. Whether you live or die, war is coming. Do you imagine your fight will be against the Ashlords alone? No. You will face all the power the gods can summon across the barriers and into this world. Surely you know this?"

I nod. "We are ready this time."

The god's face twists into a smile. "So your father thinks. Let me add my strength to yours. Let us see how ready you are, then."

"In exchange for blood? Servitude? I haven't come this far to bow to you."

"Partnership," the god corrects. "Between equals."

That pulls a laugh up my throat. "I don't trust you. None of our kind do."

"Allow me to offer the first sign of faith between us. Your father has thrown you into the fire, Adrian. He did not accept my trade. So allow me to offer my protection freely."

He unfurls his left hand. My grip on the knife tightens, but before I can do more than unlatch it from my belt, he blows powder from his palm. It flashes out like smoke and fills the room in less than a second. I hold my breath, but the substance coats my skin, tingles down my spine. I do everything except pinch my eyes shut. I don't want to lose sight of him in the haze.

"Calm down," the god says. "It is a boon. This will help you survive the Races."

I wave my free hand to clear the air. It slowly starts to thin until I can see him again.

"What did you do to me? What is this?"

"Caution," he answers simply. "You think they come to bruise and break you. You're wrong, Adrian. They are coming to *kill* you. The blessing I just offered will bring swift healing. Sturdier bones. Less bleeding. It will keep you alive. You're welcome."

My eyes sharpen. "I didn't ask for your boon. We have no agreement. Understand?"

"For now." The god nods a concession. "But you'll see the truth in a few nights. This is just a fraction of my magic. If you find it is useful, imagine what else might exist between us. I am a patient god, Adrian. You might not want me today. You may not even want me a year from now. But I will wait for that fateful day to arrive, because I know I'm your best chance of winning the war that's coming."

He starts to rise. Instinct brings my knife around. He's

already violated me. I have no idea if he's telling the truth, or if the spell he's put over me will ruin everything. I'm not about to risk a second mistake. The knife flicks from my hand and shivers through the air. My aim is true. It hits right where the beating heart of his priestly vessel should be. I'm expecting the tear of flesh, the spurt of blood.

Instead, the Dread vanishes. Like he was never there.

The smoke clears. I sit there staring, and it's like I imagined the whole thing. My eyes turn back to the door. It's closed. The windows are shut, too. It takes a while to steady my breathing and shake off the effects. I am not here to parley with gods. I am here to start a rebellion. I am here to change the face of the Empire.

I'm here because Daddy sent me.

A shiver runs down my spine. The Dread lied to me. Nothing but lies.

It takes a little muscle to pull the knife free from the upholstered chair. I go through my normal routine before dousing the lamps and crawling into bed. I pretend to be calm—just in case the gods are still watching—but inside, my heart hammers in my chest. It takes hours to finally fall asleep. I drowse with one hand under my pillow, tight around the grip of my knife.

When I finally sleep, I dream of the sea.

17

SCREAM

PIPPA

You planned every single detail to perfection.

And ever loyal, Bravos follows all of it step for step. The night of your tour through the Hall of Maps, he calls you from the mobile he has registered with the city. Your scripted conversation is brief. He says he didn't want there to be any hard feelings. You say there aren't any, that you're too focused on the Races to feel anything else right now. He says that he misses you. You whisper a goodbye. It takes the hackers about five minutes to post the entire conversation onto the Chats.

You know gamblers and fans will devour every word and gossip with their friends about all the *nothing*. It has you smiling. Some things about Furia are just so remarkably pre-dictable. Fifteen minutes later, you hear a chirping sound from the corner of the room. You retrieve your unmarked mobile and answer it.

"Well done, Bravos."

"You know me, love. A slave to details."

"Tell me, did you enjoy your stroll through the Hall of Maps?"

"You know history bores me."

"How about making history? Does that bore you?"

He laughs. You can't help but imagine the *perfect* flash of his smile.

"You're sure about all of this?"

The question has you rolling your eyes. Ever since you told him you wanted *him* to win, he's been fighting against the idea. It's just like him to act so sacrificial. Like he's never imagined taking first. You suppose it's possible that he never has. After all, the Empire has basically crowned you already.

"For the last time, Bravos, I'm sure. I want to *marry* the winner of the Races."

You hear him smiling. "You're seriously amazing. But we still have to win, right?"

"Right. Let's talk about the course."

"You saw something? You had that triumphant look on your face."

It's your turn to laugh. "Triumphant. That's the whole point."

"Very much the point," Bravos replies. "All right, what did you see?"

"A secret. I want you to let your phoenix startle out of the gate."

"Startle?" He echoes the word. "Really? Come on, Pippa. I was five the last time my horse startled out of the gate."

You sigh. "Just do it, Bravos. I'm going to let my phoenix

startle, too. The other racers won't think twice about it. They'll all thunder off and forget about us. They'll think the pressure got to me and that I've lost my nerve. After the dust settles, follow me."

Bravos hesitates. "You're sure it will work?"

"Trust me. We're going to be first and second. Just like we planned."

"What about the Longhand? Did you see his interview?"

Of course you did. You watched Adrian Ford unbutton his shirt during a live interview and grin like a fool for the entire Empire. You know he's the biggest threat, but there's no point telling Bravos any of that. "You're as big as he is."

Bravos laughs. "I'm really not."

"But the two of us together? He doesn't stand a chance."

"Right. Together we win." Noise sounds in the background. You hear Bravos call a muffled answer back to someone. "Time to go, love. Can't wait to throw you some brooding looks during the Longest Ride. This is what we've been waiting our whole lives for."

"Good night, Bravos."

The call ends. You turn off the lights and lie back, eyes searching the dark. You've been nervous until now. All the expectation and training and attention. Father's constant devotion and Mother's constant affirmation. All of it has built up to a boiling point. Now you're sinking into the pillows and squirming beneath the blankets. They can have their dreams, and you can have yours. For the first time, you're starting to believe they'll actually come true.

It's all so exciting that you just want to throw your arms around Bravos before the Races start and kiss him for everyone to see. But you've been too careful to slip up this late in the game. Everyone else thinks you are blood-sworn enemies. And everyone knows how alliances can impact the Races. There are so many unpredictable twists awaiting the riders. Having someone you trust can absolutely mean the difference between winning and losing.

And *no one* will expect you to let Bravos win. That will be the brilliant and final twist to the story. You'll ride hard to the finish line and, at the last minute, your phoenix will fade. Bravos will win by a few lengths because you let him win. You will be the one to crown a new champion. The world will see that you worked together and that the two of you are meant to be. Marriage will guarantee an extension of celebrity. You'll live happily ever after.

Those are the bright hopes that have you drifting off to sleep. You dream that you are sailing. The sun chases unpredictable patterns over the water. A southern wind stirs the waves. You admire the horizon until arms wrap around your waist. A kiss lands on your cheek.

You look up.

And Adrian Ford is the one smiling at you.

The shock of seeing his face makes the noise that drags you out of sleep even more startling. You're still blinking away that image of the Longhand as reality's greedy claws strip away the dream. Why is your door open?

Light pours in from the hallway. A shadow waits there.

"Pippa?"

Your mother's voice. What's she doing up this late?

"Are you awake?"

You sit up. "Mother?"

"Come. Quickly."

You obey her with an urgency you haven't felt since childhood, rising and following without question. The halls are lit only by spare window candles. Mother leads you down the stairs, careful to skip the step that always groans underfoot. You skip it, too. There are no obvious signs of danger, but she's moving with such deliberate quiet that you're drawn to do the same. Past the foyer, the dining room, the kitchen. You realize the servants are all gone. Dismissed for the evening. Mother never does that.

She opens the stone door that leads into the wine cellar. Reaching back, she takes your hand and pulls you into the dark. For the first time in years, you feel like a child. You get a death grip on her hand as she leads you down, one step at a time. A few times you stumble, but she's there, braced to keep you upright. Sightless, your other senses start to sharpen. There's a smell like cinnamon. Your mother's fragrance. Occasionally, your arm rubs against the bracelet of obsidian symbols that always dangles on her wrist. The air is damp.

But it's the sound that sends a chill down your spine.

Rising up from the very stones, you can hear a distant *howl*. It sounds like it's coming from another world. Mother's grip on your hand tightens, as if she senses your desire to run. She keeps hold of your hand and leads you through a section of the house you never knew existed.

After several more passages, she stops and lights a candle. She sets the light in your trembling hands and kneels. Squinting, you finally see the obsidian knife she's carrying. She speaks in a whisper. "This way is now yours to travel."

Your eyes widen as she slips the sharp point over her palm. Blood drips down to the eager stones. Blood sacrifice is common among your people. How often have you seen gods and their vessels walking the streets or crowded around their temples? It isn't uncommon, but you've never heard Mother or Father talk of the gods as anything more than allies. Before you can figure out what's happening or what all of this means, the stones at your feet groan to life.

The floor—blank just a moment before—blooms with pattern and color.

You nearly drop the candle as your mother moves back to your side. Both of you watch invisible hands finish their ancient pattern. Fractured light shivers over the symbols; then the circle coughs smoke into the air. You watch as the floor *vanishes* and reveals a secret passage. Mother leads you down it with an undeniable sureness. She has walked this path before.

You also have the sense that the air has gone *silent*. Just seconds before, it must have been filled with noise, but now the quiet has taken its place, and the quiet is somehow louder than any noise could ever be. You follow her until your candle casts its light on an altar.

A figure waits beyond: The Madness.

You would know the three-eyed god of death anywhere, but down in this deep dark place, he looks like an actual nightmare. A great wolf's mask sits unnaturally over the proxy's human head. At the neck, hair weaves itself into skin, sealing the man inside. As the Madness's chosen vessel, the priest will never show his face again. He wears no shirt, no shoes. His pants are dusty and stained. His entire body looks emaciated, ribs as pronounced as the bars of a cage.

The sight of him redefines your fears. You do not ask why he is here. You do not ask why *you* are here. All the pieces of this dreaded puzzle are falling into place.

Mother says, "I would ask the blessing you gave me be extended to my daughter."

The three wolfish eyes leer in her direction. You fight back a shiver as the Madness inclines his head, taking in the request. A rasping voice echoes, "A drop of your blood."

She starts forward, bloody palm held out.

The Madness growls at the sight. "A new wound is required."

She hesitates, then takes up the obsidian blade again. She calmly slits the opposite palm and shows it to the god. He gives an approving nod as she holds it out over the altar. In the light of your candle, blood drips over the stones. The Madness licks his lips, tongue slavering.

You know he is the god of death. He is the way between the worlds. Some call him the Bridgekeeper. Nothing passes up from the underworld without his approval. You cannot fathom why he is here tonight or what Mother could possibly be thinking. This is not a path you ever imagined walking. It is the fool's way forward.

"The girl now," the Madness says. "Her blood must surround the altar entire."

You watch in horror. She cleans the knife and turns. She offers it to you.

"Take it," she orders. "Pippa. Do as I say."

There's no room in her voice for argument. You exchange candle for blade. The Madness has started chanting and moving. He speaks in an inhuman tongue. The words start out as words, before echoing like the rattle of bones, bounding between worlds with dangerous reverberation. And then the Madness dances around the altar, lost in the chaos of his spell. You take the distracted moment to ask the question that burns brightest in your mind.

"What is happening?"

"Trust me," she whispers. "I'm offering you a gift."

She shoves you forward. The Madness continues to dance. You step up to the altar, carefully clear of his circling path. Your hands shake as you take the blade and press the black tip to your palm. The sharp pain makes you gasp, but a bloody streak appears.

The Madness stops. "Let it encircle the altar. The spirit must attune to you."

You eye him before walking in a circle. You let blood drip down in a staggered loop. Twice around before the god lets out a bone-chilling howl. You drop the knife and dart back to the safety of your mother's arms. His howl does not stop. It grows, pulsing in your chest, and shaking the stones, and calling your spilled blood into the air.

And then the noise cuts off sharply.

Mother gasps as a violent slash of blue light tears through the dark. You watch the bright ball glow, trembling form-lessly above the raised altar. It shapes itself into a spirit. You see the face, the torso, the legs. The spirit leaps to the right, but an invisible barrier knocks it back. The Madness watches in fascination as the creature beats blue fists against the walls. He howls again.

The spirit panics. Lashing out again, failing again. But the walls are closing in around it. As the Madness continues to wail his horrible noise, you realize that it's *your* blood that is pinning the spirit to the altar. There's a horrible writhing and everything goes black.

The world dances away from you.

Until it stops dancing. You're back in your room, safely under the covers. You have no idea how you got here, or what's happening, until Mother sits down on the edge of your bed. The secret room and the Madness and the summoned spirit burn back into your mind.

You wait for her to speak.

"The gods move between our world and the one below," she says. "You have always known this, dear. You were not born into war, but you were created for it all the same. The gods derive their power from a trade between worlds. In the underworld, our blood gives them power. They take our sacrifices and use them to rule those forsaken lands. In return, they offer us the powers of their world. Invisible armies. Fire that rains from the sky. The Madness, as you know, controls the passage of spirits into our realm. That has always been his trade. He has the ability to bring souls from that world into ours."

You nod mechanically. Your head feels ready to spin from your shoulders.

"One of those spirits will be gifted to you. For the race."

Hearing her words, a truth settles into your mind, a

realization about her brilliant performance in the Races all those years ago. Your mother was not simply the most talented rider. No, the truth is far less pretty than that. She *cheated* to win.

"You had a spirit for your year, didn't you?"

She catches the accusation in your tone. "As did many of my competitors. I was the only one who understood the power I wielded. By the time the others realized what could be done, I'd already run circles around them. It is not cheating to use the tools you've been given."

"Then . . . the years of the Madness . . ."

"Are the years in which the god of death and passage involves himself. He offers gifts in exchange for blood. The gift will come at the start of the race. Command it well."

Your heart is pounding. The Madness is something you've always dismissed. It's only happened four times in the history of the Races. The odds were against it until Mother invited the fickle god into *your* year. Now everything feels like it's slipping from your grasp. The Madness will bring events you cannot predict or control. Those under its effect have won the Races easily, but others imbibing on his power have lost the Races just as tragically. Your jaw clenches as you realize the risks Mother's created with her meddling.

It could ruin *everything.*

"Others will benefit from this?"

She nods. "The Madness will seek more deals tonight. He favors no one."

"Then you are a *fool.*"

Your mother flinches. Even you are surprised by the

venom in your voice. She has invited chaos where you had created order, but what is worse is that she treated you like a child.

"Think," she replies desperately. "Who is the one rider the Madness will *never* help?"

Realization washes over you. The burning rage fades ever so slightly. You know that she's right. There is one rider that no Ashlord deity would ever consider helping. The only rider who belongs to a group of people who refuse to worship any of the pantheon.

"Adrian Ford."

Mother nods. "We're not in front of the cameras now. Be honest with yourself: He's the greatest threat you will ever face. Before he joined, I would have never dreamed of inviting the Madness. It's possible you could have won. Consider the spirit another tool in your arsenal."

The final realization hurts most of all. She didn't trust you to win on your own. The daughter of champions, destined to follow in their footsteps. It doesn't matter that you've won every single amateur race or that you train harder than she ever did. At the end of the day, your mother thinks that Adrian Ford could beat you.

Driven by that unnamed fear, she might have ruined everything. It takes effort not to shout at her or to dismiss her coldly. The die has already been cast. There's no fighting it now.

Your voice is iron. "Tell me what will happen."

"The spirit that comes will want one thing from you: freedom. It has lived its entire life bound to the gods in the world below. The Madness transferred that ownership. It is bound to you. All you must do is make a deal with it. Offer freedom in exchange for victory."

You nod to her. "And then what?"

"Then you ride, sweet girl. Use the spirit wisely. Beat the Longhand."

She pauses meaningfully before taking your hand.

"And win the Races."

18

WHISPER

IMELDA

Martial appears an hour before I'm scheduled to leave.

Yesterday was my last day with all of them. Farian and I walked around the entire city, laughing and eating the kind of food they would only ever serve in a city like Furia.

After, I sat down with Martial and Ayala. A final strategy session. They both had some great ideas. I let them talk me through it even though I have my own plan now.

Change the game.

If I'm going to win, I have to win *my* way.

Ayala is scheduled to escort me in thirty minutes. She's the last person I'll talk to before the Races begin, which is why I asked Martial to wake up early and pay me a private visit. I can't share my plan with Ayala. It would break her heart, and I've actually started to like the woman. But Martial? He'll understand *exactly* what I'm going to do and why I'm going to do it. And I need him if my plan is going to have any chance of working.

"Good morning," he says.

"Morning." I usher him in and lock the door. I'm about to unload my plan when he shakes his head. Quietly, he leads me into the bathroom. He runs the dueling faucets in the massive bath, filling the room with noise, before giving a nod.

"Never know who might be listening."

I lower my voice to a whisper. "I need your help."

"I figured you had a plan of your own."

"I know where the course is."

He lifts an eyebrow. "Is that so?"

"During the revelation, I kept getting distracted. I was seeing the edges of the map and not focusing on the high-lighted course. It just looked so familiar." I pull the folded map from my back pocket and point to a western corner. "It looked familiar because it *is* familiar. My cousin married a girl in one of these mountain villages. We all had to travel there in secret for the wedding." I trace a section of the map with a finger. "This is the course."

Martial looks at me uncertainly. "That's great, Imelda. I hate to be the bearer of bad news, but most of the other riders will know that, too. If they don't know where it is, they'll probably have redrawn the course from memory. That's how the Ashlords are trained. Most of the good ones can take mental pictures. They go home after the revela-tion and draw the whole thing. Some of them are trained so well that they don't even have to draw it. They just have it in here." He taps his temple. "It's a standard talent among their kind."

I shake my head. "My advantage isn't knowing the course."

He frowns in confusion. "Now you've lost me."

"My advantage is how well I know the outskirts. The Gravitas Mountain chain, Martial. I rode through these areas during the week of my cousin's wedding. The two families rented out phoenixes from a nearby ranch. Weddings are boring, so I spent most of my time riding. I've been through some of these passes before. I know the terrain."

Martial frowns. "Look, Ayala should have told you this. . . . Really, you should know this from watching it every year. The course is enclosed. They raise these huge metal barriers around the whole area. From start to finish. So you can't get out. And what good would it really do to get outside the walls? The paths on the course are always more direct than going around."

"Not for what I have planned."

I reach into my other pocket and pull out a small square of paper. The instructions I've written on it are absolutely thorough. I hand the slip to Martial and watch as his pale eyes scan the contents. The longer he reads, the wider his eyes get. When he reaches the end, he sets a hand on the marble frame of the bathtub to keep himself steady.

"You can't be serious."

"It will work. I just need your help."

He's stunned. "You're asking a lot of me, Imelda."

"Don't just do it for me, then," I reply. "Do it for my family. Do it for Farian."

He takes a few steadying breaths and finally nods.

"I'll send the letters today. What happens if they figure out what you're doing?"

"They won't. It will work. Trust me, it's going to work."

"Great. Then what? What if it works?" he asks. "Ashlord law . . ."

"Is *very* clear on the subject. The crime I'm committing can't be extended to anyone but the person who commits it. I spent half the night going through their standard book of laws just to make sure it wouldn't echo back to my family."

The water's still running loudly behind him. I hate asking this of Martial, but if there's anyone who will understand what I'm trying to do, it's him. He reads the instructions two more times, shreds the little paper, and tosses it into the bath. We both watch the flowing water snatch the paper, curling and darkening it before sucking it down to the sewers.

"It's risky." He smiles, looking ten years younger. "But if anyone can do it . . ."

We go over a few more details before he leaves. His absence makes me nervous. All that's left is execution. No more planning or dreaming or hoping. I just have to do the impossible. I have to make something out of nothing. Farian's always called me the Alchemist.

It's time to take the title seriously.

Ayala arrives. She spends five minutes fluttering around the room like a mother hen. I smile at her. It's the closest I've come to feeling affection for any Ashlord. She's nervous. Today marks the last ceremony before the Races begin.

Today is the Longest Ride. It's a classic Ashlord tradition. The one time in this whole process where cameras aren't permitted. It's a raw moment of showing strengths, revealing weaknesses. All the riders are packed into a massive carriage and ushered to the racing location. Ayala explains that conversation inside is forbidden. It's a sizing up, a staring down.

Who will break? Who can't handle the heat?

She explained that it's symbolic. Ashlord myth claims the bravest warriors used to ride in carriages that took them through the underworlds. For that reason, our ride today will have no windows. That way the symbolic warriors will not have to see how vast and dark the underworld really is.

I take my box of ashes and follow Ayala through the streets. I've put on all the provided gear she gave me, except the boots. Farian will get a good laugh when he sees that.

I should be nervous about the crowds that watch us march past, about the voices that call out my name. But I'm more worried about making my plan work. I've only been riding with my horse for six days. There's a relationship now, but that doesn't change the fact that he could spook over something completely random. My plans should mitigate some of the potential damage.

But there are still so many ways to fail.

The crowd of reporters parts for us. Ayala walks proudly at my side. She's all confidence, even though I've given her no reason to believe I can win. I smile to a Dividian reporter and give a polite wave to everyone else. Most of the other riders are already standing in the great square. The temple bells ring out from their gilded towers. The waiting carriage *is* massive. Everything about it screams opulence. As I eye the riders, the crowd, I realize how normal all of this is for them. They're accustomed to riding in finery. They've never known a life without riches. Each of them had one hundred thousand spare legions to spend on this event. My family would kill for that kind of money. I stand there in line with the others, and I have never felt so sure of myself.

Pippa's the last to arrive. For the first time since meeting her, she looks disheveled. Nothing horrible, but her hair's not perfect, and her eyes are a little bloodshot. Her mother and father stride beside her, unblinking as the cameras turn their way. I watch Pippa for a little longer, and it's clear she's not at the top of her game. That's a good thing. Ideally, the eyes of every spectator will be drawn to an exciting, competitive race. Distractions will help me.

The Brightness doesn't appear this time, but an official opens the carriage door. Her voice rings out over the gathered audience. "Bravos. Enter!"

The strapping rider raises a fist to the cheering crowd and ducks inside the carriage. Its frame shakes as he vanishes from sight. The official calls another name and I know mine will be called soon.

Ayala leans close and whispers, "I believe in you, Imelda. Show them what the Dividian can do."

I don't nod or whisper back. Instead, I stare at the gathered crowds and wonder what she means. What the Dividian can do? How will the world ever know what we can do? We're made poor and her kind keep us poor. We're supposed to do as much with half as the Ashlords do with double. I find the face of a young Dividian girl in the crowd. She's standing with her father. He wears a finer suit than my father ever wore, but even these city-born Dividian observe the gathering of Ashlords with awe. The Races have always been a spectacle. One more chance to see the glory of the people we are made to worship. The Ashlords and their gods.

"Imelda Beru."

I smile as I walk to the carriage. It is not forced or fake. I'm seeing the undeniable righteousness of my plan. I'm going to break their rules. I'm going to win their precious spectacle my own way. Maybe then they'll see just what the Dividian can do.

19

SILENCE

ADRIAN

I find myself in another box, but this time I'm surrounded by enemies. They seat us in the tightest, most uncomfortable circle imaginable. Not a window in the place. It's only worse once we've started moving, as everyone's jostled into everyone else. The cabin is heat and hatred and little else. I sit there and smile as the Ashlords take turns staring at me. It's good to know just how far under their skin I've managed to dig.

The Ashlords put down the Rebellion on the backs of their gods. They've always been competent fighters and expert military strategists. But they called for fire to rain down from the skies and buried whole cities in ash. That's what really won the war. And it took sacrifices, the blood of thousands. In the arena, the riders won't have gods at their beck and call. It takes effort to push my memory of the Dread's visit aside.

No gods now. It's just me against them.

Looking around, there's only one real bruiser in the bunch: Bravos. I've seen some of his gladiator vids. He's strong and quick and brutal, but I still like my odds if it's a straight-up fight. The problem is it won't be. The back-end riders are always teaming up. The Races have a strange history when it comes to teamwork. Duos are well loved. Some of the most famous winners worked their way through the first legs together, then split at the end and raced each other for glory. Two is acceptable. Three's a crowd. Four is a desperation worthy of shame.

But after my interview with Cassiopia, I know I have a target on my back. Most Ashlords won't risk being embarrassed in a fight, either. They'll come, and when they do, they'll have friends with them. It's just a matter of figuring out which crew hates me enough to make the first move. As the Longest Ride begins, I drink in all the details.

There are four racers who never look my way.

Pippa shut her eyes the second she sat down and hasn't opened them since. She's going to that place that only champions can go. Pushing everything else out except for the idea of winning. She takes one breath after the next. Her hair is drawn into a perfect racing braid. I memorize the details because I have a feeling that's the face I'll be looking at coming down the homestretch.

An Ashlord four seats to my right ignores me as well. I recognize him from the amateur circuit: Revel. He's a burner if there ever was one. Even the purest phoenixes can't sprint the whole race. Revel pushes up against those limits more than the rest. Fast and reckless, but he looks incapable of true violence. Even if he chases out to a lead, he'll be lucky to keep it.

The Dividian sits on Revel's right. She's a quiet girl with a wide-set face and a determined look. She was all smiles in her interview, but she's not smiling now. I can see a patient anger burning to life. I'm not worried about anyone teaming up with her, though. No self-respecting Ashlord would ever let a Dividian share their fire.

The last person who ignores me is Etzli. The experts describe her as consistent. All my research echoed that. There's nothing flashy about how she fights or how she rides, but sometimes all you have to do to win is be careful. She picked a spot on the ceiling and has been staring coolly at it ever since. People like her worry me more than most. Not hot and not cold. It's the lukewarm ones who can swing either direction. It makes them unpredictable, dangerous.

Once I've eliminated those four, I start to assess the other potential teammates in the carriage. Bravos might pair up with someone, but I can't figure out who. It's hard not to notice the dynamic happening with a trio to my left. Almost everyone in the carriage is tense. Tight jaws and taut shoulders. Not these three. I find myself blanking on one of their names. He's from out on the coast. Very precise, good fighter, uncreative. And clearly not very memorable.

I definitely recognize Capri. A former prodigy who peaked when he was seven. It's been nearly a decade since he actually did anything impressive on the back of a horse. But the one who really has my attention is Thyma. Her head is completely shaved and her eyes look like dark pits. She answers every glance her way by baring her teeth. The third time she does it, I can't resist winking. The look she sends back promises blood.

They're going to kill you.

The Dread's warning echoes. His accusation of Daddy is there, too. I choose to dismiss both. Let them try. I wait and watch and by the time the carriage stops bouncing us into each other, I've recalled the names of the riders she's teaming with. I memorize their faces and try to remember all the pre-race research I did. How do they fight? How did they ride?

When they come for me on the first night, I'll be ready.

The whole group is led out into the scorch. There's desert for miles in every direction. I breathe it in because it's the closest I've felt to home all week. Every rider carries their ashes, their locked set of first components, and a regulation riding sack full of clothes and gear.

The riding location treats us to an iconic view of the Gravitas. The mountain chain cuts across the breast of the Empire like a scar, or maybe an open wound. Hundreds of years ago the Ashlords defeated the Dividian. Later they did the same thing to the Reach, but they've long ignored the people who call the Gravitas home. The lower mountain villages are full of outcast Ashlords and escaped Dividian rebels. Most of them still bow to the Empire when necessary, but travel deeper in and you'll start running into the kind of people the world prefers to forget.

We walk forward until a row of buildings cuts off our view of the mountains. Temporary fences connect the barracks to familiar metal barriers enclosing the entire course.

I can't quite see the starting gates from here, but it's still nice to get a look at the size of our cage for the next five days. The officials start herding us to our assigned buildings and a chill runs down my spine.

Everything after this is real.

No more games. No more practice rounds. Blood is going to spill and bones are going to break. I remind myself that if I go in there and do my job, this will just be the beginning.

War is coming.

Generals will look at the Gravitas on carefully etched maps. We'll consider where to send troops, how many to send, and how many are likely to die in each engagement. A small voice inside of me begs for peace. Daddy's voice echoes louder. He showed me the truth. The peace the Ashlords offer us is a lie. We exist at their mercy—and the mercy of their gods. My victory will be a sign to every Longhand across the Empire. Rise up and take what is ours.

The Empire's fate is in my hands now.

Time to bloody my knuckles.

I'm directed by an official to the building on the far right. Bravos and Imelda Beru walk with us. There's a few sideways glances, but for the most part we're too focused on our own thoughts to say much to each other. The interior of the building is plain and undecorated. It's similar to the temporary barracks used during wartime. Something that's quick and easy to put up and take down. They're only meant for a night or two.

Officials flock around us. They take our bags and start rifling through the contents. Our ashes are confiscated for inspection, too. I smile a little, seeing Bravos treated with the same lack of dignity that I am. The Ashlords revere the Races as a sacred event. It is one of the many ways they honor their gods. The only possibility more distasteful than a Longhand winning is one of their own cheating and getting away with it.

We're taken into private bathrooms, strip-searched, questioned. The other officials circle like hawks until I'm given the all clear. They look a little disappointed at finding nothing. Like I'd be foolish enough to cheat. Dressed, I return to the main entryway. Imelda Beru stands off to one side. Bravos returns a second later, still tugging his shirt back over his head.

"Bravos, you'll be on the far left." The head official points to that door. "Imelda, you'll enter the center door. Adrian, you're on the right. Once you enter and close the door behind you, the only way out is forward. Do you understand?"

We all nod.

"You'll find three separate rooms in your section of the building. The first room is your sleeping quarters. The second room is a hallway that provides access to the Powder Room. There you will order the five components you intend to use during the Races. Our officials will be available in that room to you before dawn tomorrow. You just need to knock on the glass.

"The third room is an open stable for your phoenix. You'll arrange your ashes now, using the components you've previously requested. Sun will strike the ashes at dawn and the Races will begin just an hour after first births. Do not attempt to take *any* components other than those that you receive from the Powder Room. Any attempts to smuggle components into the Race will result in an immediate disqualification. Do you understand?"

Again, we nod. The official smiles at us now.

"Then you may begin. An official will monitor your first alchemical attempt. Once you're satisfied with what you've done, you will be briefed on other aspects of the Race, including the use of your distance bracelets and switches. Enjoy your privacy tonight. Once you've passed the starting gates, every move you make will be monitored by the Empire Racing Board. The general public is watching, too. What you do and say can be held against you in a racing tribunal. Thank you for listening and good luck, riders."

He looks squarely at Bravos when he wishes us luck. No luck for the hated Longhand or the forgotten Dividian, I suppose. The three of us exchange glances as an official opens each door. I walk forward without looking back. An official follows, closing the door on the others.

"The ashes?"

She gestures to a door on the opposite side of the room. I allow her to lead me through consecutive doorways and into the open stable. It's a simple, square room, roofless to allow sunlight in. The angles are wrong right now, though. The setting sun's already scaling the walls and half faded to the color of rust. My horse's ashes sit in their box at the center of the room.

I make my patient way through the hanging gear first. Officials have slung my saddles and straps over temporary pegs. I carefully inspect all of it. The other riders aren't the only ones who hate me. Antonio didn't think officials would try anything, but Daddy taught me to be cautious. Most everything's in order. Nothing suspicious.

The official watches as I cross back to the center of the room. Three cubes sit beside my box of ashes. I snap open the lids and inspect the components inside. All three look fresh, clean. But as I dump my horse's ashes out on the floor, my fears are confirmed.

The ashes look normal, except for a handful of tiny, crystalline specks. I spread the pile out in a perfect square, my preferred rebirthing shape, and start picking the crystals out.

I wouldn't have noticed them if I hadn't been expecting some kind of sabotage. Powdered glass. Not particularly potent on its own, but combined with the onyx I planned on using for my first summoning, they create a combination notorious for birthing hobbled horses. This isn't an accident. It's a carefully planned betrayal, involving officials no less.

It takes me an hour to find every single crystal. Seventy-three miniscule grains. I stand when I'm sure I've plucked the last one. Walking over, I hold the little grain out to the waiting official and smile.

"Strange," I say. "I don't recall putting powdered glass in my ashes."

She shifts uncomfortably but says nothing. I wink at her and flick the last grain away. After that, I can't stop grinning. I set the components for my phoenix's first birth and retreat to my sleeping quarters, making sure the official retreats with me. She takes her seat in the corner of the room.

I guess she'll just watch me awkwardly through the night? How comforting.

First they tried to poison me. Now they've tried to poison my ashes. I turn my back to the watching judge and like my chances of winning more than ever. The Ashlords don't want me in the Races because they know I might actually win. I am something to be feared.

Good.

In the morning, I'll give them a few more reasons to tremble.

20

A DOOR LEFT OPEN

PIPPA

You don't sleep well. You're still hearing the howls.

The benefits of the sacrifice ritual haven't manifested. You wanted more of an explanation from Mother about what to expect, but Father's presence the following morning made that impossible. You're left with a lack of sleep and an empty feeling inside. It took most of the night to figure out that you're not even mad that she cheated. A tool is a tool. Mother is right. Other riders in her year had the same benefits that she did. No, the part that makes you angry is that she didn't give you a choice. She forced you to play the same hand that she did.

You deserved better than that.

The unfairness of her decision has you leaning more than ever toward Bravos. A new life is waiting in the distance for both of you. It feels like the only way forward now is *together*.

It's a blessing when the official knocks on your door to announce the coming dawn.

You dress in sponsored racing gear and head for the second room. On your left, a glass partition reflects back your image. You cross the room and knock twice. There's a flicker of movement behind you in the mirror. Ghost and gone. You look back, but no one's there.

Before you can start feeling like you're going insane, the glass wall grinds to life. It lifts, revealing a second official who's haloed in blinding light. "Step forward, contestant."

White briefly scalds your pupils. You blink through the blind and find yourself staring into a room of white walls, white lights, white storage units. Seven cameras watch you step into the Powder Room. The feeds go straight to a vigilant team of infraction judges. It's their job to make sure no one cheats during the crucial moments before the Races begin.

The official waits at the edge of a silver barrier. When you're in position, she offers you the race-standard cubes. Five black boxes linked together, each about the size of a clenched fist. You inspect the container and nod your approval. The official takes it from you and inserts the plastic into fitting grooves along the fixed, circular railing. As it clicks into place, a series of automated systems hum to life inside the room.

"Five powders," the official says. "You have five clock-turns to decide."

In the white cabinet grid behind the official, vibrant colors stare back at you. Thousands of powders sit in thousands of compartments. Every imaginable substance in the Empire can be found in the Powder Room. Each one collected, ground, and refined. You step up to the barrier and inspect the seemingly endless list inscribed upon the surface.

Some are so common you can find them in fields outside the city, but others are so rare that they're nearly worth the cost of the entry fee. Endless combinations and endless rebirths. It makes the competition even more unpredictable. You know that the alchemy will matter as much as the riding. A rider can't just be a horseman and a warrior. They have to be a scientist, too.

In spite of your anger, it's Mother's advice that echoes in your head: *You get five choices. I've always believed in combination riding. Pick the two component combinations that make the most sense to you. I'd choose something reliable and consistent, something that fits the challenge of the course. But the fifth component should be your wild card. If all hell breaks loose, what's the one component that could turn the tide in your favor? That's your fifth choice.*

You've doubted your combinations all morning. You calm yourself by quietly going back over the facts. There will be four rebirthings. And you know the route you intend to take if everything goes as planned. All you have to do now is trust you're making the right choices.

"Gasping Mercies and Lingerluck."

A grinding click sets the rows of components into motion. Compartments shift in and out of gridlocked patterns until a baby-pink powder appears in front of you. The sealants of the container whisper open as the entire shelf frees itself from the surrounding compartments. It tilts, pouring fine powder until the first cube in your utility belt's filled to the brim.

Those choices won't surprise anyone. They're the most reliable components for long-distance riding. Gasping Mercies grow healthier lungs and a healthier heart in a phoenix. Lingerluck pushes horses past their natural limitations. It's the kind of combination that will have you carving out an excellent pace on what you're hoping will be an unexciting second leg of the race at Bravos's side. You wait as a golden powder filters into the second compartment.

When it finishes, you give the next order. "Fearfell and Rainroot."

The mechanisms rumble to life again. Those two will raise a few eyebrows. Separate, neither substance is very powerful. Combined, however, they create the most sure-footed phoenix imaginable. The path you want to take Bravos down on the third and fourth legs is far from straight. It will require consistency. You want to feel fearless as you forge a path to the finish line.

The first four choices were easy. It's the last one that has your stomach turning. Mother's advice makes sense, but it's hard to imagine what possible disasters can strike. You let your eyes wander through the lists of components and you feel more unsure than ever.

Waterlily? But how useful will it be for your horse to run on water? Most of the rivers you saw ran left to right, not forward. Onyx is interesting. Scaled armor might prove useful against the Longhand. There's Nocturne, too, but a horse with night vision? Useless.

"You have one clockturn remaining, contestant."

Closing your eyes, you draw on the memory of the map. You see the twisting roads and slashing rivers, the narrow forests and open plains. What do you *really* need? Your eyes open at the memory of the caves. The fastest route in this year's Races goes straight through the dark underground.

If something goes horribly wrong, that's the route you'll need to catch up.

"Sunscape. I need Sunscape."

The machine obeys your command, adding the final component to your remaining cube. A second later the judge walks over, seals the box, and waves you out of the room.

"Good luck, contestant."

The glass door closes as you return to your quarters. You take a moment to adjust your hair, fix your collar, and then you're striding into the open stable. It's a wide, square room without a ceiling. Sunrise lights everything in pinks and golds. On the far end of the room, a narrow break in the walls shows an open-faced tunnel that wasn't there the night before. It will lead to the starting gates, naturally. Your phoenix stands at center, tethered to an iron stake.

Never before has there been a more majestic creature. Sleek, gunmetal gray, and a few hands taller than any of the other competing phoenixes. A champion, born and bred. Hearing your footsteps, his ears cock and his eyes roll back toward you. Both irises smolder as he lets out a snort and shakes that lovely silver mane.

You smile as you dig a hand into your pocket. Most horses love apples or oats, but your phoenix has always favored ripe tomatoes. It's your tradition, a reminder of all that's come before and all that will come after. You cross the room and hold the treat out. An answering snort has you laughing. "Hey there, Flicker. Today's the day, boy."

You like the name. It's the five hundredth title you've given the horse, a lucky number. True riders know better than to rely solely on technique and strategy. The evolving relationship between the rider and horse matters just as much. Every time a phoenix is reborn, the connection built in former lives has to be seized again, restored into quick and painless trust.

Most riders use constants. A saying or a snack or a noise. Something that echoes throughout the many lives and deaths of the phoenix. But you've always seen naming as the quickest way to establish trust. A *true* rider sees the subtle differences as clearly as the surviving similarities in their horses. They use the knowledge to give true names to each new phoenix.

It all matters, because the slightest distrust can ruin a race.

You untether Flicker before running a hand lightly down his left flank. The phoenix jigs in place, snorting pleasantly. It has you smiling again. "That's right, Flicker. Today's the day."

Taking a fistful of silver mane, you slide your left foot into the stirrup, hop twice on your grounded leg, and swing to mount. It takes a moment to shift clothes and adjust your riding belt before you can take the reins. A click of your tongue has the phoenix turning. You start nosing him toward the narrow opening before catching sight of someone else in the room.

A girl. She wears dark leathers and looks soaked to the bone. Which is strange, because you haven't seen a rain cloud in days. Ratty hair hangs in dripping tangles across a pale forehead. A very pale forehead. You've never seen someone with skin so pale in all your life. Her eyes are like a pair of mismatched moons. You can't help noticing how chaotically the girl's chest is heaving, how insubstantially thin she seems compared to the solid wall behind her.

"Lost, sweetie?" you ask.

The girl ignores the question. "Who are you?"

"Pippa, of course."

She squints at you. Then notices your horse. The sight of it widens her eyes.

"This is the world with the horses."

All you can do is stare. The world with the horses? What is she, a fool?

"I'm sorry, but who let you in here?"

"The gods left the door open. I was the first one through."

She grins at that, like she's done something marvelously wicked. The words make so little sense that you find yourself repeating them slowly. "The gods left the door—"

But then you cut off as understanding strikes. Whatever your mother did. Whatever deal she struck with the Madness. This girl is the spirit your mother spoke about. She is here to help you if you're wise enough to guide her into it.

"What's your name?"

She stares back. "Quinn."

"How'd you get here, Quinn?"

"I rode the lightning," she says, like that makes all the sense in the world.

You remember the words your mother said. You remember what the spirit wants.

"Freedom," you say softly. "Help me win, and I'll give you your freedom."

There's a flash of bright blue. The girl vanishes from where she's standing and appears on the back of your horse. She wraps her cold, ghostly arms around you.

"Deal."

21

DISTRACTION

IMELDA

I stand, stretching my arms and shaking my legs loose. The attendant is waiting in one corner, gear piled in her arms. I look through my gear before nodding to her with satisfaction.

"I'm ready."

She opens a lacquered wooden box. The inside's been carved to make space for two particular items. Ayala explained both of them before the Races. One is less familiar than the other. The Ashlord lifts that object up. A sleek, black wristlet. It's made of some kind of flexible leather. It stretches to slide over my hand before gripping back against my skin. I turn it around my wrist until the digital standings are faceup. Three empty slots glow in the early light:

1. _____
2. _____
3. _____

"Once the Races begin, you'll find the leaders' names listed on your wristlet. Our generators and data should be updated every few minutes. Distances should be listed beside each name, indicating how far ahead of you they are on the course. If you invert the bracelet, the numbers should indicate how far the leaders are from the finish line. Understood?"

How far ahead of you they are . . . Naturally. Her assumption is that I will be well behind the leaders. That has been their assumption from the beginning. I bury the brief flash of anger, though, and ask the only question that matters to me.

"So you use these to track us?"

She nods. "The same energy field we use to broadcast the Races is used for keeping your locations up to date. It tracks all movements inside the boundaries of the course."

When I don't respond to that, the official reaches inside the box again. The second item is painfully familiar. Polished and flexible wood about the length of my arm. It rests in the shape of that baton the Ashlords are so deadly with. One end is padded with fine leather.

"Your switch." The official watches me for a moment. "Do you require an explanation?"

I give the grip a quick double-squeeze. The Ashlord magic snakes through the material and the wooden frame retracts as a leather whip shakes out to the floor. I give the tongues a dance before squeezing the grip again. There's a *zip* noise as the whip returns to baton form. I show the Ashlord the standard weapon.

"I think I've got it."

The Ashlord nods. "The Powder Room is open."

She leads me forward, knocks twice on the glass door, and leaves. There's another Ashlord waiting to give instructions from within a bright, blinding room. I can barely pay attention to a word she says. Something about holding the switch in my hand and slapping the bracelet on my wrist has added a new weight to my shoulders. The burden of what comes next hovers overhead like a death sentence. The plan is the plan. I know it's the right thing to do, but my life will never be the same. There will never be a chance to go back to normal.

Anger thrums in my chest. I can never go back to less. I can never go back to being buried before I'm born. I can never go back to bowing and scraping for what they give us. I will not be their pretty pawn in this year's Races. I will show my people that we are more than that.

"You have five clockturns to make your decisions."

I stare at the woman. Five clockturns? I barely need five seconds.

"Ivory of Earl, Gold, Revelrust, Kisspowder, and Silvertongue."

The official eyes me with curiosity as the machines start fetching the powders and dumping them in my waiting cubes. I resist the temptation to glance over at her, or clear my throat, or scream at the top of my lungs. This is the beginning of *everything*.

Some small part of me expects Ashlord officials to enter the room, shake their noble heads, and disqualify me from the Races. It's an irrational fear. I am allowed to pick whatever components I want to pick. Those are *their* rules. I wait for the woman to comment on my choices. She doesn't speak, though. And no one comes to arrest me.

Five of the most priceless powders in the world slowly siphon into boxes that will soon be strapped to my belt. I just hope the officials and the gamblers look past how much my cubes are now worth. I'm sure they'll have the value listed somewhere on the Chats, but I need them to focus on the idea that I've got some ancient and brilliant alchemy planned for each substance. In every interview, I pretended to have something up my sleeve. It's not a lie, but it's not the truth, either. They think I'll be making my horse teleport between canyons, race through walls. I can already imagine the gamblers discussing all those sparkling possibilities.

Once the cubes are full, the official walks over and seals them. She hands the belt to me. Her silence is a dismissal. I glance up at the cameras, nod once for Martial, and leave.

My phoenix is waiting in the open stable. She's a gorgeous blood bay, prettier than any of the horses I've seen on Martial's ranch. Even after a week, the two of us are still far too new to each other. More acquaintances than friends. She's almost ready to trust me, but I still waste a good fifteen minutes getting her settled and fitted. It's just one more sign I never could have won. In the Races, Ashlord riders need a minute at most to settle their rebirths. Their restarts are quick because every minute counts.

The unfairness of it digs under my skin.

I take a deep breath and remember my purpose has changed.

I'm not here to win the Races. I'm here to break them.

I mount when she's finally calmed, sliding feet into the

stirrups and urging her toward the opening. She's the big-gest horse I've ever ridden, but we find our rhythm as the path funnels out into a wide, red powdered canyon. In the bright morning sun, everything looks vibrant.

The rumps of seven other horses are already waiting. I catch sight of Adrian on my right. His horse is a massive thing, several hands bigger than the one I've been gifted. Each rider is positioned in separate, silver gates. The course stretches out in front of us, winding like a red-bellied snake into a blinding dawn. As I trot to my numbered starting gate, my eyes flick over to our right. A silver barrier borders the course. They built the wall fifty feet high. It would look impossibly tall if not for the looming Gravitas beyond it. Those familiar iron-scaled mountains rule the western sky. Seeing them gives me hope.

It starts here. It starts now.

A new world is waiting for me with open arms.

22

THE BEGINNING

PIPPA

You're expecting the girl to slow you down, to be an uncomfortable burden, but she fits to your back like a summer cloak. There's a here-and-not quality about her that unsettles you.

"So," you say quietly, "you're not the only spirit."

The other riders wait inside their silver gates. You spy two horses that are sitting more than one rider. On each one, a solid figure holds the reins and a ghostly one clings to their waist. It's a lower number than you expected. You have to squint to figure out who else traded the Madness their blood for this favor. One is Etzli. That worries you. If Adrian is the loudest threat, Etzli is the quietest. Your eyes find Adrian next. He's mounted in the gate on the far right, but as your mother predicted, no spirit rides with him.

"They're from my world," Quinn says. "The brave ones."

You don't know what the girl means, but you note that Revel is the other rider with a spirit. In the amateur circuit, he's always been the one to get a lead and lose it. You can't help wondering if the guidance of a spirit will force him to be more disciplined. It makes him more of a threat. On your right and left, towering metal barriers narrow the course to a handful of twisting canyons. Applause and shouts thunder even louder as *you* trot to the starting gate.

Quinn tenses. "What is that noise? Where's it coming from?"

You nod to the barriers flanking the course. "See the faces there?"

Circles cover the entire surface of the massive metal barrier. It's almost like looking into thousands of glass mirrors. Instead of reflecting back the canyon, each circle features the face of an individual spectator. Supposedly the simulation gear makes the audience feel like they're standing right on the course and watching the Races. All the highest bidders appear on the top row. Only good money gets full access. Those spectators can cycle from rider to rider with less than a click. Some of the recent riders have claimed to feel a skin-tingling sensation as thousands of viewers move through the digital air around them. Just one more distraction to consider.

"Are they demons?" Quinn asks. "Bound for eternity for their sins?"

You can't help laughing as you turn a curious glance back to her.

"Demons? No, those are all my fans."

You wave once and the roars boom even louder, the cheers grow even more obscene. Flicker noses into position and a series of metallic snaps lock in around you. Inside the silver stall, bright-red numbers tick their dramatic way down to zero. Quinn's breathing heavily. You can almost feel the panicked thoughts as they whip through her head.

You lower your voice to a whisper. "Hey. I'm not sure how all of this works, but follow my rhythm and movements, all right? Leave the riding to me. It's what I do best. Hold on tight at the start. I'm going to startle our horse out of the gate."

Quinn grunts an affirmative, but the noise is swallowed as thunder roars out from every direction. The sound refines and snaps into the crisp boom of a gunshot. Metal catches release all eleven horses into the dusty mouth of the desert. Your horse jolts clear of the gate, but a quick tug of the reins stutters him, and you hold on tight as Flicker rears up on his hind legs.

Quinn's nails dig into your side as his legs kick wildly. And then you land back on the earth. Ahead, there's horses and dust and distance. Except for one other rider. Bravos's horse comes out of the gate frantic and unsettled, too. He leans over and whispers to calm the creature. When he rights himself, you can't help but grin. He's done up his hair for the event. Intricate braids on one side of his head, all clasped with silver jewelry. He looks so perfect it hurts.

None of the other riders will see that you've both stayed behind and that you're riding together now, but the fans certainly will. It's the only thing any of them will be talking about after the first day. They'll see you working together, and how well you've hidden your plan, and the crowds will obsess over every single detail.

"Convincing enough?" Bravos calls.

"More than enough! Let's ride."

Eyes along the metal barriers follow the interaction hungrily. There's anger and astonishment and triumph. You gather the reins and urge your horse into motion. Bravos follows. You can feel Quinn shifting her body against yours, falling into your rhythm. The first hundred lengths give you a view of the valley below. The other riders have a massive lead on you.

"We're losing," Quinn points out.

"For now," you reply. "Watch and learn."

Ahead, there's a pair of towering weathered stones. Quinn's grip tightens as you pull Flicker into a sharp turn. Tucked just behind the boulders is the hidden trail you spotted at the map unveiling. Mother's advice is already paying dividends. It winds you closer to the metal barrier along the course's western flank, close enough to see the curious expressions and hear the hungry cheers. You can't help smiling. Is there anything better than leaving people stunned?

It takes half an hour to reach the open plains and increase your speed. The pace you set is far from gentle, but you know it's not enough to just find the secret trail. A champion takes advantage of every stretch, every second, every opportunity.

Once the path widens, you urge your horse into a full gallop. It's an easy route that winds slightly uphill. Untouched, your horse starts to build momentum. Your father's favorite alchemical combination—Vibrancy—is working exactly as planned. It's just you and Bravos out here. No one's harassing your flank and you can feel the top speeds getting faster and faster. Bravos would fall behind, but his horse is designed for the hunt. As long as there's something to chase, it can burn hard and fast. Take the lead and the horse gets bored.

You glance back. He looks so stark and handsome in action. Dark strands of his hair catch and toss in the wind. You can't help loving how much he looks like a *champion*.

The first leg couldn't have started any better.

23

CHANGING SKIES

IMELDA

One thought pulses in the front of my mind: *survive.*

I remember enough of the map to know that the first day has us winding down a single, narrow valley. The riding was always going to be tight, but the presence of so many other riders has the first few sprints feeling claustrophobic. Adrian shouldered into a lead right away. Even through the growing cloud of dust, I'm close enough to see Etzli and Revel nipping at his heels. I do my best to follow all the little rules Martial has taught me over the years. Tight on the turns. Pressing my horse out of the shade and into the sun to increase endurance. It's a little harder, though, with company on your heels. A trio of riders have started closing in.

My phoenix's rebirth is designed for evasive maneuvers, but their horses are designed for stamina. I can tell because as they trade trots for gallops, each of their sprints lasts a little longer than mine. The thought has me fired up again. *Must be nice to choose rebirths knowing no one's going to try to put you into the wall.* It's a classic example of an early alliance. I shake my head because no one approached me about forming an alliance. And why would they?

I'm just the Dividian.

"Let's show them who we really are."

We burn around corners and dig deeper with each stretch. An hour passes. A second hour. I can see the surprise on the faces behind me. I have to remind myself that this was always the part where I could hold my own. I am as fine a rider as any of them. It's what happens at night—on foot and defending my ashes—that separates me from the rest. That truth is a good reminder of my goal for the first leg: survive at all costs.

A particularly long straightaway comes, and that's when they catch me. I nudge my phoenix to the right as I hear the approach of their beating hooves. A girl name Thyma leads the pursuing pack. I recognize her from all the pre-race activities. Her eyes swing over to me with every promise of violence. Riding in her shadow are two others: Capri and Darvin. I'm half expecting them to just skip past me. We're behind the leaders. Swinging in for contact with me will only slow them down. But after a brief and silent exchange, their riding formation shifts.

Thyma commands her horse with a firing get-get.

All three of them glide slowly across the canyon. The threat almost has me fumbling the reins. I've logged thousands of hours at Martial's ranch, but I've never had someone actually press me like this. It takes all of my focus to push that fear aside. I have to remember why I was invited here. I have some tricks these Ashlords have forgotten.

Thyma pushes the pace. The control she has over her phoenix is impressive. I watch as her horse noses slightly ahead of mine. Both of them are pinning ears at each other. There's still a gap—four or five widths—but the distance keeps shrinking. I'm so close to the right wall that my riding pants are almost scraping the stones. I'd be worried about my phoenix spooking if it wasn't designed for this exact moment. A turn is coming up and I can see what's going to happen as clearly as any prophet.

The angle will tighten. Thyma will force me into the wall and the two other riders will swing in to finish me off. None of them wants to kill me, but this ends with me spinning from my saddle and landing in the dirt. They want my race to end here and now. The thought has me smiling. It's the same mistake Oxanos made.

He walked in the room and saw one possible outcome.

Time to teach them a new dance.

Thyma drifts closer. I can hear the heaving breath of each horse. The fire in their voices. The flexing of their hands on the grips of their switches. Time shrinks down to a grain of sand. At the very last moment, I swing my phoenix straight into the wall.

Gravity spins in a different direction.

There's no collision. Instead, my phoenix shifts. Its hooves find the sidewall and we sprint onward in complete defiance of gravity. It took forever to find and perfect the Changing Skies rebirth, so my heart pounds with relief when it *actually* works. The ground becomes the sky. Thyma's eyes shock wide as I drive us farther up the wall, higher into the air. She lashes out with her switch, but far too late. We keep on sprinting, sideways to all the Empire's viewers, and I take some pride in imagining the face my brother's making right now. I can almost hear thousands of Dividian cheering me on.

I finish the trick by pressing my phoenix up to the top of the canyon. Gravity shifts again and now we're sprinting atop the raised shelf—a section of the course that I'm certain the Racing Board never intended for riding. I grin a little for the cameras and push the pace.

I'm just the Dividian.

I can only hope they keep thinking of me that way.

My plan depends on it.

24

RAVENOUS

ADRIAN

One former champion described the Races as the brief existence of another world. He claimed that the first leg acted like a purifying flame. It burned the rules. Set a torch to expectations. Each new race created a world in which the riders—like risen gods—could determine their own fates. And the other riders make the mistake of letting me rise first.

I don't hesitate to teach them the rules of my new realm.

Only Revel and Etzli match my pace out of the gate. As the miles stretch and the sun glides overhead, the three of us leave the rest of the field behind. I keep eyeing my bracelet for signs of Pippa, but she never appears. Her absence is strange, but I don't have time for curiosity.

Etzli's the first to test my lead.

I'm a little surprised at her boldness. She takes a sharp angle on one turn and starts gliding up my right flank. I can hear the eagerness in my horse's answering growl. It's been hungry for contact. That's the nature of a Ravenous rebirth. I keep a tight hold of the reins, trying to check its hunger, until Etzli is almost neck and neck with me.

A quick flick from me gives permission.

My phoenix's head snaps up immediately. Sun glints off the wild fangs. It lunges over, but Etzli's pretty damn fast, too. There's a strange flicker of blue light as she instinctually tugs the reins. My horse's teeth scrape across the protective scales on her horse's neck. It takes us both a few seconds to regain control, but she doesn't test my lead again, falling back to a safer distance instead.

The course starts the first of many descents. I remember that this gentle slope leads to a straightaway, and that straightaway pours out onto the plain we're all supposed to reach tonight. I'm thinking through strategies when my horse's eyes snap up, suddenly alert.

I was distracted for a second.

That's all it takes for Revel to make his move. He's leaned over his horse like a dancer and the two of them come storming up the right side of the valley. I fire off a command and my phoenix answers. Revel can burn faster than the rest of the field, though, and I know if he clears us, he'll take a big lead into the first night.

My switch flicks into the shape of a whip. The world shrinks to numbers and distances. I use my free hand to drag my phoenix in their direction. It obeys—liking the possibility of spilled blood—but the angle of our approach gives Revel the lead. I have just one shot at it.

Luckily, I am a true son of the Reach.

We are rangers and herders. The whip is an extension of

my arm. It snakes through the air and snaps along the back of Revel's neck. He pulls out of his determined stance—a cry of agony on his lips—and the movement is enough to pull his horse out of stride, too. It lifts its head and my horse pounces, teeth bared.

We collide—our legs smashing between flanks—as my horse rips into the neck of Revel's phoenix. The impact shoves us back apart, but not without blood. It sprays through the air and my horse trembles with excitement. Revel spits a curse, but a few more strides and I'm back in the lead again. My eyes dart back to the east. I thought Etzli might take advantage of our slowed pace, but she doesn't test my lead. Instead, she slows her own horse and wisely trails me.

I can't help smiling. No gods in this valley. Only riders and horses.

Now, that's a race I can win.

25

VIBRANCY

PIPPA

Every twenty minutes, you bring the horses back to a trot. But five minutes later, you urge them back into a gallop. It's a race-standard pace, slightly slower on day one than it will be on the last. The phoenix's sides burn beneath you at the perfect race temperature.

"Won't the horse get tired?" Quinn asks.

It had been quiet for long enough that you'd forgotten about her.

"You don't have phoenixes in your world?"

"Phoenixes," Quinn repeats. "We call them horses. Are they a certain breed, then? Clearly they run farther. . . ."

"As long as the sun is out, they can keep running. Don't worry. I've been doing this my entire life. Most people would say that I was *born* for this."

"What?" Bravos calls from behind. "Everything all right, Pippa?"

You glance back. "Yes, I was just explaining . . ."

"Explaining what? Were you talking to me?"

Your eyes dart back to Quinn. Both of you raise an eyebrow at the same time. You could see the other spirits, but clearly Bravos can't see Quinn. And it makes sense. None of the viewers could see the spirits in the years the Madness intervened. Only people connected to the spirits can see them.

That could make things interesting.

"Sorry, love. I'll explain when we stop for the night." As you settle back over the horse, you speak in a whisper for Quinn. "The Madness years make so much more sense now. Seeing random competitors talk to no one. Watching riders fall from their horses for no reason. It's such an amazing advantage."

Quinn says nothing. So you ride. Cycling between gallops and trots, pressing deeper into the red-bellied course. The sun rises high and quick, backing the desert ground and blurring the distant landscape. Both you and Bravos pull riding hoods overhead to shield yourselves from the pressing glare. Even for an Ashlord, it's a bright and burning world today.

As the sun starts to set, you check the leaders on your bracelet:

1. **Adrian: 403 paces**
2. **Etzli: 370 paces**
3. **Imelda: 225 paces**

Only Imelda's name surprises you. Adrian and Etzli were always going to be in the thick of the action. You're certain that Adrian is glancing at his own bracelet and wondering where you are on the course. A quick mental picture forms of the map.

Even if they're in the lead now, night is coming.

The other riders will be staggered through the strangled valley below. Some of the leaders will reach the open plain, but no one will be completely safe. Tonight there will be fights and poisoned ashes. Bones will break. Riders will lose their chance at glory through the smallest mistakes. But the secret route saves both you and Bravos from all of that.

You'll make good time and not have to worry about other riders until the third night. And at that point, the others will be bloodied and tired. Both of you will be fresh. You can almost hear the odds on you winning the Races ticking higher and higher.

Overhead, the sun falls quicker and faster than usual. The mountains to the west start siphoning away the light. As it staggers down the horizon, the two of you push your horses a little harder. The path leads to a sprawling plateau that overlooks the narrow canyon valleys, but even up here the light is fast fading.

Only when the last golden streaks abandon the upper crags of the distant Gravitas Mountains do you slow. Bravos does the same, reining in beside you to dismount. All your recent training has been for multiday races, so you both know the routine. A ritual removal of saddles and gear, paired with quiet encouragements for the horses as you do.

Quinn stands off to one side and watches curiously. You realize this must all be so very strange to her. If she's truly a slave, what must she think of your freedom?

Bravos digs through a sack before removing a hand-length sword. If he used it against another rider, he'd be imprisoned for the rest of his life, but officials still allow them in the competition for phoenix deaths. It's a more brutal, archaic way of doing things. Bravos has always preferred it. He starts forward with the weapon in hand, and you're surprised by a flash of blue light. Quinn darts between the two of you, hands held out protectively.

But a second later the spirit sees his true intention. He turns the steel not on you, but on his horse. He sets a trusting hand on the creature's neck and puts his full weight into a deadly thrust. Metal bites through muscle and past bone, finding its mark.

There's a single, terrible scream. Bravos holds his horse's gaze and twists the blade once before dragging the weapon free. You can feel Quinn's shoulders shaking. His phoenix stumbles and slumps as blood starts to pool.

"Gods below, Bravos. Do you always have to be such a *butcher* about it? You do realize we're not fighting in the Helio Wars, don't you?"

You leave Quinn's side and approach Flicker. Bravos shrugs back at you.

"Dead is dead. We're riders, Pippa. Faster is always better."

"Boys and blood." You reach up and offer a handful of berries to Flicker. The phoenix snorts twice before snapping the offering up. Bravos has already turned his back on his own dying horse as it heaves its final breaths. Flicker is busily munching on the offered poison when Quinn slides quietly over to you. Her voice trembles.

"Why would he do that?"

"Phoenixes die. And what dies can rise."

A burst of flame tears through the night. It scorches the air and forces both of you to shield your eyes. Fire streams over the corpse of Bravos's horse. You watch Quinn closely. She's fascinated by the flames. It takes less than a minute for the unnatural fire to consume everything and turn the creature into a pile of ash.

Quinn's still looking lost when your horse starts to slump. Shallow breaths tremble out before an agitated cry scrapes the back of Flicker's throat. You don't turn away from your horse the way that Bravos did. You kneel down and set a comforting hand on the side of Flicker's head. You want Quinn to see. This is your partner, your best friend.

Flames burst to life. You keep your hand pressed there. Quinn rushes forward to pull you away from the danger, but you hiss a quiet warning. "Don't touch me. This is our tradition."

Fire rushes through and over the corpse, and you pull your hand away at the last moment. The heat is like a snake-bite against your palm. Eventually, it forces you to take a few steps back. Quinn stands quietly at your side.

"Do they have to die?" she finally asks.

"Yes, they die so that they might become something more."

26

NOISES AT NIGHT

ADRIAN

The sky's rusting overhead, nearly night, as I break out of the valley and onto the open plain. In the failing light, I see a stretch of hills that roll on for several leagues, with a series of canyons waiting beyond them. Focusing, I bring up my memory of the map. I trace those trails and set myself down on the right plain. I know we were never meant to clear this section of the course on the first day. The Racing Board knew we'd all close the first day out in the open. First blood will be drawn here with our ashes scattered in the moonlight.

I'm in the lead. A glance at the bracelet shows the nearest rider is about one hundred paces back. After Revel's horse faded, Etzli stayed in sight but decided not to test her luck by coming any closer. Not like I'd risk knocking her off her phoenix this early in the Races. Too easy to accidentally break a neck and end my competition before the first day's done. Besides, she's the epitome of caution. I know she won't approach now unless she has to.

I'd feel good about having the lead if I'd seen Pippa or Bravos at all today. Coming out of the gates was chaos. I remember getting an almost flawless start, seeing Bravos startle on my left, and pushing past the Dividian.

All day I expected Pippa to catch me. Her name never appeared in the standings. I'd have liked to take her measure early on. A sizing up in the valley would have been preferable. Bravos never showed, either. It's hard to imagine both of them made mistakes on day one. I'll have to keep an eye out. Maybe they both decided to fall behind to avoid the fallout of the first night?

It'd be a surprising choice.

Their absence doesn't change much. My plan is the same it's been since the interview. Prepare for the worst. Fight through every night. Survive and advance.

With the sunlight failing, our phoenixes will die bold and bright. It'll be nearly impossible to hide the fires from the riders behind me. Deaths never last longer than thirty seconds, but that's more than enough time for trailing riders to figure out where I am.

As soon as they settle their own ashes, they'll come for me.

It makes my decision easy. Instead of riding deeper into the course, I cut east along the raised mesas. Keeping my phoenix tight to the rocky formations, I use what little lead I have to push wide of the pursuit. Etzli will hit the open plain right after me, but I know she'll see my horse's tracks and head in the opposite direction. Always out of trouble.

It's the pack behind her I'm worried about.

So I gallop along the towering rock faces, searching for clefts and clearings. I need a place that will shield my first fire from sight. A good place to put my back up against a wall and make a stand. The first cave I find is about perfect. Stone juts out before carving a neat opening in the side of the canyon. I take a good look at the spot before trotting my phoenix past. Two minutes later, I find a second one. Not nearly as big or nice, but secluded enough, and the fire of my phoenix will look vague in the growing light of the stars.

It takes a handful of minutes to unsaddle and put the horse down. I set my body in the entrance of the recess, shielding the light of the fire from prying eyes. When it finally burns its way to ash, I start creeping back along the canyon, following my own footsteps. I know I have just a handful of minutes to make this work and I know it'll be lucky if it works at all.

Off to the west, there's a second fire.

It's as far in the other direction as possible. Definitely Etzli.

All around me, night noises. I stay hunched as I hustle back along the staggered stones, searching for the first recess. The stars and moon are out, washing everything in weak light.

It's easy to see about fifty feet in every direction, but outside of that, the dark plays its tricks. I spy a handful of figures pouring out of the course's first valley. Riders on slumping horses. I watch them dismount before I reach the first nook. I left it as bait, and sure enough, I've caught something. Movement in the vague shadows has me pressing back against the stones.

Whoever the rider is has settled in, half hunched over their ashes.

My eyes flick back to the valley. Four fires spark against the night, all circling the same encampment. I'm surprised by how many have chosen to team up. At least three of them will go hunting. At least one to defend the ashes. I know I'm running out of time.

Shielding my eyes, I glance back inside the nook. There's a shift of shadows. Someone's kneeling over their components. I can't help but wonder how they killed off their phoenix without me seeing the flames. Back in the valley, there's shouting. The pack's starting their hunt, searching for me. It's now or never.

I take a solid grip on my switch. Leaving it in baton form, I dart into the opening. The light of the stars gives me a perfect view of the surprise on the Dividian's face. Imelda Beru staggers up from a knee, hand reaching for her own weapon. My first blow hits her right in the stomach. I hear the breath snatch from her lungs as she doubles over, helpless against the pain.

"Sorry about this," I grunt. "I wanted it to be one of them."

Before she can respond, I bring the switch across her temple. It's far from a killing blow, but more than enough to spin her unconscious to the ground. There's barely time to feel bad about it. I make my way carefully around her ash pile and drag her limp form deeper into the recess. Around a little outcropping, there's a second nook. I settle her into it, pushing her legs out of sight. "Sorry again," I say. "Hope you have some absolution for whatever they use."

I return to the ashes. She was starting her rebirth. A few components are already sprinkled in the ashes. It couldn't be more perfect. I knew I couldn't win tonight, but now I won't consider what happens a loss. I stand over the pile and wait for my guests.

Shouts sound in the distance. Wooden clacks announce fighting. Maybe the group that's after me has targeted someone else. Maybe they're just letting me know they're coming.

Even if it takes them all night, I know they'll eventually . . .

Noises. Footsteps. A few muttered words.

All three of them wander in front of the opening. I see them before they see me. I square my shoulders and step around the Dividian's ashes protectively, hoping to make it look like they're mine. The movement has them pausing. Their faces stand half in shadow, but their intentions are more than clear. I raise my switch and point at the clear leader of the pack.

"Evening, Thyma."

They spread, taking a few steps forward, widening their stances. It's clear they've all been trained for engagements like this one. They know how to fight in formation. They know how to use their numbers. There's no way to win this, but the point of the first night was never to win. The point is to cut away. Take out one enemy at a time.

"Going to kill me?"

Thyma laughs. "You've forgotten your place. We are here to teach you."

"Good of you to bring so many instructors."

The circle's closing. Muscles flex and grips tighten. It will come soon, and it will happen fast, but my goals are straightforward tonight. The two flanking Ashlords keep their switches in baton form. Thyma has shaken hers into a whip.

"You never should have entered the Races," she says.

She lets the lash cross the distance. It's damn near textbook. A flushing blow that's meant to move me right or left. It doesn't matter how I dodge the strike, the others will move to hem me in with reaching blows of their own. But I don't do what she expects. I don't dodge. I let the whip catch me across the shoulder as I step into a brutal strike of my own. Thyma's eyes widen, but she can't transform her switch fast enough to get up a defense. My blow crushes the side of her knee, and there's enough force behind it to shatter *everything*.

Her screams tear the night in two, but there's no time to savor them. The other Ashlords press me, undistracted by their fallen partner. My first strike leaves me vulnerable, and both of them punish me for it. Two shots to the ribs, another glancing blow off my shoulder.

But I'm bigger and stronger than they are. I parry a fourth shot, strike low, and spin away. I catch another lash to the kidneys before smashing the knuckles of the Ashlord on my right. It's a cheap shot, but he cries out, fumbling his switch. Behind him, Thyma's started struggling back to her feet, even though I know her knee's a nightmare of pain.

I trade blows with the third Ashlord, and he's smart enough to set his feet in a defensive stance. His face is that perfect display of angles every Ashlord has. He's shaved fancy slits in both eyebrows. I'm close enough to feel the heat of his breath. It takes a second to recognize that it's Capri. The former Ashlord prodigy trying to prove his worth.

Unfortunately, his footwork is as smooth as a dancer's. Every one of my blows rattles his forearms, but by the time I have him backing up a few steps, the other Ashlord has started lashing at me with his off-hand.

I can feel my arms getting tired from the prolonged fight and the sweat running down my forehead. Desperate, I decide to finish things. Do what they won't expect. Recklessly, I shoulder past both of them. The decision earns me a pair of wicked blows on both sides, but it exposes Thyma again. She's finally back on her feet, and her eyes go wide when she sees me coming. She thrusts her baton up, but I sweep low and smash her knee a second time.

Whatever didn't break the first time does now.

She screams. This time I'm trapped. The other Ashlords are methodical in how they put me down. I'd never seen them before the Longest Ride, but both of them punish me like this is all *personal*. It's when I finally hit the ground that they become artists. A shot to the head, quick and dazing. A second to the ribs, a third to the knee. They can't swing as hard as I can, but that doesn't stop them from turning me into something small.

I'm expecting them to stop. The rules are clear. Murder is illegal. Their race will end if they keep going. Their lives will be reduced to a poorly lit cell. But down on the ground, surrounded by darkness, I'm conscious enough to feel fear for the first time.

Neither of them stop. The blows keep raining down. Bones are breaking.

I am going to *die*.

Darkness comes.

I feel life slipping out of my grasp. There are distant noises. The Ashlords move away to help Thyma. The girl is weeping and cursing my name. I do not move. I cannot move. It feels like I'm falling through the earth itself. But then a set of hands holds me steady. Adrenaline spikes in my chest. I can feel every wound pulsing like it's a living thing. I'm still careful not to move, but I know with strange confidence that I am not going to die.

Someone—or something—is pulling me back into the land of the living.

"I think he's dead."

"No one's come. Dead or not, it doesn't matter. He won't win the Races now."

"Use the wormwood," someone says. "On his ashes . . ."

I am not going to die. That hope beats in my chest. I can't lift my head to watch, but it's not hard to imagine them leaning over the Dividian's ashes and poisoning them. I'm starting to feel each individual wound. A few broken ribs. A swollen eye. My clothes are slick with blood, but at least the plan worked. My attackers will walk away thinking they've ruined my chances, but my ashes are waiting in the next recess, untouched.

"Welcome to the Races, Longhand."

I can hear them at the entrance helping Thyma. I'm sure

they know what I know. She's a burden now. They'll honor their pact, return her to her ashes, but in the morning she'll be left behind. Even through the pounding pain I can't help smiling: one down, three to go.

Black threads spin in my vision. I know I need to stop the bleeding. Get back to my saddle and treat the wounds, bandage them. But I spend the next thirty minutes trying to breathe as I stare at the stars. The night grows lonely and quiet. Before long, the world is so still that the only thing I can hear is the pounding in my head. . . .

The stars snap back into focus. It's not dawn, but it's getting close. An hour or so has passed. I sit up—half groaning—and realize the pain is bearable, which seems impossible. I thought my ribs were broken. Death was close enough that I could feel it breathing along the back of my neck. I sit up and rub the sorest spots and realize the wounds are all gone.

This isn't normal.

A figure stirs within the recess. I'm thinking the Dividian has woken up and is coming to take her own vengeance on me. Instead, moonlight traces over reptilian features.

"Could you hear it?" the Dread asks. "The wild beating of their hearts? They were going to kill you, Longhand. Almost did kill you. My gift is the only thing that kept you breathing."

I spit blood on the ground. "I would have survived."

He grins. "Would you have? Remember, Longhand. This is but a taste of my power."

"A power in decline," I whisper back. "By your own admission. Aren't you afraid the other gods are watching? The whole Empire can see us right now."

"They see you," he replies. "Muttering to yourself after nearly dying. I've obscured the words. I am the god of caution. I did not come to be seen by them, but by you. I wanted to tell you that most of my boon is gone. Please use more restraint in the days to come. Unlike your father, I need you *alive* at the end of all of this."

Before I can lash out in anger, the Dread vanishes. I curse the god's name before tracing my footsteps back east. His words trail after me like ghostly things. *Unlike your father.* I want to dismiss it as a lie. Daddy has plans for me. I'm the face of his revolution. I'm a general in his army. I am meant to march on the Ashlord capital and lead us into a new era.

But he also taught me to be logical.

In the back of my mind, doubts loom. Daddy sent me here knowing what happened to the last Longhand. I've avoided poison. I've escaped a beating that should have killed me. What if the Dread's telling the truth? I know Daddy wanted me to win, but I know him well enough to know that he's planned for *both* outcomes. If I die, will he shout my name in the streets? Will my spilled blood be the fire that spreads like flame across the Empire? The truth leaves me cold.

I know my father better than anyone. He will have plans ready for any outcome. And that means he knows I might die down here; he knows I might never come home.

I reach my ashes. There's no sign of movement in my chosen nook. My ashes haven't been scattered or poisoned, because the crew that came for me thought they'd already done the job. Careful not to let my own blood drip down, I unlatch the cubes and start my first alchemical mixture. My body feels fine, but my head is still spinning. Looking down for too long just makes it worse. So I take a few pinches of the right components and scatter them blindly. It's easy alchemy. After the work's done, I clean the wounds that haven't unnaturally healed already. Some sting like hell, but clean is better than infected, and bandaged is better than bleeding.

As dawn comes, I set my back to the stones.

It takes effort to remind myself that Daddy doesn't want me to die. There's a difference between planning for my death and wishing it into existence. I know the Dread is right. If the Ashlords actually killed me, Daddy would have wasted no time using my death to start his revolution. That realization almost knocks the breath from my lungs. All the years together, and it is the first stain painted over an image I've held of a flawless father.

Knowing is living.

I steady my breathing. None of this matters. Not right now anyway. I carefully set those thoughts off to one side and focus on what *does* matter. Pretty soon my phoenix will burst free of its ashes. I'll saddle him and we'll ride. I survived the first night. The pack stalking me has one less member. Now I get my turn at being the hunter.

I spit out a mouthful of blood, gargle water from my canteen, and start arranging my gear. The first night couldn't have gone any better.

27

BLINDING

PIPPA

"Your ashes are ready, Bravos."

The coming dawn gives only enough light to see shapes and outlines in the dark. The heat of your own phoenix has long settled, and you've performed some quick and easy alchemy. It's a standard rebirth. Far more difficult rebirths are waiting ahead. You'll have to do alchemy while surrounded by enemies. But on this first night, you have enough space to time-control the burns and get your mixtures just right.

Bravos leans over his pile. "Not quite ready. I don't like to add components until they're on the verge of re-forming. They're more powerful that way."

You can't help grinning at him. "Been reading more of Azlo's theories?"

"They're convincing," he replies. "I've seen some good results in my training."

"Fair enough. What component combinations did you go with?"

Bravos sets down his cubes and slides the locking dials. They open with consecutive little snaps. Over his shoulder, you notice Quinn moving through the camp. You watch the spirit inspect your saddlebags before forcing attention back to Bravos. You're still not sure what to make of the girl, or what to tell Bravos. Maybe it's better to leave it unspoken.

"Lingerluck and Gasping Mercies for the first leg," Bravos says.

"I went with the same."

He points to the next two. "Then Iron and Latchlock."

You make an appreciative noise. "That's not a mixture everyone knows, Bravos."

"Thanks, love. Means a lot coming from you. I thought about a handful of speed combinations, but the forest paths in that last leg will be tight. If we're riding against Adrian or Etzli, I wanted a confident phoenix that can do some damage. I used it a few times in my training. The spikes are pretty wicked."

You nod your agreement. Iron and Latchlock is one of the few purely physical mixtures. Bravos doesn't realize *you're* the one who put the idea in his head. You even underlined the two components in a textbook on his desk as a hint. It offers his favorite tool—dagger-sharp spikes—but adapts the horse for tighter turns and trickier footing. It'll be perfect if the two of you have to go up against Adrian Ford down the stretch.

"What's the last one?" you ask curiously.

Bravos frowns. "I'm not too happy about that choice, actually. I picked it before I knew we'd be off on our own like this. I thought we'd be down in that strangled canyon, de-

fending our ashes all night. I should have guessed you had
something up your sleeve. Anyway, I grabbed a few doses of
Absolution in case our ashes get poisoned."

You squint at the substance. "Absolution? I didn't know
it was such a dark powder."

"Me neither," he says, snapping the case shut. "Feels like
I wasted one, though, doesn't it? I just hope our final leg
doesn't depend on it. I'll feel like a fool if we lose because
of that."

Absolution is the only known cleansing powder. A
healthy dose added to ashes will birth a horse without any
increased or decreased attributes. Some more defensive alchemists even know how to add the substance to remove
negative effects *without* negating their original combination.
It's useful in the Races, especially if someone manages to
taint your ashes with a poisonous component. You've never
had your ashes compromised, but you've seen enough footage of horses tainted by wormwood, or rend, or powdered
glass to know the damage they do to a racer's chances.

"Having a fail-safe is smart, Bravos. We have no idea
which riders we'll run into on the second or third legs. Absolution might be what wins the Races for us."

"Speaking of other riders," Bravos says. "We've got about
thirty minutes before sunrise hits. Want to scout out the valley? I'd love to know who survived the night."

Your camp is set alongside a rising shoulder of rocky
spires. Above, the plateau runs flat and far until dead-
ending. In the valley on the right, all the campsites of your
competitors will be waiting. The light isn't perfect, but you
know anything you learn could be valuable in the next few

days. Your eyes are drawn to the waiting spirit. You'd like a moment alone with her.

"I'll go," you offer. "Guard the camp while I take a look."

Bravos nods. "Just don't take too long. I want to ride at first rise."

It's funny, hearing him push you on timetables and logistics. He said the sun would hit the ashes in thirty minutes, but you know it will really strike in forty-four. Still, it's nice to see him acting so professional and focused. You lean down and kiss him on the forehead.

"I'll be back soon."

Carefully skirting the ashes, you head for the upper plain. You give Quinn a little wave and you're pleased to see her stand and smile. It's hard not to like her a little. Together, you make your way through the vague morning, sidestepping knuckled stones and stopping at the cliff's edge. Only as the lower valley comes into sight does the girl speak.

"You like him."

"I want to marry him."

"I'm surprised he can't see me." Quinn makes a thoughtful noise. "Better not to tell him."

"Why not?"

"I'm *your* spirit, not his."

You swallow your instinctual response. What is yours will be his. You know the girl is here to help you win, and the reality of that has you worried again. What if she mistakes Bravos for a target? What if she can't stop herself from taking action as you come down the stretch?

"Bravos is not an enemy."

Quinn nods. "Understood."

You let out a little sigh of relief.

"Well, Quinn, I don't really know how all of this works. I can tell you that you're with one of the best phoenix riders in Furia. I have the map memorized and we're in a great position. But . . ." You hesitate. "What do you actually get out of all this? What's in it for you?"

The girl doesn't respond immediately. In silence, the two of you stare down at the unlit valley below. You can just make out the silhouettes of four riders there. All grouped together. Teaming up for the first night, only to betray each other at sunrise. You can't help wondering where Adrian Ford and Imelda Beru are camped. The shadows are too thick to pick them out.

Quinn answers, "This is the only chance we have to escape our bondage."

"But haven't you already escaped it? If you're here?"

Quinn reaches out and sets a cold hand against your cheek.

"Feel that?" she asks. "I'm here and not. Alive and dead. If I can help you here, I'll go back to our world as one of the *revived*. The revived have power in our world. Some do not return. The rumor is that they go on to other worlds. But I will not do that. My friends and family are waiting for me. I will return and I will stand up to our former masters."

Masters. It's not hard to figure out she's referring to the gods. In this world, they're powerful allies for you and your people. Quinn doesn't see them that way. She clearly thinks them cruel. You imagine they are. A shiver runs down your spine as you recall the Madness.

"So we finish the Races. And then you . . . go back?"

"I *revive*. There are only twenty or thirty revived ones in our world. Some end up joining the masters. The taste of power is too tempting. But there are some . . ." She pauses, and it's like she's looking down into her world. "Some fight for the enslaved. I intend to join them."

You nod, even though it makes as much sense as the stars. Deep down, you realize you're afraid of Quinn. You remember the footage of other Races that involved the Madness. Some riders performed impossible feats. Others were shoved over cliffs. You know your mother's gift will likely prove useful, but until then, you're just hoping to keep her happy and on *your* side.

"And your world, is it really so bad?"

"My world . . ." Quinn shakes her head, struggling. "I've been a slave all my life. Your gods? They are cruel to us. They use us. The place we live is nothing like this one."

For a time, the two of you are silent. First light is striking the mountains, working its way over the great iron shards, dripping down into the waiting valleys. The two of you leave the lovely sight and start making your way back to camp.

"Your days are shorter here."

"Are they?"

Quinn nods. "Your nights, too."

"We're a fast-moving people. I guess the world is just trying to keep up."

She smiles at that. You're almost back to camp when sunlight spills over the plateau. Bravos is separating his equipment, getting ready for the second births. Beyond him, you see light catch the ashes. The wind whispers of creation. You pause at the edge of camp and watch as the ashes turn and stir, then whip up with devilish force. Quinn watches beside you, fascinated.

You can't imagine what it's like to see the magic for the first time. Somewhere along the way, this all became normal to you. It would be nice, you think, to see it again for the first time.

Dark forms rise out of the storms and sunlight fractures against the swirling wind, bright to the point of blinding. Quinn shields her eyes. You do not.

Both phoenixes stagger free, glorious and full-formed.

You're surprised to see that your horse has a slightly darker coat than it did the day before. Normally, their color doesn't change unless you drastically alter the alchemy. It's still silver-maned, but the rest of its coat looks closer to char than the usual cloudy gray. Bravos's horse stomps and snorts until your phoenix startles. You watch as it trots a safe distance away.

"That's amazing," Quinn says.

"It's my favorite thing in the world."

Bravos looks over. "What?"

You shake yourself and remember he can't see Quinn. "Nothing, love."

He raises an eyebrow before crossing over to his horse. You can hear him whispering the same phrase over and over as you sort through your own supplies. When the creature is finally calm, he hefts up a saddle and sets to work on the girth and then the bridle. You've unearthed your own saddle and started walking over as he mounts. Those gorgeous arms flex as he swings gracefully onto the phoenix's back.

Bravos adjusts his hair before glancing your way. He's

got that determined look that you're so proud to see. He's a champion craving victory, and your first step toward that victory couldn't have been more perfect. Your mother would caution you. It is called the Races for a reason. Champions aren't crowned at the end of the first day.

"I'm going to scout the valley," Bravos says. "Get a look at who has the early lead."

"Go ahead. There's a pack formed. It'd be good to know who's in it. Looks like Etzli is starting out in the lead today. I'll catch up to you in a clockturn or two."

He nods back, and urges his phoenix into a trot. Dust trails him, rising like smoke. There's nothing finer in the world than a man like him on a horse. After a few seconds, you turn back to the task at hand. Your phoenix has wandered off toward the nearest cliffs.

You click your tongue in greeting. It's a sound this phoenix has heard in every life, through every death. Digging into a pocket, you hold out a baked-red tomato. But when you set a probing hand on the horse's wide flank, he startles. A series of unsettled snorts follow. Even his ears are swiveling. "Whoa, boy. It's just me, boy. Just me."

Carefully, you circle round and approach from the front. It's a bright morning, and you have to squint as you walk into the sunlight, letting your eyes adjust. But your feet stick to the ground. An unconscious hand drifts up to cover your mouth. *No, no, no.*

Quinn takes an instinctual step in your direction. "What's wrong?"

The fruit slips from your hand, kicking up dust as it falls and rolls.

"He's blind."

"You can tell that just by looking at him?"

Tears streak down your face. "His eyes. He has no eyes, Quinn. I must have . . . Somehow I must have messed up the mixture. The wrong components or added them too late. Quinn, I blinded him. We can't ride blind. That's not—I've never trained for that."

The horse is feeding off your distress. It's impossible to calm down, though. You're finally in the Races and you made the biggest mistake of your life. The horse neighs, but you don't have any words of comfort to offer. This is un-thinkable.

"So what do we do?" Quinn asks. "There has to be some-thing we can do."

Bravos. Of course. You need Bravos.

"My horse can follow his," you say, turning. "We need Bravos."

The resurgent hope brings you stumbling back to reality. You ignore your unsettled phoenix and start walking toward the open plateau. Quinn watches with narrowed eyes.

"I've seen them do that with blind horses before. They use mates or companion phoenixes. They trust the scent and fol-low. We just have to slow the pace a little, but not by much. We can make decent progress before nightfall that way."

You've been distracted, so you haven't been watching. As you stumble past the staggered rock formations, you get a clear view of the empty plateau. And even as you strain your eyes, there's no sign of Bravos. You blink, trying to clear that impossible vision, but he's still not there when the dust and sunlight settle.

So you call out his name. Again and again, ignoring the sudden clench in the pit of your stomach. You shout your voice raw, stumbling through the scorch and ignoring the truth:

Bravos is gone.

28

WORMWOOD

IMELDA

I claw my way back into the waking world. My breath comes heavy and it feels like something's been sitting on my chest all night. I stare at the approaching light, the rock formations, and none of it makes any sense. I was doing my first mixture. . . .

The Longhand. I scramble to my feet and go light-headed. Weak-limbed, I stagger right into the nearest outcropping. Pain lances through my hip, then connects to the pulse at my temple, and all I can do is let out a groan. It's like I'm still getting hit by the blow.

"Dammit."

At the end of the first day's ride, I had let myself dream for just a second. I thought that maybe I really could win the Races outright. Now I have a knot on my head that's the size of an apple. I rub at it and wince. Still light-headed, I stumble over to my ashes. Morning light's coming on quickly, reaching its claws across the valley, and I realize I'm way too late to do anything. The Longhand scattered flakes of green through my ashes. I lower my head, wincing with the pain, and take a whiff. The smell is one that I know well.

"Wormwood," I say to no one. "That jackass used wormwood."

I stand, noticing the bloodstains for the first time. *That's strange.* They streak the entrance to the recess in dark and faded pools. I have a wicked bruise, but there are no signs of blood. My mind starts playing detective, but I know I don't have the time for mysteries.

Furious, I turn back to my things. They're piled in the opposite corner and I've got about twenty seconds to prepare for the rebirth that the Longhand saddled me with. I start sorting through my gear as the dust swirls.

Sunlight creeps across the entrance. Bright fingers grasping for my ashes. My mind is racing. Wormwood. It's a psychedelic poison. The symptoms are straightforward. With a heavy dose, a phoenix starts to see visions. Some people think the visions are real, that the phoenix is getting glimpses of the veiled underworlds controlled by the Ashlord gods. I couldn't care less about the philosophy behind it. All that matters is that when my horse is born, it's going to be seeing demons and monstrosities. It will smell them, too. I can soften the fear at the start, but there's only one eventuality for a horse that's been poisoned by wormwood.

They run and they run and they run until they die.

I curse, hearing the rebirth begin. Dust spins violently around the recess, sudden wind knocking me back a step. I brace myself and keep rooting through my packs. When everything's arranged, I shove the sack over one shoulder and lift my saddle from the ground.

A glance shows the chaos settling. A bloodred horse strides out of the scattering dust, new to the world and not. I unlatch the third container and dip two fingers into my stores of Revelrust. I didn't want to use any of the stuff— every gram of it is worth a fortune—but I know the addictive substance will buy me the time I need to saddle the phoenix.

She's already stomping, testing her new legs and snorting wildly. She starts toward the entrance and I dart forward. Three strides have me in front of her, cutting off the exit, hands raised and fingers powdered with Revelrust. She huffs at me, but then catches a whiff of what I'm offering. There is no component more addictive for a phoenix. Her whole body shudders and I sprinkle a pinch of it down to the ground. She can't resist. Lowering her head and sniffing, her eyes go wide and unfocused. I slip past as she tries to gauge the strange substance, confused by how badly she wants the stuff.

I'm quick on the saddle and with the straps, slipping around her frame with as much precision as I can manage. I have to go fast, but if I miss something, I'll break my neck just the same. She finishes the Revelrust and turns, sniffing and searching for more of it. I let her snort against my fingers, and use the other hand to work on the harnesses, getting everything in place. She gets bored with me and starts moving toward the entrance again. This time, when I get in her way, she snorts and stomps. I stand firm until she settles; then I slide past to tighten the final buckle.

Sack still bouncing against my shoulders, I swing up to mount. My head spins with pain, but I keep a tight grip on the reins as she begins forward. I know the visions will start soon. Wormwood starts fast and stays strong. Its effects won't fade until her heart bursts.

I've never used the stuff, but I've read about it a few times now. She'll smell the blood and the rot and the ruin. She'll see twisted demons. All of it is in her head, but she'll *bolt* the second she notices any of them. I set her on a northeast path. The edge of the course, and the mountains beyond, are in that direction. Once she bolts, I'll have no control over where she goes. All I can do is hold on for dear life.

The day's warm and the sun's bright. I send a little curse in the direction of the Longhand, wherever he is, and then remember I need to name the horse. It's better to die on a horse I named than on one I didn't.

"Burn," I say as calmly as I can. "That's what you'll do, isn't it? You'll burn bright and hard and fast before you go out. Just try not to take me with you, all right, Burn?"

Her coat shivers with light. She snorts pleasantly, too, like she likes the name. But before I can take much pride in getting that part right, she flinches. A second flinch is followed by stamping. Her head shivers, eyes swinging and rolling wildly, and then she breaks.

I tighten my grip and she's from trot to gallop in heartbeats. Her hooves thunder against the packed hardpan and wind comes howling from all sides. I try to match her rhythm with my body, but it's a jolting and terrified sprint. I end up more focused on not being thrown from her back.

The sprint doesn't stop, because the demons that Burn is seeing don't stop, either.

The course looks empty. This route isn't one the real riders will choose. It's the long way around, winding on the eastern side nearest the mountains. Before the Longhand poisoned my ashes, I intended on taking this path, flanking the barrier, and executing my own plan.

Now I just have to hope Burn doesn't run us off a cliff or right into a wall.

It's not a pace that can last, but a phoenix pushed by fear and powered by the sun can still perform miracles. A glance at my bracelet shows we're in the lead after an hour.

A second hour passes, and even though she's sweating and frothing, Burn never slows. We tear through the vast, clay-caked valleys and it's pure luck that most of the way is straight and safe. I glance at the standings on my bracelet and see the impossible: I'm leading the Races.

1. Imelda: 0 paces
2. Etzli: 573 paces
3. Bravos: 701 paces

Naturally, that's when Burn's heart gives out.

I feel it a second before her forelegs snap, and her front end drops. Momentum whips my feet out of the stirrups and sends my body straight over her lunging shoulders. I scrape my way, rolling and cussing, some ten paces past her. Pain sears along my waist and arms and shoulder. I'm still groaning and spitting out dust when the flames course over Burn's sides. It was a short life, haunted and unfair, but she'll work her way to ashes and rise stronger. I glance up at the sun and know the other riders will keep moving for another few hours.

My lead will vanish. They'll be so far ahead that I'll never have a chance to close the gap.

"You were never in the lead," I remind myself. "You came to break the Races."

It helps to say the words out loud. It was nice to flash a little alchemy the day before. It was nice to hold the lead for a few hours, but the ease with which Adrian poisoned my ashes echoes the truth of things. I was never going to win the Races. Not their way.

Eyes to the east, I measure the distance to the course's metal barrier. A little over half a mile. The sun's moving, but I have time to get where I need to go. There's a danger in moving ashes after sundown. As long as the sun's still up, I can keep moving.

The spectators will wonder what I'm doing, what I'm thinking, but they won't figure out the plan until it's too late to stop it. As long as they keep believing in the myth of the Alchemist, the girl with the magic plan, I'll be fine. So I carefully scoop my ashes into an empty, race-standard container, and when I'm sure I've got them all, I start jogging east.

The silver bars of my cage are waiting.

29

HUNTING GROUNDS

ADRIAN

The second and third days of the Races are about separation and distance.

The Racing Board defines each course by rhythms. Yesterday, they had us snaking through a narrow valley, fighting for room in the most cramped section of the course. Today, there are seven different routes forward, each with its own advantages and pitfalls.

I always knew which way I would go.

A hunter follows its prey.

Instead of riding off at first breath, I waited. Saw the Dividian first, hurtling off on her poisoned horse. Heading down the longest and slowest trail—to the east—but that's not something she could have helped if she wanted to. Wormwood's nasty stuff. I find myself praying she doesn't get herself killed. Honestly, I'm impressed she even decided to mount the thing. That took iron sides.

Next off was Etzli. She's building on her day one lead.

I sat there waiting, horse tethered and settled, until I see three riders make their way into the yawning canyons.

Thyma isn't with them. I smile at that and follow. I made the switch from the Ravenous rebirth to a hunting combination. I actually saw Bravos was going to use the same one for his first day of riding. Today is all about the chase.

As the pace picks up, I'm still a little stunned at how completely my pain has faded. I'm a long way away from trusting the Dread, but at least his magic works. It would have been a long day's ride after the beating I got last night. The thought has me eager to pay them back.

It's not hard to shadow them. I ride faster and harder than they do, but pull back on the straightaways, keeping out of sight. This section of the map has us fording a few rivers, cutting through the heart of everything, and moving gradually into territory where the most important decisions will come into play.

I'm not surprised to see Imelda rush out to an early lead. Riding breakneck like that can't last forever, though. Behind her on the bracelet is Etzli, followed by Bravos. That's a surprise. I didn't even see him yesterday. It has me wondering if he went a different route altogether, but I don't remember one on the map. It also has me curious about Pippa.

Where is the Ashlords' prophesized champion?

There's forest on the western side of the course. My kind of terrain, but it'll be a hotbed for the other riders, too. I remember the cave route, but I didn't choose the components for it. Didn't want to test my luck in a place like that. On the east side of the course there's the long way around, but I know that anyone who goes that way can't win the Races.

The way forward is west. If I want a chance of surviving on the forest paths, I'll need to clear out some competitors.

So I hunt. The pack ahead of me is making decent time, but it's not surprising when one of them splits into a separate canyon. I think I recognize Revel's wild ponytail. It's only a small betrayal, and one that shouldn't surprise the others. After all, this is the Races. No one can stay friends forever. I direct my phoenix to the right, following what I can only guess is the duo I met the night before. Capri and the coastal Ashlord. They fought well together, but that was with me cornered and facing three of them. Tonight's story will be written in my handwriting.

I lean over my horse as the canyons slip past, as the sun sweeps overhead, and I can already taste vengeance in the sun-struck distance, waiting like a promise.

30

BLINDSIDED

PIPPA

Where are you, Bravos? Where are you? Where are you?

You continue shouting his name, stumbling over stones, your voice piercing the rising clouds of dust. There are no trails, though, no flashes of movement on the empty plain.

He doesn't come back for you. You're afraid to look at your bracelet, afraid of what it might show you. Quinn's voice sounds behind you, but you ignore it. You need Bravos.

"Pippa." You hear the unsteady breathing. "Pippa, stop."

You don't turn back to look. "Stop? You don't get it, Quinn. We *need* Bravos."

"No," she says. "We don't."

You spin back, a curse on your lips, but the sight silences you. You can't fathom how, but the girl somehow saddled the blind phoenix. Your eyes run through a standard equipment check. Knots tied correctly along the halter, saddle pad centered perfectly, and even the girth cinched properly.

The horse nickers as Quinn traces her fingers lightly along its neck.

It's impressive, but all you can do is shake your head.

"That's great, Quinn. But we still need Bravos. Another horse is our only chance."

Quinn digs in. "He's not coming back."

You want to shout that she's wrong, that you and Bravos are *in love*, but instead, you turn around and let your eyes trace the endless plain. He must be waiting for you, ahead somewhere. If you can just make your way to the descending valley, you'll find him, waiting like he promised he would. What does the spirit know about love? How could she ever hope to understand what you and Bravos have together? He would never leave you behind.

"You're right," Quinn says. "He's up ahead. We have to ride, Pippa. Catch up to him."

You stare back at her. "What if he comes and we're not here?"

The girl's voice is steady. "You said to meet up ahead. Let's go meet him."

Her calm echoes inside of you. Her voice steadies your shaking hands. You nod.

"Right. You're right. We have to start. He's waiting for us."

"Good," Quinn says. "What next?"

"A name. We need to name him." A harsh laugh claws out of your throat. "Gods, everything that comes to mind is so bitter. Just look at him, Quinn. Look at what I did. What do you call a horse you've betrayed this way? Ruin? Prodigal? Lost?"

"Trust," Quinn replies firmly. "You call him Trust."

To your surprise, the horse's coat flickers brightly in response to the name. He nuzzles down at Quinn's shoulder. "Trust," you repeat numbly. "Trust works."

You reach a hand out, but the horse startles away from your touch.

"See? He hates me. He knows I'm to blame. He can *feel* it."

Quinn takes your hand gently in her own. She feels cold and ethereal, but she leads you patiently over to the horse. Together, you stroke its neck in small, circling patterns. Over and over the two of you repeat the horse's name, allowing it to hear your voices, the single-syllable sound. Before attempting a mounting, Quinn casts a sympathetic glance your way.

"Are you sure you're okay?" she asks.

"Yes, I'm fine. I'll be fine."

"You're crying. In our world . . ."

You nod. You can feel the tears sliding down your cheeks. "Bravos is really gone, isn't he?"

Quinn's face is a mirror of your sorrow. "Yes," she says. "He's gone."

She flashes into the saddle and helps pull you up. You're not sure you could have managed it without her help. You don't object either when she sits in front, taking the reins. It's hard to think straight because it feels like your whole world has slipped mercilessly out of reach.

A glance at your bracelet shows Bravos's name in third. The distance between you grows with each passing second. He's gone. He left you. He *betrayed* you. In this condition, you're not sure you could direct any horse, blind or not. Besides, it's clear to you that Quinn has a better bond with this rebirthing. You search the blurring plains, but each time you find them excruciatingly empty. How did Quinn know?

How could Bravos do this?

Understanding comes slowly as you cover the plodding, sunlit miles. The first realization is that you never messed up the components. It isn't *your* fault. Bravos must have poisoned the ashes. You trace back through his words: *I figured a few doses of Absolution might be useful.*

In the concealing darkness, he baited you into believing his fifth component was something it wasn't. You *knew* Absolution isn't a dark powder. Any other rider and you would have questioned that fact. But it was Bravos, spinning pretty lies through pretty lips.

He poisoned your ashes.

Everything feels broken now.

The phoenix stutters forward and you ride lifelessly with your hands grasping Quinn's waist. The girl clicks her tongue, mimicking your invented commands. You feel admiration for her for picking it up so quickly, but that dies away a few seconds later.

There's little room for anything but the looming defeat.

It's clear why he did it. He didn't trust you. Even though you made promises, time after time, he didn't trust you enough to hold to your word. He chose to betray you and destroy his strongest competitor. All for a taste of glory. All to cross the finish line alone.

Trust picks his cautious way through the canyons. The girl's not the smoothest rider, but Trust isn't exactly the ideal horse for learning how to ride. Changes in elevation startle him. Missteps cause him to snort and cower. Quinn's quick to stop the phoenix's progress, whisper firmly, and prod him back into motion. An admirable effort, but you know the truth. You've fallen too far behind. The distances will only increase. There's no way of getting Trust up to a full gallop. By the time night comes, the Races will be all but lost.

Eventually, the plateau narrows into a winding descent. Trust gains a rhythm as the sun starts to sink, broken only once by the anxious flight of a pair of dark desert birds.

You hate how often you find yourself searching the distance, looking for some sign of Bravos. It's a foolish and pitiful hope. Especially with the numbers ticking on your wrist. You hate how accurate the measurements are, how Bravos's name appears there next to them:

1. **Etzli: 1,803 paces**
2. **Bravos: 1,502 paces**
3. **Revel: 1,238 paces**

For the first time, you imagine your parents reacting to what they're seeing. The hidden alliance likely surprised them, but now you're certain this failure is a crowning embarrassment for them. How will you ever face them again? The perfect little girl who made a perfect little mistake. Too long you've imagined how this race would be the foundational piece in a prosperous future. You never imagined a failure so full, so final.

"Pippa."

Quinn's voice drags your eyes to the present. A river flanks your path, dirty and sluggish. Ahead, the rust-red walls of the canyon divide. Two paths slither their separate ways.

"Which way?" she asks.

Unbidden, the map rises in your mind. You see all the trails and rivers and passes. Go left and you'll follow the course most of the other riders will choose. The forests wait that way. You're sure Bravos is already halfway there, and any other rider worth their weight will follow.

Go right and you'll end up traveling almost due east, across the face of massive canyons, and eventually around to the safest roads the course has to offer. The safest and slowest.

"Left," you say. "He—The rest of the riders will be that way. Go left."

Quinn clicks her tongue, and Trust allows himself be pulled in that direction.

You watch the canyon faces grow nearer, towering to block out an already setting sun. The other riders will reach the forest paths soon. Bravos has a head start on most of them. If he rode well today, he'll have the advantage as night falls and the second rebirthings begin.

Not too many surprises in that section of the course. And Bravos has the ability to hold his own whenever night comes. The winner will need to race hard and have an iron will. It's more clear than ever that Bravos possesses both.

"Wait," you call suddenly. "Go to the right. Quinn! Go right."

The sudden shift and shouting unnerves the blind

phoenix. You slow, cutting across the rising face of the canyon and slipping into the shadows of the second valley. You see now that you were right. Only one other pair of tracks leads this way. A backward glance shows a chaos of footprints heading the other direction.

"Why this way?" Quinn asks. "Why'd you change your mind?"

For the first time all day, you smile.

"The caves are this way."

"Caves?" Quinn calls back in confusion. "And?"

"And it's the only way to catch up."

Quinn glances back. An understanding passes between the two of you.

This isn't over. Not yet.

As the sun sets, you hold your pace. There's one unintended advantage to Bravos's betrayal. Riders can push a phoenix in sunlight, recklessly so. Something about daylight regenerates and renews the physical body of a phoenix. Hearts that should burst don't. Bones that should break remain whole. Most riders still pace their horses, trading gallops for trots, because even ancient magics have their limitations.

But Trust hasn't worked up to a gallop all day. So even as the sun sets, you know he'll be able to ride well into the night. Somewhere on the course, Nelli is doing the same thing. You haven't seen her name in the standings, and strategists have long refuted any benefit to slow-riding. The pace that resurrection riders can set is impossible for a slower horse to recoup in those brief hours of ashes and stars.

Tonight, though, you'll slow-ride as far as you can. You're pretty sure you can at least reach the entrance to the caves.

"I like that idea," Quinn says. "It's a good plan."

You blink, a little startled. "Was I saying that out loud?"

The spirit shakes her tangled hair. "No . . . I . . . I somehow heard it, though."

"Good. That's the plan. I hope you're not afraid of the dark."

Quinn grins back. "Afraid of the dark? The dark is all I've ever known."

You return a grim smile. Darkness comes, a hanging black that's pinpricked by glinting stars, a darkness made soft by the fading glow of day. What waits for you in the caves will be more complete. You measured the route carefully in the Hall of Maps. You know a solid run will have you through the caves and out the other side with plenty of time to spare.

But that's the danger in cave riding. A phoenix can't be reborn without sunlight. So if it dies in a cave, it's up to the rider to carry out the ashes and let it be reborn again. There's always a risk in going somewhere that's cut off from the sun's light. But at this point? Risk is all you have left. You follow the stars for hours until the canyon begins to narrow and the path grows more treacherous. Rather than risk the footing, the two of you dismount.

You set up camp as Quinn removes Trust's saddle. When the phoenix is stripped bare, you see the spirit hesitate for the first time. It's easy to read her thoughts.

"I'll do it if you don't want to."

Quinn shakes her head. "It should be me. He followed my lead all day."

Nodding, you dig into a pouch and hand her a helping of fellfall seeds.

"Feed him those. It will take a clockturn or two."

She rolls the little seeds in her hand before turning back. Trust snuffs at the offered treat, ignoring them until Quinn whispers quietly, her opposite hand stroking his neck softly.

It doesn't take long for him to die.

Once the fire's gone out and the ashes have cooled, you set out the components. This time you carefully explain how it all works to Quinn, just in case.

"I always flatten the ashes. An even spread, and almost always in a circle. People have some *ridiculous* theories about placing components and how to do it. The only thing that matters is what mixes and how much." You pinch two components between your fingers and let them trickle into the ashes. "Gasping Mercies and Lingerluck. They're the main components we used in the last rebirth, although the poison Bravos used negated both of them when he put it in the ashes. I'm just using a few dollops this time, because they're not the main component."

Quinn nods. "What is?"

"When you're going in a cave, only one component helps." You pour out the pure-white substance, watching as it suffuses the night with a gentle glow. "We call it Sunscape."

PART THREE

STORM

The best way to weather a storm is to
become a mountain.

—Dividian proverb

31

ENEMIES

ADRIAN

They make camp along a raised ridge.

It's an almost flawless position. It nestles against a second, higher ridge that looks like it can only be accessed from some other section of the course. The only safe path up to them is narrow and straight, which means they'll get a good look at anyone who's trying to join their party. It's such a defensible location that I actually consider leaving them be, but I know I owe them for the night before. It's time to eliminate some of my opponents.

Once I've got my own ashes settled and safe, I start the climb. In daylight it'd be hard enough, but in moonlight it's about impossible. Twice I lose my footing and almost go flailing back into the valley below. Once I reach the point of no return, a new focus grips me. I wedge myself up one ridge, then a second, slowly working my way back over to where they're camped.

There's a pair of uncomfortably large gaps to leap, but I

make the jumps and go quiet as I reach the section of stone that I know borders their camp. Moonlight hangs above everything. I flatten myself to the stones and start crawling. Wind snags at my hair and cloak, but at least it hides the sound of my progress as I work slowly over to the ledge. A glance over the lip shows the two of them are there, eyes on the valley below, hands ready on their switches.

"Bravos made an appearance."

One nods. "Revel's up there, too, the traitor."

"But no sign of Pippa?"

The other makes a noise.

"She has to be up to something. She's too smart to fall back."

"Well, if she's out of it for some reason, I like our chances."

"Bravos will fade, but Etzli? You know she doesn't make mistakes."

They go on talking like that for a while. Daddy taught me patience. I didn't risk my life climbing up here to waste my chance. They're both competent fighters. Maybe I could take them together, but it'll be far easier if I can isolate one of them, quick and clean.

The conversation drags. One starts to nod off before the other slaps his shoulder.

"No sleeping, Capri," he says. "Not tonight."

"I'm going to take a look at the valley, then."

I watch as Capri takes his feet, eyes the two piles of ashes, and steps toward the precipice. My moment comes so quickly that I'm almost not fast enough for it. Both forearms flex as I push up, a silent shadow in the midst of other shadows. The one sitting sees the movement, but there's nothing he can do as I get a firm grip on my switch and leap.

The impact shakes my legs hard enough that I stumble. The motion sends me sprawling into Capri's back. It's clumsy contact. My lowered shoulder shoves him accidentally toward the edge. He screams and I reach for him in a panic, trying to keep him from falling, but his riding scarf slips through my fingers. He vanishes into the night with a scream.

Cursing, I turn to face the other. My baton barely catches his first strike, and his second, and his third. He's good, and this time he's on higher ground, but with each new blow I can see his forearms trembling more and more. I am too strong for him.

My switch starts to move faster as his moves slower, and he opens himself up with a wide and tired strike. I sweep the blow left with my off-hand and punch my own baton into his throat. The wood catches him hard and folds him in on himself. My second swing takes out his legs and the third has him raising his hands for mercy.

"Please," he says. "Please don't."

He wants what he would never give. That's the way of all Ashlords.

I bring the switch down on his knee, then his hip, then his nose. There's no mercy in the strength of my arm or in the accuracy of each strike. I don't take pleasure in giving pain, but this is a necessary message, to him and to all of his kind. I'm playing by their rules in the Races, but there will come a day when we are no longer at their mercy.

It's possible they'll be at ours.

I leave him unconscious in the dust. I don't bother using wormwood. That's their kind of poison. Calling forth demons to haunt horses. I flip the lid of my fifth cube and take a pinch of the fine, white powder there: Rend.

It's a substance most Ashlords know, even if they pretend it's beneath them. Some use it in training to better understand the true limits of a phoenix's heart and body. It's an effective poison. Get their horse up anywhere close to a trot, and the heart will burst. I've always liked it because it cuts away the core of what a phoenix is: blood and bone and sunlight.

Both riders will be able to walk their horses tomorrow, and little else.

I give both sets a healthy dose before remembering the Ashlord I shoved over the cliff. The second is still knocked out, but the first hasn't climbed back up looking for a fight. And no officials have thundered out to punish me for murder, either. Silence has my guard up again.

I slink down the narrow path. It curls slightly, feeding back into the main valley. I glance in both directions. The moon's bright enough to show just how empty the valley is. A pair of dark wings stir to the west, but otherwise? Completely still. I make my way back along the canyon to the spot where the other Ashlord would have fallen.

At first, I think he's run off somehow. I'm eyeing the place for blood or footprints until I see the body. A shelf of raised stone caught him in the air. He's lying about chest high, back broken against the stones, blood pooling on his right side and coloring everything. His eyes are closed and his mouth is slack. Nothing looks right or alive about him.

The truth trembles through me. My race is over. He's dead.

So why haven't the officials come?

He must be alive. Our bracelets monitor heart rates. If his stopped beating, I'd already be surrounded and ready to be taken into custody. I move closer and gently set both forefingers to his neck. The beat is still there, but for how long? Even in the moonlight I can see how bad the injury is. The fall mangled his back. A sharp point of stone punched through the meat of his right side, too. I actually impaled him.

Blood pools around the wound. Dirt and dust are fouling the thing. He'll be septic by the end of the next day, if the blood loss doesn't kill him first. Maybe he's paralyzed? The way his body just dangles there isn't the best sign.

I pace, thinking and thinking. If he's paralyzed and he's dying and he's losing blood, can I get to the finish line *before* he goes? So long as his heart's beating, my race eligibility remains. The second it stops, though, I'll have officials riding out to arrest me.

But if he dies *after* I cross the line, there's nothing illegal about it.

Leaning close, I eye the wound again. The spike of rock is blade thin. Like a little knife punched through the skin. I wouldn't worry about it, but if he's paralyzed, he can't treat the wound or drink water or anything. And I've already seen what these Ashlords do with their wounded. His friend won't help him. He'll saddle up and cover him in dust as he goes.

"Damn."

I tuck the switch back in my belt and lean over him. I'm not sure how to help him without doing more damage, but I set a hand under his back and another right beneath his hip. Wedging both hands as close to the stone as I can, I lift him away from it. The blood sucks and smacks and the pain snaps him awake. A protest escapes his shaking lips. Blood pours out from the back of the wound as I get him free. He passes back out a second later.

I've got a head of height on him, so it's easy to tuck my head over one of his shoulders and bear-hug his chest to mine. I get one hand pressed over the wound and the other tight against the base of his neck. Careful to not let his head bounce or his spine shift, I stumble back through the valley. He's not light by any stretch, but it's only a few hundred paces. I set him down beside my ashes and rummage through saddlebags. There's not a whole lot of light, but I practiced enough that I could stitch a wound in the black of a cave.

I clean it out first, wasting my own bandages on him. I'm thankful he's blacked out from the pain, because this would be a nasty welcome back into the world. The entry point is easy, but the frontal wound ruptures twice while I'm patching him. Cursing, I waste even more of my bandages to finish. When that's done, I wash off my hands and put my back to the canyon wall. I sit there, eyeing a gap in the raised mesa where the sun's supposed to come.

Before sunrise, I know I'll have to wake him. If he's paralyzed, I'll have to take him with me. It's far from ideal, but it's also the only way to guarantee he stays alive long enough for me to reach the end. Leave him behind and helpless and it's likely he'll die the next night. In fact, I wouldn't put it past the Empire Racing Board to lure something over that would finish him off and get me disqualified.

This is an unexpected complication. I can almost imagine Daddy pacing through his study as he watches me, a hundred strategies spinning through his head. But that thought chains itself to an image of the Dread offering to protect me, and Daddy rejecting his offer. I shake my head and know that out here, no one can help me.

I'm my own general now.

Every choice I make is not just a choice for me. It will echo back to the Reach. Feeling the weight of all that on my shoulders, I take a second to close my eyes.

32

BARRIERS

IMELDA

The bordering wall of the course is some thirty lengths high. It'd be impossible to climb if not for the raised, metallic circles covering the entire surface, the help of my switch whip, and some fancy alchemy. There are eleven rows from top to bottom, and they stretch left and right as far as I can see. Each circle contains a face. Dividian faces, Ashlord faces, Longhand faces.

Thousands of fans that weren't content with watching the government's public cuts of the footage. They want to walk the course and follow their favorite riders. I don't understand all the tech, but I know folks on the bottom row purchased vid packages that follow a single rider. Maybe they're obsessed with Pippa, or a fan of mine, or viewers from the Reach. But each row up the wall gives viewers more access to more riders. I'm not surprised to see the top row filled with Ashlord faces. The only people in the Empire who can afford to pay for full access to all the riders, all the fights, all the tense moments we see every year in the Races.

Ayala explained that it's a technological *grid*. Whatever that means. Apparently between the two metal barriers, the Racing Board's got eyes and ears on everything. They miss nothing, and neither do the fans who subscribe for the extra services. Previous racers have claimed they could feel the viewers walking around. A strange, hair-raising chill in the air.

All it means to me is that people are watching. They see me now, at the edge of the course. They watched me walk my ashes here in the night and I know both fans and officials are curious. What's the Alchemist going to do next?

The answer is simple. I plan to do what any good alchemist would do.

I'm going to make something out of nothing.

Night burns its way into dawn, and I sit beside my ashes, in the shadow of the metal barrier, staring at the faces. Are the Dividian watching me? Will they take hope from what I'm about to do? Are Father and Mother somewhere in the vast rows? Maybe on the opposite wall? I hope they didn't waste their money, because they'll only get half the show they wanted.

My eyes drift to that upper row. It feels appropriate to see Ashlord faces filling it. They're so fond of putting their own kind above us. And now it just means they'll have the best view of my rebellion. *Witness me,* I think. *Watch as I break every one of your precious rules.*

I hope the Dividian see this, too. I don't know if what I have planned will actually change anything, but it's a message at the very least. It is a bold cry to our rulers that not all

Dividian will be made to bow and serve their purposes. We will not continue pretending. We are not small. We are not to be swept aside. Amaya was right. It's time to outdance a few more Ashlords.

Sunlight streaks across the upper sections of the canyons back to the west. I wait to start my alchemy until the sun's leaking across the lower plains. Instead of reaching for the cubes on the front of my utility belt, I unclip the set hidden behind my right hip. Anyone watching will know something's wrong. Fans will flock to the Chats and shout about infractions. I just have to hope the judges won't disqualify me before I can disqualify myself.

I glance up at the faces. Some of the eyes are focused on me now, watching curiously. I smile up at them like Farian's filming me behind the camera. I think of him, and my family, as my rebellion begins.

"Good morning. My name's Imelda Beru, also known as the Alchemist. I wanted to thank you for watching my recent videos, but I've saved the best one for last. You've probably seen this trick by now, but today it's got a new name. Today it's called the Shattering."

I kneel down and take a healthy pinch of locust dust. I let the powder feed between my fingers and highlight the border of the ashes with a deep, tan color. Next, I take the gypsum and limestone. They pile up fine and high before I use both fingers to mix them together. Any fan of mine will know this is the Trust Fall mixture. I smile up again once I've added the unborn ashes.

"Now we need sunlight."

It creeps over the ashes just thirty seconds later. I step

back and admire the magic as it summons my phoenix into being. She staggers free, proud and beautiful, snorting like the world is hers to conquer. We're of a mind today, so it doesn't take me long to saddle her and get the straps tied right. Once I've got her done up, I look back at the admiring fans. More and more of them are watching me, drawn to whatever stunt I'm about to pull. It's exactly what I wanted. I needed them to see this. I need them all to know what the Dividian are capable of doing.

"If you're going to *shatter* something," I say with a smile, "it helps to have a Hammer."

The horse's coat shivers with light. She takes the name and I can't help smirking as I imagine Farian rolling his eyes at the lazy joke. But what comes next isn't a joke.

I let the humor fade from my face before looking right into the imaginary cameras. I try to picture my features written brightly and boldly across thousands of screens. In one swift motion, I mount Hammer. She stamps her feet before accepting the prodding of my knees. I get her striding forward, parallel to the metal barrier. With a gritty determination lining each feature, I ride her as close to the wall as I can before standing in the saddle.

Every eye follows us as we make our quiet way down the edge of the course. They watch with hungry eyes as I mimic the movements I did in the video that made me famous. My feet slip the stirrups and I'm up on her back. She's a little unsettled by the movement, but I flex my legs and leap before she can startle. It's a short jump, but the impact shakes through my arms and legs. I hit the wall hard, but don't drop. I keep my grip on one of the raised metal circles and get situated.

There's a flush of wind behind me. When I look back, Hammer has vanished from sight. It takes ten seconds to scurry up to the top of the wall using the circles as handholds.

At the top, the view of the Gravitas takes my breath away.

But I'm only halfway done with my trick. I remove the switch from my hip. Carefully, I squeeze the grip twice. The wood unfolds and the whip shakes out. I knot the material around the top of the barrier before lowering myself down. This side doesn't have metal circles. Fewer places to set my feet or get a solid grip. I'm about halfway down when I see the dust rising. To the north and to the south. A pair of officials ride out from both directions. Every second matters.

I resettle my equipment, eye the drop, and let go of the switch.

Air whistles up as my body *smacks* back into the saddle and my hands scramble for the sudden mane and I'm laughing as Hammer comes flashing back into existence. The fans will get a final glimpse of this, and they'll see me laughing as I escape their precious Races.

"Get, get! Let's ride, girl!"

Dust plumes around us. I shift my utility belt, waiting until I'm beyond the sight of the course's cameras, and then I let the precious set of black containers—full of the world's most expensive components—fall to the ground. Hammer pushes into a gallop, making a line toward the distant mountains. The officials chase, all four in pursuit, but I know it will take them all day to catch me. And even if they do, they'll return empty-handed. All I have to do is escape.

All I have to do is reach the mountains.

Eyes to the great, iron rises, I ride.

33

SETBACKS

ADRIAN

"I can't feel my legs. Why can't I feel my legs?"

The Ashlord hasn't stopped talking since he woke up. He's got their dark skin, their dark hair, their dark eyes. During our first fight, I thought he'd shaved matching notches in both eyebrows. But up close, I can see they're scars. Surgically perfect cuts. Some kind of blood sacrifice when he was born. The kind of Ashlord blessing that's supposed to protect him from moments like this one.

The worst-case scenario is playing out. He can't move his legs. His upper body isn't doing much better. He can make fists with both hands, but moving them functionally is a stretch. I've used up the last of my bandages on him. At least the sutures are holding. He stares up at me, and his face is full of hate—but also touched by a growing fear.

"It's temporary," I say. "You fell. You're lucky to be alive."

"You pushed me," he says. "You pushed me off the cliff. If I die . . ."

"You're not going to die."

"I can't feel my legs."

I nod again before glancing up the canyon. The sun has already stirred my ashes back to life. I made a last-minute adjustment. Needed a phoenix that could carry a little more weight. It trots nearby, sniffing loudly and stomping its feet. I realize I'm losing precious minutes. Time that will matter as we race to the finish line on the final day. And I'm wasting it on someone who beat the hell out of me two nights ago. The Ashlord's dark eyes trace my movements around the camp, following as I gather my belongings.

I broke him. He didn't fall on his own. He didn't trip. I pushed him, and the Racing Board will know that. It means I have a decision to make. Either I take him with me and keep him alive, or I race his death to the finish line. Annoyed, I spin the cap of the canteen off and set it down next to him. His eyes flick to it and he licks his lips.

"Drink."

He's pushed up on his elbows. I watch him reach and fumble the canteen. He tries to open his hands, then tries to close them around the body of the container. He manages enough force to almost knock the thing over into the sand. There's no chance of him lifting it up and taking a drink.

There are three full days of riding left. I consider the odds of him surviving in the shadow of these cliffs, without water or food, his infected wound attacking him from the inside out. I look back down at him and he looks like he's considering the same odds as me.

"Don't leave me," he says. "Please. Don't leave me."

I kneel down next to him and heft the canteen. Carefully, I tilt it so water runs down into his mouth. He drinks, half choking, but when I tilt the canteen away, he looks relieved, like the water is my promise to stay with him. "You left *me* the first night."

His eyes widen. "This is different."

"How?" I ask. "You didn't know if I'd survive or not."

His chest heaves now. He understands I could really leave him. He understands, maybe for the first time in his life, that his decisions have consequences. The utter surprise there makes me want to leave. It is the Ashlord way to rule without looking down.

I turn my back on him and start saddling my phoenix. He moans the whole time. I ignore his pleas, letting the fear steal through him, letting the Empire see one of their blessed ones beg for his life. The noise goes on and on until I've pulled the final strap tight.

"Your name is Capri, isn't it?"

He nods at me.

"Capri, if I leave you, you'll die. Agreed?"

He bites his lip and nods again.

"If I leave you, no one will come for you. They could send help. But I think they'd rather see me disqualified than see you live. Agreed?"

A third nod. The Ashlords have no mercy for their weak and wounded.

"There are three more days of riding. I'll take you with me today. Once someone crosses the finish line, they'll come to get you. Two rules. You keep your mouth shut. Not a word. To me or to anyone. Just because I'm riding with you doesn't mean I want to listen to what you have to say. Second, don't touch my horse. It's a purebred. I'm guessing you know what purebreds do to horse thieves?"

He squints past me like he's trying to figure out if I'm telling the truth about the horse.

"They burn them," he says finally.

"You've been warned. Try to steal my horse and your death is on your head."

It takes some work to get him up on his feet. I wrap his arms around my neck and turn so he's leaning fully against my back. Taking the rope from my pack, I loop it around the two of us until we're tied together tight enough to be hostages.

Luckily, I'm taller than him by about a head. His face is pressed into my right shoulder, and his feet bounce off the backs of my calves. He could try to choke me, I guess, but he doesn't have enough strength to light a candle right now.

It's easy enough to lift him. Thankfully he's light, but like most Ashlords, his skin burns a little hotter than normal. The heat has me sweating as I struggle to get the two of us onto my phoenix's back. His legs are the hardest part. They flail and bounce and disagree. I can tell he's at least trying to help. He pulls up with his arms, but it still takes a few minutes to get us situated in the saddle.

My horse doesn't love the extra weight, or the scent of the Ashlord, but I get him settled and trotting. We make it out of the first canyon and we're looping through a second when I finally hear the Ashlord muttering into my back. He says it just loud enough that I can hear him, but not loud enough for the audience to catch the words.

"Thank you," he says. "Thank you for saving me."

I give a grunt and push our pace a little faster. He stays quiet after that. Maybe he's thinking what I'm thinking. If the rules were any different, I'd have left him in a heartbeat.

34

CAVES

PIPPA

You watch light sift through the staggered stone shelves and rusty pillars. It raises your horse out of the bright dust. Quinn makes an appreciative noise at your side.

"You set the ashes here on purpose," she says. "So we could start as early as possible."

"When you've been riding as long as I have, it's the first thing you learn."

Even in dark of night, you knew how to find the location the sunlight would strike first. You've always had an instinct for the little pieces of knowledge that separate great riders from good ones. And you let your love for Bravos blind you to all of that. It is not a mistake you will make again. The newly born horse has a coal-black coat, dappled by thousands of ivory specks. Quinn might not notice the changes, but you see how much shorter and thinner this version is than the previous two. It's just as healthy, with just as much fire, but you groomed the ashes so it'd be easier to navigate any narrow tunnels in the cave.

"Live or die," Quinn says, "I will never forget the sight."

You look over and know that you need to thank her. It's embarrassing to remember your own weakness, but today is a new day. You will never make the same mistake again.

"I needed you yesterday. I'm so thankful. What you did was nothing short of a miracle. But today, I'm the rider. If we want to win, it has to be me the rest of the way."

"He's all yours," Quinn says.

Determination burns across the link between the two of you, from flicker to flame. You came into this race with a confident swagger, but Bravos's betrayal stole that. You're stunned to feel recovery so soon. It's not hard to figure out that the spirit's presence is helping you do the impossible. It also helps that you've realized something about men like Bravos—men like your father. Their need to be first place is a weakness. Their desire for you—or your mother—to be less so that they look like more is a *weakness*. You realize they're afraid of you.

They fear anyone who can rise higher than they can.

So that's what you plan to do.

You and the horse get reacquainted. It's like two old friends learning a new dance. Once you're mounted, Quinn appears behind you in a flash of blue light.

"What will you name him?" she asks.

"Trust." The horse's coat flashes brightly and you know the name's taken. "I've never repeated names, but that name means something different today, doesn't it? Yesterday, he needed to trust us. Today, we have to trust him. Ready?"

Quinn tightens her grip on your waist. You tighten your grip on the reins. With a little click, Trust starts picking his way through staggered stones, winding down a narrowing section of the valley. It falls away, cutting to the left and fanning out into three separate roads.

The middle section dives down into the dark heart of the cave. You're not afraid of the darkness, but that doesn't mean where you're going is safe. You feel the same fear from Quinn.

"Remind me," she asks. "Why didn't any of the other riders choose this path?"

"Because caves are dark and scary?"

"That's all? Really?"

"And you've seen the rebirthings. We need the sun to make it work."

"So what happens if we don't make it out the other side?"

Your voice is firm when you finally answer. "We'll make it. I won't fail again."

Before you enter the cave, you glance down at your bracelet:

1. **Etzli: 1,402 paces**
2. **Revel: 1,100 paces**
3. **Bravos: 1,023 paces**

If Trust fears the dark, he doesn't show it. You hold the gaiting rhythm and he snorts loudly before diving into the abyss. Your pupils expand and every darting look gives no return. Still, you do not slow the pace. You keep Trust trotting forward as Quinn clutches anxiously to your waist. The path winds to the right, descending gradually. As expected, the footing feels smooth. Your eyes are getting used to the dark. You see shadows and shapes now, sharp outcroppings and distant turns. The deeper you ride, the brighter the surroundings appear. You sense Quinn's question before she asks it. Her curiosity has you smiling.

"Sunscape. It gathers the sunlight and releases it from within the phoenix."

Trust's coat glows now. The thousands of white specks suffuse the tunnel with a brilliant sheen, casting thin beams of light in every direction. It makes Trust look like a puppet, strung to cave walls by thousands of bright threads.

"I still don't understand how we're moving so fast," Quinn says. "It's like you've been down here before. Almost as if you know the way."

You smile at that. "It helps that I memorized the route."

"The whole thing?"

"Every single turn. I am my mother's daughter."

"Brilliant," Quinn says. "That's brilliant."

"It was easier than you'd think. This is a mating tunnel."

Trust nickers before rounding another curve. The path leads slightly uphill before cornering and diving deeper again. Quinn asks, "What do you mean, a mating tunnel?"

"See how smooth the walls are? Not exactly a natural passage."

"Meaning what?"

"Sun wraiths," you answer. "They're an interesting breed. Big, obviously. And their mating patterns are *really* cute. When a female finds a male, they run away. The male just sits there, shut off from the world. Sort of like a game of hide-and-peek. He doesn't move until the female calls for him. Then he goes to her. No matter what's in the way."

Quinn glances over your shoulder. "A creature made this. . . ."

"Actually, a creature *ate* this. It burns and devours its way through mountains or hills . . . even buildings, occasionally. The Meridian Towers collapsed because of a mating tunnel in 731. Most of the legislation about sun wraith breeding grounds came from that little accident.

"But here's where it gets cute. The female goes to him, too. She matches his movements by reading the heat signatures. So there's this perfect, mirrored path that cuts through the ground. They meet in the middle of whatever they're going through and *burrow.*"

"So . . . ," Quinn says, thinking, "we're going to ride through their *breeding grounds.*"

"Ideally, no. We'll ride *to* their breeding grounds and tiptoe our way around the burrow. Trust me, it's safe. Sun wraiths bury themselves pretty deep, and they're usually a little distracted. Unless there's a jilted lover down here, we're fine."

You get the feeling that this news isn't comforting. You remember what she said about being trapped and imprisoned by the gods. It's not hard to imagine what horrors that kind of life could hold. Eager to keep her distracted, you keep talking.

"Any rider worth their weight should have seen it. No cave trail is perfectly symmetrical by accident. And it obviously makes for good, steady riding. Sun wraiths melt the rocks and . . . well, you know. Leave them behind. It's kind of like compost. Good idea to clean your shoes afterward, but otherwise it's relatively easy riding."

Quinn nods. "So why wasn't this your original plan? If it's the fastest way?"

"Honestly," Pippa answers, "I didn't think the horse Bravos rides could handle caves. And . . . I didn't know that I'd have you with me."

Eventually the quick, chopping turns cease. The path grows straighter and you can tell you're close to the breeding burrow. The cave itself narrows slightly, as if the creature grew frantic by the proximity of its lover. So eager that it squeezed through the final boundaries of rock, ignoring the pain. A primordial scent clings to the air. Heat washes up from the unseen dark. Bellowing rumbles shake the cave walls, a vibration that feels like it's coming from the center of the earth.

"It doesn't sound as romantic now," you note.

Quinn laughs. "No, it doesn't."

"All right. We're halfway through the cave. Here's where we tread carefully."

You dismount and she follows. It takes a minute, but you rig a lead rope and use it to steer Trust along the ledge. You don't mind wasting a minute because you know this path might save you half a day's delay. Quinn follows a few paces behind. Trust's coat casts dull light into the wide, molten chamber. The walls are scorched black by the collision of the two sun wraiths.

You notice long marks clawed in quick succession. A

perfect circle pits the stone floor, stretching almost the entire length of the room. You lead Trust and Quinn around
the ledge that's no wider than Trust's rump. A glance into
the abyss surprises you. In class, your teachers made it
sound like an endless fall. But a foul broth sluices up from
below. The slop boils with heat, squelching against the sides
of the newly made burrow, smearing the air and everything
in it. You hold your breath, but that doesn't keep your skin
from feeling soiled.

"Hello?"

The word chokes into the air. Your head swings back to
Quinn, but you know the noise came from the dark morass
below. Quinn's eyes are the widest you've ever seen them.

"Do wraiths talk?"

You shake your head, terrified.

"Who's there?" the voice asks. "Revel? Is that you?"

Definitely from below. Quinn kneels. Trust's coat suffuses
half of the room, but the surface of the pit hangs in vague
shadow. It takes the two of you a minute to locate the source
of the voice. Just a mouth and a nose and a pair of eyes.

"Please," it says. "Please help me."

For the first time, you recognize the person the voice
belongs to. "Etzli?"

She tries to answer, but all you hear is a nasty gurgle.
You watch the mouth spit and gasp, barely holding above
the surface. "Please. Please help me."

"What happened?" you ask.

"Didn't see this. My phoenix is dead. The ashes are gone.
Gregor too. My . . . my spirit . . . he saved me by sacrificing
himself. Please, don't leave me."

You feel a flicker of heartbreak. You confuse it for your own emotion until Quinn's voice trembles out, full of pain. "Gregor?" she asks. "Gregor was with you?"

"Yes." Etzli spits out bubbling mud. "Gregor. I'm so sorry. He's dead. I thought no one would ever come. I thought—"

For a long time, the spirit just stares. You watch her, but a range of deep emotions flicker past in quick succession. It's staggering to feel someone else's heart break. You realize that's what Quinn must have been feeling from you after Bravos's betrayal.

She turns to you. "Do you have rope? In your bag?"

"Of course I have rope." But you don't move. "We don't have time, Quinn."

The two of you stare at one another in the half dark. All the connection, the back-and-forth emotion, vanishes. You have no idea what the girl's thinking, or what she expects. You don't want Etzli to die, but this is not your fault and it's not your problem, either. You have a competition to win. "If we don't get out of the cave by the next sunrise, we lose."

"If we don't help her, she dies. This is more important than a race."

"Quinn. I get it. You want to help, but we *have* to go. I've made my choice."

"And I've made mine," Quinn says. "Leave me the rope. Go on. Win your race."

"We had a deal."

Quinn's shoulders are set, though. You hiss in frustration. She's clearly not going to change her mind. Annoyed, you dig through a saddlebag and toss her the rope.

"Have it your way."

Without another word, you turn. Trust snorts uncomfortably before easing back into motion. You slide along the wall, a soft glow marking your progress. Quinn follows, but only so she can get in position above Etzli's floating head. You hear the shallow and desperate breaths, but you ignore them because you have to ignore them. This is the Races. It's not a charity event.

"Hello?" Etzli calls up. "It's getting warmer. Please help me!"

You hear Quinn answer quietly, but you don't wait to hear how it plays out. Your heart is hammering in your chest. Beneath the bright anger is another emotion you don't recognize. You push it off to the side, gritting your teeth and leading Trust deeper into the caves.

With each step, you try to ignore the fact that somehow he looks a little less bright than he did just a few minutes before.

35

THE MOUNTAIN REBELS

IMELDA

They're close enough now that I can hear the rhythm of their hooves, the firing *get-get* of their voices. This was not the plan. The sun should be gone. The mountains should be closer. I didn't expect the officials to be this fast. I'm leaning over Hammer and digging in both heels and pressing her to go faster than horses were born to go. At least four of them trail me. Sideways glances show an Ashlord wide to the left, and another swings out on the right. The other two must be riding on a line directly behind me. They're still a hundred paces back, but they're out far enough that I can see dust rising up and the steady, knowing expressions on their faces.

Even at a distance, I can tell which rebirths they're using. The phoenixes have the telltale signs—inflamed nostrils and razor-thin eyes—of a Seeking rebirth. The Empire's favorite breed of tracking horses. The only rebirth that can follow a scent through multiple lives, which means even if I make it to the mountains, they'll still have the trail.

I am their legitimate prey.

I have stolen from the Empire.

Behind me, the hunters ride wide enough that if I tried to swing west or east, they'd have the perfect angle to end this chase in minutes. So I keep straight. I know there are two other Ashlords riding directly behind me, closing the distance one mile at a time. I know the sun will set in forty minutes and I know they'll catch me long before then. The worst part is that I can feel Hammer struggling. She's frothing and sweating and there's that telling scent of burning flesh in the air. It's like her insides are already working their way toward an inferno. I keep pushing her because she was born to push, born to die in flames, and born to rise with tomorrow's sun.

I just want to be alive and free when she does.

I hear the shot long before I see the smoke.

It's followed by others. Little, distant snaps of gunfire. Smoke curls in the vague landscape ahead and I hear one of the sets of hooves behind me stop. The rider falls. The second trailing Ashlord shouts out quick commands. Her flanking riders angle inward. They're still a hundred yards back, but the noose is getting tighter.

More shots ring out. They sound closer this time. But these Ashlords are military trained. They swing their horses, making moving targets for my unknown saviors. We're close enough now to see the slight distinctions between landscape and man. There might be twelve of them, all dressed in drab gray outfits, all reloading rifles as I bring a storm to their doorstep.

The sight of them gives me hope. This is what I asked Martial to do. I needed him to whisper my plans to the mountain rebels. Spread the word. Tell my cousin I'm coming. The Gravitas are full of Dividian, and rebellious Ashlords, and insurrectionists. They'll have watched the broadcasts. They'll have seen my rebellion, written bold and bright against the backdrop of the Empire's most cherished tradition. I just have to hope they think I'm worthy of joining them. A handful of desperados firing on my pursuers is a great start.

We're still a hundred yards from their front line when Hammer's shoulders start to slump. Shots ring out again and this time the Ashlord on the far left goes down. His scream is swallowed by the spinning dirt. All the triumph of the shot vanishes, though, as Hammer staggers again. My whole body *clenches* as one of the trailing Ashlords closes the gap. My eyes swing back as she lets loose a war cry and stands in her saddle. She's holding a switch, but it's not modified for safety like the one I left behind. Her leather grip extends into steel. The blade swings in an arc as she passes. The silver streak promises death.

I don't react. Time doesn't slow. The only thing that saves my life is Hammer's collapse.

Her blade whistles overhead and my body hits the ground with an air-sucking *smack*. The landing shakes me from toe to hip, a numbing blow that leaves me helpless as Hammer rolls onto my legs. The weight's not enough to break bones, but it's more than enough to pin me.

Everything moves around me like a storm. I watch the desperados break forward, then scatter away from the oncoming Ashlord. Her sword bites down, past a raised spear, and sends blood splaying out from the closest throat. The man dies, but the lunge costs her.

One of the other rebels catches her shoulder with a perfect jab of his spear. The blow spins her out of her stirrups,
and she hits the ground hard. To my right, the second Ashlord sits in his saddle, but he's surrounded and swinging
wildly. The rebels turn his blows aside until one of them
gets hold of his cloak. The Ashlord shrieks as he falls, as
the men surround him, as their spears dart down into flesh.

There's something stunning about the blood. Reading
about rebellions is different from living them. I watch how
the desert drinks every drop. What was I thinking?

What have I done?

My eyes flick back to the other Ashlord. She's surrounded, too, but a far better soldier than the other official.
She sweeps her sword in dangerous arcs, carving a cautious
circle around her. The rebels backpedal until one of their
number answers.

He looks like an average Dividian until his weapon
lashes out to meet hers. The Ashlord parries the blow, but
I can see my own surprise echoed in her expression. The
soldier's entire right limb is hardware. From the shoulder
down, an arm of pistons and steel and strange joints.

The second surprise is how *young* he looks. The determined look on his face can't hide the fact that he's just a
boy. I watch as he swings again and again and again, backing the Ashlord down with the strength of each blow. He
matches that strength with grace. There's something poetic
about the way his shoulders twist at the last moment. His
metallic arm catches the point of her sword and another
turn sends the weapon spinning to the dirt.

The boy moves to finish her off at the exact moment I notice the flames.

Panicked, my eyes sweep back to my legs. Hammer's heart has given out. The burst of fire courses over and through her, and I realize the flames are starting to spread to me, too. I squirm and scrape my nails into the dirt, but I don't have the strength to get out. The heat snakes through my leggings and I can't bite back the screams.

Half the rebels are at my side in seconds. I feel hands and see legs and they're pulling me free. Someone pats me down. Someone else turns me over. Beyond them, I see the final Ashlord fall. She gasps as she does, and the boy with the metallic arm kicks her aside to end it. Blood drips from his elbow joint as he sounds the next command.

"Gather the ashes," he says. "Loot the corpses. Help the girl. There'll be more."

One of the rebels pulls me to my feet. In the failing light, I can see that every single one of them is Dividian. I've been surrounded by Ashlords for so long that I forgot what it's like to have someone look my way without their chin raised in pride. There's something blessedly familiar about their casual stances, about the scent of the same cologne my father wears curling into the air. These are my people. I'm still wary as the leader crosses the distance and offers a greeting.

"The name is Bastian." We shake hands. I have never seen eyes as light blue as his. And I've never seen someone so young with so many scars. Something about my expression has him grinning ear to ear. "You must be Imelda Beru."

The others look up to smile at me as they pick the pockets

of the dead. It takes a few seconds to realize the whole crew is younger than I thought. A bunch of rebel boys and girls.

"We came down from Sickle Pass as soon as we caught wind of what you were doing." He nods back to the tree line. A figure is crossing the plain. "Your uncle even sent a familiar face so you'd know you could trust us."

It's an effort to look past the fallen Ashlords. All three are dead. The fourth is back in the desert, food for birds or wolves or worse. My eyes fix on the figure, though, and finally I recognize him. "Luca?!"

The last time I saw him he had a guitar in hand. He watched my first rebellion against Oxanos, so it's only fitting that he's here for my second effort. He's exchanged the guitar for a sword, though I notice Bastian kept him out of the action just in case. We embrace in a hug.

"You've got every village in the Gravitas stirred up something nice," he says, releasing me. "My father got your instructions. The plan worked."

"So far," Bastian puts in. "If we can help you pull this off, you'll be a proper legend."

I frown. "Help me pull this off? Isn't it over now?"

Bastian's grin widens. "You think they'll send just four of them? What's your take?"

That question has my eyes narrowing. "My take?"

"On the belt," he says. "That's what you stole, right? Components?"

I nod, but don't answer right away. My silence drags a laugh from him.

"Look, it's all yours. That's a Dividian rule, a mountain rule. Every outlaw here respects that. If you steal something from the Ashlords, it belongs to you. No questions asked. And if you think I'm going to steal something from Dig's niece, you're out of your mind."

Dig. I've never heard someone call my uncle by that nickname. Luca just nods.

"It's safe, Imelda. That's the code. The only threat to you now will be Ashlords."

A weight slips off my shoulders. "Let's just say the belt is worth a lot."

"A hundred and fifty thousand legions sound right?" Bastian guesses.

It's not a bad guess, either. Clearly he's smart. "More than that."

Some of his crewmates whistle. Bastian just keeps grinning.

"Well, you have it on you, right?"

I lift my riding jacket just enough for him to see the cubes clipped onto the front of my utility belt. He nods once before looking around at his troupe, making sure everything's in order. I glance around, too, gauging how interested his soldiers are in my take, but they look too busy looting their own treasure. Luca shakes me by the shoulders.

"That was *brilliant*, Imelda."

I smile at him as Bastian's soldiers finish their work. He orders us to start marching as soon as everything's been picked clean. I watch as he sweeps the long hair out of his face and looks back at me over one shoulder. He seems pleasantly surprised by me.

"So. You're the Alchemist, huh?"

I smile at him. "Now I am."

36

THE WRAITH

PIPPA

Another curse slips through your lips.

Why did Quinn *ruin* everything? If it had been you down in that pit, Etzli would have ridden by and laughed as she did. That's how Ashlords work. Another person's misfortunes only mean your gain, your victory. Quinn's apparently never learned to live by those rules.

Frustrated, you give Trust's lead rope a sharp tug. The horse protests before picking up his pace. The light from his coat casts a soft glow a few feet ahead. Enough to be sure of your footing, but little more. Above and beyond, the darkness of the tunnel unsettles you, especially now that Quinn isn't at your side.

"And *then* she guilt-tripped me, Trust. Like I was this awful person for not stopping to help out, even though *my entire future* is on the line."

The horse follows in silence. You let out another frustrated noise and continue to make your patient way through the narrowing cave. The air fills with vibrant heat. You let your eyes run ahead, searching the darkness for signs of movement. You're not sure what you'll find. You're not even sure why you're doing something *so stupid.*

"All this for some random spirit."

You can hear the grunting noises. Heavy breathing echoes from the tunnel ahead and you finally spot little Quinn. She's rigged the rope around an outcropping of rock. She has half a length wound around both hands and she's nearly horizontal as she tries to pull, inching the rope away from the distant pit. Etzli's pitiful moans echo from somewhere below.

Quinn's face is streaked with sweat and her arms and wrists are singed red by her efforts. Either the light or Trust's clomping footsteps catch the girl's attention. She doesn't loosen her grip, but her dark eyes burn in your direction. The look she gives you is furious.

"What?" she snaps. "Are you lost?"

"Look, you were right. I'm sorry. Let me help."

"Why?" Quinn asks. "Why come back? Figured out that leaving made you a horrible person? Or maybe you came back for some selfish reason? Can't go on without me?"

You came back because it felt wrong. That natural impulse that's been carved into you for your entire life. In the quiet whispers of your proud parents. In the heart-pounding cheers of full stadiums. Always reinforcing one truth: Win at all costs. Be the best. Fight hard and burn brighter. You have never doubted the righteousness of that feeling until now. So you came back.

Once, you'd have been too proud to admit that.

"I was wrong. You were right. Let me help."

Quinn's eyes narrow, but she gives you a conceding nod. You lead Trust forward and attach a line to the back of his saddle. Quinn uncoils the rope around her wrists and edges her way forward, allowing you to work with the slack. Calmly, you tie a pair of riding knots. After giving each of them a testing tug, you turn Trust around. Quinn doesn't let go of the rope until she sees the light moving up the tunnel and Etzli's body lifting slowly from the nightmare.

The two of you kneel at the edge of the quagmire together.

"I'm sorry."

"I know," Quinn replies. "Just . . . I know."

Etzli dangles and bounces until her arms are in reach. Both of you lean down to help pull her up over the ledge. For a second, you imagine the shock Etzli will feel being pulled out by Quinn's invisible hands, but then you remember she can see Quinn, too. The same way you saw hers and Revel's spirits.

Etzli collapses face-first, heaving thick breaths. You stop yourself from groaning at the slick smears of mud she's leaving on your brand-new leggings. Instead, you kneel down and push the girl's hair away from her face. Each ragged breath beats back your disgust. She might be dirty, but at least she's alive. Quinn was right. Abandoning Etzli would have been the same as signing her death sentence.

The room gives a shuddering jerk. It rocks you to your feet, sending both arms out for balance. Quinn's hand catches your forearm and pulls you back to the safety of the wall. You both notice the pit below begin to move and glow. It's like watching ocean waves during a storm. Something dark is rising up and you know it's coming for you.

Quinn shoves you back toward Trust and helps Etzli to her feet.

"They're resurfacing," you shout. "We don't want to be here when they do."

Another tremor shakes the tunnels. Debris flutters down from the makeshift ceilings. A violent splash of heat sears the air behind you and a glance shows shards of light fracturing the black. You curse, knowing the wraith is breaching. You mount Trust before turning to help Quinn get Etzli in the saddle. Fire scorches upward. A golden, sunlit claw appears along the rim of the pit. Blackened nails dig into the ground as a shapeless head rises, eyes bright with wanting. Etzli's body fits against you with a slap of mud and heat. Quinn blinks from the floor to Trust's back and you whip both sides of the horse, urging him into motion.

He bolts, almost rocking you off one side, but you clench your legs and hold tight to the reins as the wraith gives chase. There's a press of heat, a scrape of claws, and then Trust's hooves pounding over both. The creature follows. Its mate howls in the distant dark.

Trust nearly startles when he hears the noise, but you click a command to keep him calm, feet moving. No matter how quickly you take the turns, the heat trails and grows. You thunder through the mirrored route, hoping you can survive, hoping you can make it out before the sun rises. By your measure, night should be working its way to dawn.

There's a final turn before you burst free of the cave, out into a weak, pre-morning light. Quinn slides from Trust's back and helps Etzli to the ground.

You free the switch from your belt and squeeze twice. The whip slides out as the wraith appears, burned body framing the entire entryway. Another scream sounds somewhere deeper in the pit. The great creature cocks its pitted head, listening and eager, but you've stolen its attention. You've interrupted the mating cycle. Its mouth opens in a fiery snarl.

Trust obeys the press of your calves. A few strides puts you between the wraith and Etzli. The wraith snarls, its beaded, black eyes narrowing. A hole opens in the center of the flames and you see a flash of massive stone teeth. Before it can lurch out into the light, you brandish the whip. A crack sounds as the blow lands just above the wraith's right eye. It snarls again, but you twist your wrist and land another blow. Twice more it feels the pain of your strikes, and twice more it hears the call of its lover within. It looks torn, but you watch as it scrapes the walls angrily, then turns. You crack the whip one more time and the beast disappears from sight.

Turning back, you find Quinn on the ground with Etzli. The girl looks like something out of a nightmare. Her shirt is ripped, her eyes are wide, and she's soiled by streaks of drying sludge. She watches you and it's clear as day that she's shocked you came back for her. Ignoring that, you dismount and start removing saddlebags and gear from Trust's back. Quinn takes the canteen.

"Make sure she drinks."

Quinn nods in the direction of the mountains. "Do you have enough time?"

She understands what's happening as well as you do. The sun is almost up. It's almost the start of the third day and gods help you, you don't have enough time. You're not *ready* for it. The death will have to come quick. The calculations will be a nightmare. You steel yourself, though, because if you can go back and save someone's life from a sun wraith, you can damn well do some fast-fingered alchemy.

"Let's win this thing," you grunt.

Trust is down and dying. You set your hand on his heaving neck and watch as his eyes spin with fear. For the first time in all his lives, you don't whisper quietly for him to enjoy the peace you think he deserves between this death and the next life. Instead, you're begging the flames to burn quick and hard. When they finally start to race over his body, you tear your attention away to focus on the components. Ashes are gathering on the ground and you're scrambling to figure out how the hell you're going to summon a horse in such a tight window.

Quinn leaves the canteen with Etzli and joins you. She's like a beacon of ghostly hope at your side. You stand there, thinking and panicking, but she whispers fiercely, "You can do this."

Nodding, you kneel over the components. Your mind races in twenty different directions.

"Sunlight will hit in about thirteen clockturns. Some of my components need at least ten with the ashes to take in a rebirthing. So we mix them in the next three clockturns or it's a wash. *But* the ashes are still cooking. Scorching hot ashes burn away components faster. Same result: a wash. So I have to overdose them without *over*-overdosing them."

"Keep calm. Focus," Quinn says. "What's the first step?"

"I'm thinking."

You're not thinking, not really. You're drifting into instinct. Equations flash through your head, but they're coming too fast, too unsettled. You take a deep breath and run them again. Lingerluck has resistance qualities. It won't burn as fast, but it'll still diminish. You double the typical amount before sifting out a few pinches on instinct. Carefully, you add it to the ashes.

The pile hisses smoke into the air, burning a pleasant aroma that you have *zero* time to appreciate. Instead, you turn your attention to the Gasping Mercies. They're the more difficult of the two components. The side effects of an overdose will destroy your chances. Normally, you'd add the little powdered flowers last. Their burn rate is far higher than most components, but you can't remember the exact number. Panicked, you glance over at Quinn.

"I can't remember."

"Talk your way through it."

You nod. "Gasping Mercies are a wildflower. They only grow in cemeteries."

"Keep going."

"The component breeds a horse with healthier hearts and healthier lungs. Side effects of overdosing are asthma, heart murmurs, and collapsed lungs." You strain mentally, but the words of old texts are blurring. "The Gasping Susan . . . it burns. . . . If ashes . . . Dammit!"

"Gasping Mercies burn faster than most," Etzli recites. "By a rate of 3.84."

Your eyes flick her way. You can't fight your natural Ashlord suspicion. Etzli is one of your competitors. You are the reason she always finished second. Is she telling you the truth?

"You saved me," she whispers. "I vow on my life. The rate is 3.84."

Trusting her is like breathing in a new kind of air. You nod your thanks, siphon out the powder, and start sorting through the other components. Vibrant streaks are coloring the horizon. It won't be long now. You do the final calculation, siphon the powder into an open palm, and flour it along the edges of your pile. The second it's finished, you almost collapse from the stress.

"Did we do it?" Quinn asks. "Did it work?"

You laugh, sitting back and lowering your head onto her shoulder.

"You just *had* to save her."

Quinn sneaks an arm around you. The two of you sit and watch the sun rise together. You're still nervous as the ashes stir beneath the first touch of sunlight. Nervous that you got the calculations wrong somehow, that all of this will be for nothing. But the horse that comes striding out of the storm looks healthy and whole. All three of you breathe a sigh of relief.

You and Etzli exchange a look. An understanding passes. You saved her, but now you'll go on without her. She'll survive—you're sure of that much—but her look confirms what you were hoping for. She wants you to ride on and finish. You nod once before looking back to the waiting course. The hard part comes next. Finishing the Races. Catching the leaders.

It makes you smile.

You were *born* for what comes next.

37

THIEF

ADRIAN

After passing Capri's partner in the morning, we didn't see a soul on the third day's ride.

Capri kept quiet, too. Not a word, except to ask me if I'd pull up his hood. Riding with him strapped to my back wasn't easy. Not on me. Not on the horse. I spent the entire day staring at my bracelet, expecting the gap between us and the leaders to grow as he slowed our pace. But the rankings fluctuated unpredictably. Etzli started with a huge lead, but all her number did was shrink until she vanished from the scoreboard entirely. Your stomach sinks a little. Something horrible must have happened.

Revel stormed out to the lead at first, but Bravos is the steadier rider. I always thought of him as a bruiser without much pacing or technique, but maybe he dated Pippa long enough to learn a thing or two. At one point, I glanced down and the third name had changed. I thought I saw Pippa's name scrawled there like an inevitability. But a second glance had me blinking. It wasn't her name. It was mine. I watched the numbers for a while after that, but it must have been a mistake. Pippa's name never appeared again.

I kept pushing deeper into the course, and the standings fluctuated only slightly:

1. **Bravos: 436 paces**
2. **Revel: 247 paces**
3. **Adrian**

Bravos had an even bigger lead for a while, but his progress stopped right before sunset. It's not hard to figure out that he caught an early burn. And the whole field is lucky that he did. I've never heard of a rider coming back from a lead over five hundred paces. But now?

It's close enough. Victory is within reach.

I glance over at Capri. He's lying in the dust and dirt. Looks like hell, but there's nothing more I can do besides give him food and water. I sit with my back to a rise of cool stone, eyes on the canyon we left behind. The way forward is a departure from the rest of the course. It will run us through the strange desert forests. It's full of crags and twists and sunstripe trees. The kind of course that demands a lot from a rider and his horse. I was lucky to stay this close to the leaders, but I'm not foolish enough to think it will happen again, not with Capri weighing me down.

He's as healthy as I can get him. His wounds look fine. Ugly, but not the kind of infections he'll die from. It's time to cut the cord. He's been watching me since we woke up.

"You're going to leave me," Capri says aloud. "Aren't you?"

I glance over at him. "Makes the most sense."

He nods. The movement is an upgrade from the day before. He might recover.

"You're just like us," he says.

"Is that right?"

He nods again, eyes on the fading stars above. "You don't feel guilty. I might never walk again, but you don't care. I can see it in your eyes. You're just doing equations and distances. Not thinking at all about what life will be like for me now. You care more about winning. That's all my people care about, too. Who wins and who loses. That's all I was ever taught."

I weigh his words. I know the Empire's listening. Officials are sitting in their camps at the start and end of the Races, ready to ride out and arrest me at a moment's notice. But I also know that Daddy and half the Reach are losing sleep to listen in, each of them hoping I'll speak with *their* voice. The Empire is watching. Most of them were born hating people like me.

It gives my voice fire. "I've trained my whole life for this."

"You trained to be like one of us."

I shake my head, knowing he's wrong. "I trained to be better than you. Faster than you. Stronger than you. At the end of the day, I trained to be more merciful than you, too."

"That's what you call this?" Capri gestures to his legs. "Is this your idea of mercy?"

I stare back at him. Anger's breathing into my bones, curling hands into fists. The Dread is right. Daddy sent me here not knowing whether I'd live or die. I'm wrestling with that, but it's still his words that come to mind. I haven't forgotten *why* I wanted to come in the first place.

"Nine hundred and seven."

Capri stares back at me. "What?"

"Nine hundred and seven. That's how many firstborns the Ashlords killed in the Purge after the Rebellion. Some were infants. Some were elderly. I had nine hundred and seven good reasons to bury you back in that canyon. You're right. I don't care what you do after this. I don't care if you ever walk again. But every breath you take from here on out? Mercy. Every time your parents give you a hug? Mercy. Every time you see the sun rise? Mercy. You're alive because of me. I gave you everything you have from here on out, and you'll never forget that."

I stand as sunlight starts edging through gaps in the scarecrow trees. We're a little higher up than we were the day before, on a little plateau that precedes the waiting forest. Sunlight cuts a path to my ashes and stirs them, drawing life into my phoenix again. I ignore Capri and start sorting through my gear. It takes time to get my horse settled and saddled.

By the time I turn back, he's started crying.

"My family won't take me back," Capri says. "Not like this."

I pause to look at him. "Make that another difference between my people and yours."

Taking up the canteen, I head toward the nearest creek. One feature of the Races is that the officials come in beforehand and treat all the rivers. They figured out a few years back that riders boiling water in pots wasn't all that entertaining. No one cares about those kind of survival skills. They'd rather watch us fighting to protect our ashes or throwing people off cliffs. I let the clean water run into my canteen until it's full. I'll leave the canteen with him. It should be enough to keep him alive until I've crossed the finish line.

As I turn back, everything inside me turns to *ice*.

Capri's grunting with the effort of pulling himself up onto my horse. His muscles bulge and I see sweat running down his face. In an impossible burst of strength, he flings himself up and over one flank. His body slumps against my phoenix's neck. His legs aren't working, so he can't hook them into the stirrups right, but he's in the damn saddle and that's all that matters.

I drop the canteen and dart after them, closing the distance, but Capri's plenty fast with the reins. The horse jolts forward, out of reach. I give chase as they trot off to a safer distance, but the horse is quicker, its strides longer. When Capri's got a decent-sized gap, he turns to get a look at me. He's all awkward and slumped, but there's a grin on his face as he meets my eye.

"Remember this," he calls back. "Remember the sight of me riding away."

"Capri." I make the word a warning. "That's a purebred phoenix. You know what—"

"Like hell it is," he snaps. "Like anyone from the Reach would even know how a purebred rides. How they look and smell and act. You think I'm foolish enough to believe that?"

I let the air rush out my nostrils. He's wrong. He's dead wrong. I look up into the air, knowing officials and fans are watching this on a live feed. I make each word loud and clear. I won't be blamed if he dies a death this foolish.

"You heard me warn him! If he dies, it isn't my fault." I set my eyes back on Capri. "Last chance. I swear to you that's a purebred. You steal it and you'll burn."

He shakes his head. "I'll be the one who beat the Long-hand. I'll be more than the kid who snuck into a race. I'll be remembered as the one who ended your race."

The sound of his whip follows the promise. I chase, but my strides can't come close to matching a phoenix's. Capri works him into motion, up into a gallop. Dust rises and my view is distorted in the bright swirls. I can't tell the differ-ence between the beating hooves and my panicked heart-beat. I shout as they reach the first forest path. Capri shifts in the saddle. There's a terrifying moment when I wonder if the old myths are just myths. Maybe my horse isn't . . .

The flames that come are brighter and hotter than any I've ever known. A god-sent storm. They break the morning in two. Everything echoes and bursts, and I can hear Capri's screams. The heat's so intense that I have to stop well away. All I can do is watch as fire consumes both horse and rider. The nearest branches catch, and before long smoke is pour-ing into the sky above us.

Capri rolls off one side, a falling mass of flames. The sec-ond he hits the ground, my stallion's fire winks out. Its eyes are ringed with flame, but its coat returns to that onyx color. I move forward to help Capri, but the flames still have him, and they're devouring everything. I know I'm innocent, but it doesn't make hearing and watching him die any easier. Horrified, I skirt the body and get my horse settled.

He's not bothered by Capri's death. It's the same way a wolf wouldn't be bothered by the last gasps of a rabbit. They're just animals acting out their nature. We leave Capri's body behind. The forest fire trails us, smoking and clouding every path. None of the riding comes easy, but we ride fast and hard because no matter how far we seem to go, the sound of Capri's screams follows.

I have to force myself to think of numbers. I keep my hands tight on the reins and look to my bracelet for distraction. Revel chases Bravos down around noon, but fades again. I can almost imagine the two of them ramming into one another somewhere up ahead, slowing down the pace for both of them. Bravos holds to a slim lead. My name hovers in third. As fast as they push the pace, I know I'm gaining on both of them.

Something about Capri's death wakens a deeper part of my phoenix's nature. On a few of the corners, I try to slow him down, but he snorts his displeasure and ignores me. It takes all of my mental effort to set the visceral memories of Capri's death aside. I know I'll never truly forget the flames and the screams, but for now I focus on what I can see in front of me.

I lean over my phoenix and clench my jaw until it feels like my entire body's locked in. I watch the gap start to shrink. We burn through corners and tear down straightaways.

I hope they see my name getting closer and closer and closer.

I'm coming for them.

38

GIG'S WALL

IMELDA

Bastian leads us deeper into the mountains.

I have only visited once, for my cousin's wedding, but I never forgot the taste of mountain air. It's sharper and colder and thinner. We start through a valley and only the risen sun can shake the night cold from our bones. No single mountain reigns in the Gravitas. They're a brooding group of iron giants. As morning sweeps the fog clear, I see their dark shoulders already surround us. The first valley looks green and healthy, but ahead are the warning signs of a stark world. Here, the Empire's rebels rule their own kingdoms.

At least, that's what I always believed.

Bastian moves us like ghosts. Two of his men range ahead, scouting and reporting back. He shuts up laughter and noise until the trees strangle any sight of the desert behind us. I can't help glancing over at him. Every stride he takes is confident, like he's always known he'd be escorting an enemy of the state through these mountain passes. When he notices me watching, I pretend to be fascinated by the metal arm pumping and gasping at his side.

"I've never seen engineering like that."

"Stole the design from the Longhands," he explains. "I lost the arm when I was a kid. Let's just say I've tested out a lot of prosthetics. This one's the most fun."

He throws a quick signal to his second in command. I watch as the man strides out ahead, taking point, and Bastian makes a deliberate effort to fall back and walk beside me. I try to bury the nervous feeling in my chest with curiosity.

"Why not ride?" I ask. "We'd get where we're going in half the time."

Bastian shakes his head. "Not all of my men are horsed. Even if they were, phoenixes leave trails we can't hide. We might raise them up as ours, but they'll always belong to the Ashlords. Sometimes it's better to go on foot if you don't want to be followed."

"And you really think they'll follow me?"

He nods. "You stole two hundred thousand legions on a national broadcast."

Hearing him put it that way makes me smile. "I did, didn't I?"

There's that grin again. "Hell of a start to your career as an outlaw."

I give him another smile, but this time there's less heart in it. The word *outlaw* isn't one I ever thought would apply to me. I always dreamed I'd be a rider, a champion. The choice I made has good and bad consequences both. My family will have enough money now to change their lives forever. I made sure to check the law ahead of time. The Ashlords emphasize personal responsibility above all else. My rebellion cannot be charged to my family.

Which means Prosper can get a proper education. Farian can study film at any university he wants. My father can stop working three jobs. It takes effort to remind myself that those blessings outweigh the curse attached to them: I'll never get to go back home.

The best-case scenario is that I survive this, settle into my cousin's village, and live life as a rancher. Martial is slick enough to help my family visit from time to time, but I'll miss birthdays and celebrations and all of it. I didn't know how much I wanted a better life for them until this moment, until I knew *exactly* what it would cost me to get it for them.

Bastian must recognize the change in my expression, because he keeps walking beside me but doesn't say a word. The quiet is enough to drive me crazy, though, so I force the conversation in the hopes of thinking about something less sad.

"Where are we going?"

Bastian nods in the distance. "Gig's Wall. It's past the first few villages. Our base of operations on this side of the mountain. We'll camp there and then move through the passes. The plan is to escort you to your uncle's village." His cheeks brighten. "Or you could join us. Always need extra hands. It's your call really."

He doesn't wait for an answer this time. Instead, he slides back up to the front of our column and leaves me to consider the life I left behind, and the life that waits ahead.

It's past noon when we reach the first village. From below, all I can see are the slanting roofs and stone chimneys. Bastian has the rest of the group march an overgrown path, well out of sight. But he walks in the open and flashes a series of signals as he does. I don't know who's watching or what any of it means, but fear settles like deadweight in my chest. I realize for the first time I've trusted my fate to people I don't know, and I'm stuck in a place I know even less. I've been trusting them because Luca is with them. And because Bastian is nice and they're Dividian like me. But is that enough?

Thankfully, the signals don't result in an ambush. Instead, a loaded packhorse waits for us at the next crossroad. Bastian looks patiently through the saddlebags, counting off items, before nodding his contentment. We watch from the woods as he takes a loaded sack from his coat and ties it around the road marker. It's not hard to understand. He's leaving payment. Some of yesterday's stolen Ashlord goods in exchange for food and water.

It's my first glimpse of life in the mountains.

We skirt the second village entirely, wind up the forested shelves of another valley, and stumble into sight of Gig's Wall. Once it might have been a marvel. A great stone wall that stretches from one side of the valley to the other, barring encroaching armies from the valleys beyond. It rises fifty feet into the air and stands three times as wide, but the decades have worn away all sense of grandeur. Great blasts of wind have swept chunks out of the wall's once-even ramparts. At the bottom, I note gaping holes wide enough to ride a horse through.

It's through one of these, and not the reinforced gates, that Bastian leads us. Everything about his posture—and the posture of his soldiers—changes once we're inside the fortress. They dust themselves off and move toward familiar nooks in a central room, looking like workers returning after a long day out in the fields. I realize, with a sense of honor and dread, that this place is home to them. One of many homes, and they've invited me into their trust. Luca and I both stand off to the side, feeling a little like intruders.

"Rest well," Bastian calls from the nearest stairwell. "We'll sleep the night here. A handful of you will move on to escort Imelda to Little Sickle tomorrow. Mattys, let's get something hearty on the stove. I'd like to have the whole group—"

His words are drowned by fire. It flashes in the air before us like a magician's trick. The blast of energy knocks everyone backward. I'm on one knee as the flames take form and a man strides out into the center of the room. He's shirtless and shoeless, wearing the dirtiest trousers I've ever seen. What catches every eye, though, is the great falcon mask sewn into the skin of his neck, enclosing a human head within. Everyone stares at the creature, the man, but his great beaded eyes swivel in my direction. He lets out a throaty cry and darts through our ranks.

The gods have come.

We all know which one this priest represents: The Curiosity.

Bastian screams, "Quit staring and kill him!"

The bird-man dodges the first lunge and slips from the grip of a second. Someone fires a pistol, filling the room with smoke and an echoing *bang.* The bird-man makes the hallway. Three of Bastian's soldiers chase, following the nightmarish screeches and answering with more gunshots from their pistols.

I ignore caution and run after them. There's another loud screech, then a *thump,* and I turn the corner to see the bird-man fall, feathers pluming out. He ran far enough to get back outside the walls. The darkened valley is quiet except for the sounds of him dying at the hands of Bastian's men. I'm shouldered out of the way as Bastian presses past to stand over the corpse.

"What was that?" I ask.

He spits down, looks at his men, then at me.

"The Curiosity." He says the name like a curse. "Their god of vision and prophecy. This is one of his priests. Whatever he just saw, they can see. It means they're coming."

"Who?"

"The Ashlords," Bastian replies darkly. "It means they're already here."

9

A SMALL REQUEST

PIPPA

The fourth day of riding is *flawless.*

You can almost see the smirk on Maxim's face as he confirms your record-setting pace to a national audience. Revel started the day impossibly far ahead of you. But as your phoenix burns down in preparation for another night, your bracelet shows that you're only four hundred paces back now. If you hadn't gone back through the caves, it's likely you'd be close to first place. But Etzli would also be dead. Quinn would have abandoned you.

How heavy would that crown have been?

There's a storm curling to life over the distant plains. You nestle in safely beside Quinn at the mouth of a shallow cave. The other riders are situated along the course's western valley, along the route you intended to take with Bravos. As rain starts to fall, you imagine the other competitors hunkered over their ashes and trying to survive the night.

This isn't over. Four hundred paces. Not impossible. In a way, you like that your name isn't on the leaderboard. It allows you to strike more fear in their hearts when it finally does appear. Deep down, you know that only two riders have *ever* come back from this distance, but you were born to break records. If a miracle is to happen, let it be one of your making.

"We're going to win."

Quinn nods. "I believe that now more than ever."

The two of you sit in silence and watch as the storm approaches. You don't have the ability to read Quinn's thoughts as she can yours, but you can feel the one emotion that's coursing through her like a river. She's been so fearless since the very beginning. She's saved you too many times to count. But now the girl who kept your chances alive is *nervous*.

"I mean it, Quinn. I plan on winning."

Her voice is quiet. "I know."

"And I intend to honor my pact with you either way."

"Of course."

You can't help scowling. "Then why are you so unsettled? What is it?"

"I want to ask you a favor."

The girl sits up. You can see the sharp outline of her spine through the back of her shirt. You've spent so much time thinking of her as a ghost that you haven't really seen her as an actual person. Someone who exists in another world. And that world has worn her to the bone.

"Anything within my power is yours."

She shakes her head in frustration. "This is not a small request."

"Enlighten me, then," you reply. "Quinn. I owe you a debt. You—"

You've opened my eyes. I am no longer just an Ashlord. I am more than what my parents would have me become. I am more than what this world craves. I am something new.

"Just tell me what it is."

Quinn turns, eyes wide and ghostly. "I want some of your blood." The words knock you square in the chest. It's the last thing you expected her to ask for. She sees your reaction, too, and it has her pushing to her feet. "See what I mean? It is not a promise to make lightly."

It takes you a second to regain your composure. The girl wants your *blood*. A memory of that dark, secret room in your parents' house flickers to life. You can see the sharp blade and your own spilled blood. You can hear the howling of the Madness. A chill runs down your spine, but you can see Quinn is not joking. It's taken a great deal of strength for her to request this.

"What will you do with it?"

Even as the words leave your lips, you know there's something cold and transactional about them. Quinn has taught you to be more than that, but beneath the newness there are still layers of Ashlord. You know some of those characteristics are good. There *are* worthy ideals that your people value above all else. One of them is understanding the *cost*. Since the beginning of time, your people have understood the trade they make with the gods: Give blood, get power.

It's a fair question.

"I would use it," Quinn says bluntly. "The gods wield your blood in our world. If you win, I will revive. I will be their newest target. A few drops of your blood will go a long way. It will help me survive their initial hunt. I cannot lead a revolution in chains."

You watch the girl carefully. There's an honesty to her that's rare in your own world. You've almost forgotten who she is, where she comes from. Quinn is from the underworld. The brutal realm of gods and demons and who knows what else. She's spent her entire life as a slave, and yet she was the one who insisted on saving Etzli. She's the one who believes in creating a better world, a better version of you. The silence stretches. Quinn takes it as rejection.

"Never mind," she starts to say. "I will still—"

You lean back and reach into the saddlebags. There's a skinning blade there. Every rider keeps one on hand for survival purposes out on the plains. You grit your teeth and transform it into a ceremonial dagger. The blade drags across the back of your finger. The blood gathers there. So little to you. So much to her. You hold your hand out to Quinn.

"Take what you need."

She untucks a little rag from one pocket. Like her, the material feels insubstantial, there and not, as she presses it to your wound. It drinks in the steady drops. Quinn tucks it back into her belt and lunges toward you. Defensive instincts almost kick in before you realize it's a hug. She wraps you in an embrace that somehow feels more real than anything Bravos ever gave you. The feeling of warmth and love almost takes your breath away. Your people do not hug.

"It's moving," Quinn says unexpectedly. "The numbers."

You pull away long enough to eye your Race-standard bracelet. She's right. Bravos's lead is decreasing. You watch the number tick slowly back toward the distance that's posted next to Revel's name. At the same time, Adrian Ford approaches from the opposite direction. You've raced long enough to know they're not *actually* riding their phoenixes, not at this hour of the night. The thought has you smiling. Adrian and Bravos have left their ashes unguarded.

"What does it mean?" Quinn asks.

You can't help grinning.

"Boys and blood."

40

THE ASHLORD WAY

ADRIAN

The rain sweeps in through gaps in the branches overhead.

I'm taking a risk, but at this point in the Races, the winners always take risks. My ashes are vulnerable. Well hidden, but I've watched enough footage of the Races to know there're no guarantees once you're in the arena. It's a risk I have to take. A glance down at my bracelet shows the distance to Revel ticking down. He's not on the move, which means he's entrenched somewhere. A second glance shows Bravos *is* moving. Backtracking toward us.

I tighten my grip on the baton.

A storm is coming.

Thunder shakes out overhead. Lightning briefly illuminates the gaps in the canopy. The desert forest is thick enough to act as a shield. Desert storms roll in quick and hard. Usually they're dangerous because they strike before the victim can find proper refuge. Rain slicks the branches and puddles along the paths. It'll make tomorrow's first leg trickier, but I shove all thought of tomorrow aside. I need to be sharp in the here and now. Tonight is all that matters.

These forests are not empty. Desert birds roost above. The rain brings out groans and protests from the smaller creatures that have survived long enough to call this place home. Every shaking leaf catches my attention. Where did Revel go? The number on my bracelet flatlines. We're standing the exact same distance from the finish line now.

I glance right, then left.

The answer comes from a dangling, half-snapped branch. It's not easy to lead a phoenix off the path without notice. Revel went that way. I slide back into motion and follow the other clues. There's still movement on my bracelet. Bravos is closing in on the location, too. I eye the forest on my right. It says he's just seventy paces that way, but the shadows are too thick.

I need to find Revel first.

Pressing through a gap in the tree line, I stumble into a clearing. The rain comes down thicker, but there's more light, too. The unveiled stars to the west offer me my first view of Revel. A single fist of stone has punched up through the ground at the far end of the clearing. The Ashlord has wisely put his back to it. His eyes tighten as I stride into the clearing, but he doesn't look afraid. His kind never learn fear.

It is hard to learn fear when you're always looking down.

"Longhand," Revel calls. "You look well."

He makes his voice louder than necessary. Even with the steady rain and occasional crackle of thunder, it is a voice that will be heard. His goal is clear. He *wants* Bravos to come.

I almost laugh. "Do you really believe Bravos will help you? We both know how you ride. If anyone is a threat to burn their way through the final leg and steal the crown, it's you."

"We are Ashlords," Revel calls back. "And you are not. It is that simple."

His words hang above us, bright as lightning. I pause in the middle of the clearing. The two of us stare at one another until snapped branches announce the arrival of the current leader. Bravos edges into the clearing. He takes our measure in less than a breath. It has him grinning.

"So it comes down to the three of us," he says.

"And if it should come down to that," Revel replies, "an Ashlord should win, Bravos. The two of us have ridden well. Let's ride again tomorrow. One final ride for glory." His eyes fix on me. "We can put down the Longhand together. He grows too bold."

Bravos considers the offer. His eyes roam back to me. It will not be Ashlord unity that sways him, though. Bravos is—first and foremost—a gladiator. He's weighing his chances in a fight. Can he defeat me *without* Revel? His assessment is quick and honest. He shifts his stance until he's facing me fully, then backpedals toward Revel.

"One final ride," Bravos agrees. "The crown goes to an Ashlord."

Revel is nodding, but he's a bigger fool than I thought if he believes those words. Bravos will use his help to put me down. And then he'll turn on Revel. His two biggest threats left weak and wounded, their ashes poisoned. Bravos smiles and I know he's made the same calculations I have. The Races are in his grasp now.

The two of them lower their voices. An exchange of whispers. As one, they shift their stances and start forward. I hold my ground, mind racing. Do I escape into the forest? There's still a chance they won't find my ashes, but Bravos is a lot stronger than anyone I've fought so far. The Dread's protection is gone. If I lose this fight, they'll leave me so broken that gaining ground on the last day will be impossible. I'm trying to calculate the best way to get distance between myself and them when Revel transforms his shield into a baton.

He's walking a step behind Bravos.

Which is why Bravos doesn't see the blow coming. Revel brings his switch around in a flawless arc. The wooden baton cracks into the side of the bigger Ashlord's temple. Lightning punctuates the unexpected blow. Bravos's body hits the ground and the pursuing thunder rings out as if his fall caused the noise. Revel and I lock eyes through the rain.

"You have two options, Longhand. First, stay and fight. I'm not as strong as you, but I promise I can make this a long night. Or you can go find his ashes and poison them. There's no way Bravos will recover from that. It'll be you and me going into the final ride."

I can't help smiling. "Option three. I fight you, poison your ashes, then poison his."

He looks unsurprised by this turn. As I start forward, he

backpedals gracefully toward his ashes. His voice is tight as he throws out a command. "Stop him."

I frown at the words and keep walking. Revel repeats his command and I'm about to point out that no one else is here to stop me when a flash of blue light cuts through the dark.

Not lightning. Not anything I've ever seen before. I shield my eyes as something hits me in the chest. I stumble back a few steps, baton raised, a little blinded by the flash. Darkness returns and Revel's standing there with a grim look on his face.

"I told you," he says. "I can make this a *very* long night for you."

I press forward again and the blue light flashes in answer. This time I see the sharp outline of a face. Not a random force then, a creature. The spirit shoves me backward before vanishing. What the hell? I circle now. Revel's eyes never leave mine. Each time I press closer, though, the blue light flashes protectively forward to stop my progress. It finally dawns on me.

"Your gods. They're intervening for you."

Revel smiles. "Are you surprised? We are the favored ones, Longhand."

"And what are you without them?" I shake my head. "This protection will fade. I hope you fear that day as much as I look forward to it. I'll see you tomorrow. One final burn."

Eyes still fixed on him, I begin backpedaling out of the clearing. Revel hasn't looked afraid this entire time, but now he looks surprised. He takes a step forward and gestures to Bravos. "But what about his ashes? We have to poison them."

"And you thought I'd poison them for you?" I've reached the edge of the tree line. "While you went searching for *my* ashes? It is a wonder the gods choose to protect such fools. No, I think I'll leave the task to you. Better hope he doesn't wake up while you search."

Revel finally sees the mess that he's in. He took a blind shot at one of his people's most famous and feared gladiators. Bravos will wake up eventually, and he'll come for Revel when he does. I offer one final wave before slipping back into the cover of the forest. Overhead, the rain has slowed to a trickle. It's quiet enough that I can just barely hear Revel's next command.

"Move him. Now."

I glance back and catch another blue flash through the canopy. Invisible hands lift Bravos up and start dragging him through the mud. It's an unsettling sight. I forge onward, eager to get the hell away. I would not risk the attention of their gods again tonight.

The gods.

I do not trust the Dread, but I do take him up on his warning toward caution. As I move back through the forest, I double cross my own trails, hoping to throw off any attempts at following me back to my ashes. It takes more time but I still reach my ashes long before sunrise. The rain has cleared. I sit down, feeling soaked and tired, but can't help grinning like a fool.

Bravos will struggle tomorrow. His lead will fade. Revel has me by a few hundred paces. There is Pippa, looming like a shadow, but I find myself unafraid. The Ashlords are not superior to us. They're not faster or stronger or wise. All they have that we do not is the gods.

And that can change.

Morning comes and revolution is on its heels.

41

THE FINAL STRETCH

PIPPA

You decide to leave most of your supplies. This is the final leg of the Races. You can't imagine needing anything but your hood and your switch from here on out. You are about to leave your mark on history. It starts now. As Quinn mounts, the two of you set your eyes *ahead*. It's a form of survival. If you're going to win the Races, you have to forget everything that's happened in the past few days. Taking the caves gave you a chance. It let you pass through the heart of a plateau that the rest of the riders had to go around. You're not in the top three, but you know the road ahead will bring back the time you've lost to the others.

You glance at your watch and eye the names: Bravos, Revel, Adrian.

The thought of meeting all of them on the final stretch has you grinning.

"Let's ride, Revenge."

The phoenix's coat flashes as the name takes and she

kicks him into motion, stirring the dust with each thundering stride. By some trick of adrenaline, you don't feel like there's a second person clinging to your waist. Instead, it's like you and Quinn are drifting into one being as Revenge presses through passes, down winding gulches, and through shallow creeks.

Neither of you speak. Instead, your thoughts echo in some impossible space.

We're making good time.

The next pass feeds into the final crossroads.

Let's ease off before the final leg.

What if we see other riders?

We stand our ground.

If we see Bravos?

We end him.

The sun burns overhead, but you refuse your hood. You want Bravos to see your face and tremble when you meet again on the final stretch. Your gut twists a little as you eye the leaderboard. Revel has taken the lead. He's burned his way out ahead of Bravos, who's barely clinging to second place. Adrian's in third, but you're gaining on both of them.

The two of you sit a little straighter in the saddle. The course is starting to bottleneck, drawing you west, back toward the other routes and riders. Ahead, you notice the metal barriers towering on either side of the final canyon. You know the faces of the crowds will be gathering there to watch. Hundreds of thousands of people, all craving a champion.

Let's give your fans a show.

You thunder around the final bend of this section in the

course. As you survey the distant plains, it feels like you're looking through two sets of eyes.

"There," you say, pointing. "Our leader."

Four paths converge from different directions to make a final crossroads. Leading on from there is a dead-straight stretch. Revel has at least a clockturn on you, if not more. A quick glance at your bracelet shows his name gleaming in first, but it also shows the gap between you and him is slipping.

You know the course and all the distances by heart. The final length of the race is a flat-out sprint. It will take nine clockturns at least. Just enough time for you to make up ground. You draw strength from the promise that the Races aren't over yet. You're in this. You're a factor.

The crowd erupts as they see Revenge barreling toward the crossroads.

On the left, Quinn whispers in your head, *another rider.*

Your eyes dart to the opposite side of the valley. Quinn's right. Another mushroom of dust gathers over the approaching form. You can tell that the two of you will converge at the crossroads at the same time, and both of you will need to make up ground on the leader.

Revenge responds with a burst of speed. The pumping rhythm brings you closer and closer. The landscape briefly takes both of the opposing riders out of sight. A handful of vaulting seconds pass before the path funnels into the waiting mouth of the crossroads. Your eyes narrow as the other rider straightens into a full gallop just ahead of you.

"Bravos," you hiss. "It's Bravos."

Instinct draws one hand to your switch. With a deliberate twist, you let the whip snake out. It tongues the desert dust, waiting to sing through the air, eager for flesh.

Bravos is using his Iron and Latchlock mixture for the final leg. On either side of his saddle you can see the ominous spikes the alchemy's known for producing. Bravos might not be a brilliant rider, but you know he's familiar with violence. Given the chance, he'll use the horse's spikes to spear your horse and put an end to your ride.

It doesn't stop you from thundering after him, teeth gritted. He glances over his shoulder when he finally hears the hooves. And when he sees it's you trailing him, his eyes go wide.

The two of you start the final stretch just a few lengths apart. Revel's a dark shape ahead. Shouts chorus their way to madness as the fans watch both of you drive your horses onward. You want to end Bravos, but the Latchlock hide has you keeping your distance.

He's smart enough to do the same. Neither of you can afford a confrontation, not while you're still trailing Revel. You feel Quinn's nails digging into your hips. There's an anger linking the two of you together, bright and burning as the sun.

Revenge rides beautifully. He's a hand longer and taller than Bravos's horse, and he continues stealing from their meager lead every twenty or thirty strides. You hold the rhythm and smile coolly when he noses into a lead. Bravos darts a worried look in your direction, but he concedes the advantage for now. Make contact and both of you will fail to catch Revel.

There's a horse behind you with a huge rider.

You resist looking back. It will only slow you down. Better to let Quinn be your eyes. You're sure it's Adrian. Knowing he's there creates a new pressure. Clashing with Revel or Bravos has direct consequences now. A crash will give the Longhand a chance to win the Races. You force yourself to dismiss that concern. There's nothing you can do about it now.

Revel's lead keeps slipping. The closer you get, the sharper the details. The lanky Ashlord sits up in his saddle. His long hair flows away from a silver-shining headband. You're close enough now to see the ghost that's riding with him in the saddle. You'd almost forgotten. He was the other rider who had help from the Madness.

Quinn's grip tightens as you press on. You can see Revel's horse struggling. The bracelet shows he's just five hundred paces from the finish line, but his horse's gait looks less and less rhythmic. A tired horse coming down the homestretch. You know you have two clockturns to erase his lead. A dark dread pulses in your head. You've seen nightmarish endings in the Races before. Bone-breaking collisions and tossed riders, crashing together as they approach the finish. Hard work washed away as some backtrotting nobody takes the grand prize through laws of attrition. The noise of the crowd falls away. Your focus narrows to heartbeats and hooves.

Something's wrong, Pippa.

You see it a second after Quinn speaks. A plume of dust fans out as Revel's horse collapses. Its shoulders clip the earth, and the riders both go skidding over the rocky soil. There's a moment of confusion; then the ghost helps Revel back to his feet. The ghost slings Revel's arm around one shoulder and keeps him moving toward the finish line. They're on foot, moving much slower, but just one hundred paces from the finish line.

Can they win the race like that?

You ignore the question and urge your phoenix forward. For the first time, you see the finish line looming in the distance. You're so focused on the sight of it and Revel's stumbling figure that Quinn's mental cry is the only warning as Bravos brings his phoenix slamming into yours. A kick of Quinn's leg is the only thing that saves you. It lands just before impact and lessens the shock of the blow. Her effort keeps the back spikes from finding flesh, but it doesn't stop the front ones. The collision is a storm of sounds and lightning-bright images:

Blood gushes from a fist-sized wound.

A scream tears from Revenge's throat.

The familiar mint on Bravos's breath.

Sweat colors his clothes.

Last, you see his massive hands come to life.

One grips his reins. The other flexes around his switch.

The impact jars your horses apart, but not far enough to keep you safe. Bravos is close enough for a single strike. It's an off-handed jab. It comes like lightning, but Quinn is quicker. The girl who rode the lightning into your world tugs you down by the shoulders. The blow glances overhead. Bravos looks stunned, but he's smart enough to stay focused. He takes advantage of Revenge's broken stride and vaults forward. The sight of him pulling away draws out every instinct. It takes fifteen years of endless training and bottles them into a single grain of time.

Mind and body move in flawless harmony. Your hand brings the whip up and around. Your tongue clicks a command that keeps Revenge moving. Your eyes find the target of your strike, calculate the distance with impossible precision, and force your shoulders to swivel for the perfect range. Revenge steadies his gait as your whip snakes through the air.

The black tongue curls around Bravos's wrist and *snaps*. You hear the bones break before he can even scream. Bravos slumps sideways, losing control of his phoenix. Ahead, Revel's collapsed horse has burst into flames. Revenge slides left to avoid the chaos as Bravos fumbles the reins. He's too late. Both boy and horse collide with the waiting fire.

There's a duel of screams. Revenge plunges through the smoke, past both of them. You do not celebrate the sight of Bravos spinning face-first into the sand because there's no time to glory in his defeat. Not until you've claimed your victory. Only Revel and Adrian exist now.

You don't have to look at the bracelet to see how small the world's become. The finish line is one hundred paces ahead. Revel's halfway there. Adrian's riding twenty paces back.

Time flexes every muscle and you feel like you're the center of the universe.

42

THE STORM

ADRIAN

You are the lightning.
  I am the thunder.
  We are the storm.

She strikes, and it's like the world's ending. Bravos nearly finished her. I had a good view of their collision. He swung his phoenix over at the perfect time. It should have ended, but then the impossible happened. Pippa kept her horse upright, dodged his switch, and somehow landed a blow with her whip before he could outrange her. I watched as she sent him spinning into the flames, as the dust of his fall clouded my vision.

It was stunning. I wonder if that's what happens to thunder, if that's why it's always a second late. Maybe it gets distracted thinking about how beautiful lightning is and forgets that its job is to make all the noise. The move is so stunning that I have to shake myself out of a trance.

I force myself to *remember*.

I'm the thunder, and thunder *always* follows lightning.

Pippa steadies her phoenix as I close the gap. I'm as far from her as she is from the finish line. Revel's ahead, but he hears the storm that's about to descend on him and turns. His expression is horrified. A man who knows he is going to lose at the very last second. Hesitation costs him everything. The finish line is too far for something with two legs to beat something with four. I'm riding up Pippa's left side, the nose of my phoenix even with the back flank of hers, when Revel turns his desperation into action. He leaps at her. Pippa rolls a shoulder and her horse flinches, too, straying just enough to send them both slamming our way. My stallion's too much of a monster to get put into the wall, so he stands his ground, but it leaves us tangled as we storm past Revel's flailing body and on to the finish line.

There can't be more than twenty strides left and our horses trade leads. It's her and then it's me and then it's her and then it's me. War and revolution wait with breathless anticipation.

We both look up. It's the unforgivable sin of riding. At the end of a race, riders should never look up. Do not look left. Do not look right. No, a rider's eyes find the finish line, and stay there until the end.

But we lock eyes instead. The Ashlord and the Longhand. Ruler and Rebel. We're close enough to spit curses or whisper secrets. Our eyes lock and there's no mistaking her at this distance. She's a champion, a queen, a goddess. The truth rides her shoulders like a curse.

And with a single, smoldering look, she ends me.

Blue light scorches the air between us. In the brief and

godly glow, I see a face. A girl's ghostly features darkened by a savage growl. I'm helpless as an invisible arm wraps around my neck, as the impact wrenches my feet from the stirrups, and *something* tears me out of the saddle.

The whole world spins as I fall.

I get a final glimpse of Pippa's hood riding the wind like fire.

Then the earth rises up and devours me.

43

VICTORY

PIPPA

Applause thunders.

You are the winner of the Races.

Revenge collapses over the finish line. And as he falls, you slip your legs free and tuck your body into a roll. All instinct. The impact of the hardpan shakes the breath from your lungs, but a second roll brings you upright. Dust is swirling as officials from the Empire Racing Board start riding out to congratulate you on your victory. But from your crouched position, your eyes swing back to the finish line for an eternal second.

There's an explosion of flame beside you. Revenge's body racing its way to ashes. In the distance, Adrian's horse has fallen to the ground. He's wedged against the silver-wrought walls of the course, bleeding and shocked. He stares at you and looks completely dazed.

Quinn stands over him. You never asked her to do it, but she leapt anyway. She risked her life in the end so that you could win. The two of you share a look of wild freedom. You notice the cloth in her hand. The same one that carries drops of your blood. Her thought echoes across the distance and it's as loud as if she were speaking in your ear.

Now I begin my own race.

The girl grins wickedly, and you feel the same grin spreading over your face. Instinctively you reach out for her, and she mirrors the motion before fire consumes everything. A blinding flash. You rush forward, half shielding your eyes from the bright reckoning that will revive Quinn in her world. But as the light fades, it's clear she's gone.

Drawn back to the underworld.

Free.

44

THE BATTLE OF GIG'S WALL

IMELDA

"God in heaven," Bastian says, still grinning. "They sent a whole company."

The Ashlords come on horseback. Fifty are mounted. Another hundred soldiers march in a perfect, bronze column up the mouth of the valley. They move with steady caution, because they know they don't need to hurry. The Curiosity's servant showed them how many of us there are. Whatever he saw, they saw. We have no horses summoned. We have few supplies.

And we have nowhere to run.

Bastian considered fleeing north and dismissed it. A glance in that direction shows how right he was. Running would have been useless. The valley stretches on for miles. We'd have to scale the cliffs and mountains flanking the valley to avoid the mounted Ashlords. Which makes the wall our only choice. A narrowing, defensible point.

Bastian quieted his men and commanded them to the

different choke points and entryways. He ordered me to stand on the ramparts with him. He tried to protect Luca, but my cousin spat on the ground, grabbed a sword, and went to join the ranks below. Bastian muttered something about mountain-raised Dividian and shrugged.

It strikes me that Bastian is the same age as the Shor brothers. If he lived in my village, Mother might try to invite him to my birthday party in the hopes of matching us up. Unlike the Shor brothers, he's not training to be a locksmith or a city clerk. Bloodshed is knocking at the door, and Bastian looks *excited*. This is what life in the mountains has trained him to do, to be.

I have to take a deep breath to stay calm. There are a handful of his men posted along the ramparts with us. I watch as they load spare pistols and polish weapons, preparing for battle. My gut clenches every time one of them glances my way. They're probably just looking to their captain, waiting for orders, but I can't help feeling like there's an accusation in their glances. I'm the reason this battle has come to their doorstep. The idea turns my stomach.

"Let me go," I say. "I'll give myself up. They'll leave."

"No, they won't."

"I'm not going to let this happen."

"Hey," he says, fixing his eyes on me. "You're not the only one who can make something out of nothing. Got it? This battle is by design, Imelda. Just stand there and look rebellious."

The words don't make any sense, but I resist asking the questions that burn to life. Instead, I stand there with my chin raised and watch as the Ashlord soldiers form ranks. A single rider separates from the company and trots forward, his ringed hand held up to signal a peace negotiation. The sight has Bastian grinning.

"The burners forget we play by different rules here," he says. "Cover your ears."

My hands are halfway to my ears when Bastian raises the pistol and powder *smokes* the air. The little trotting hooves. The shifting of booted feet. The rustle of cloaks. Every other noise drowns in the explosion of Bastian's gun. He echoes the bang with a war cry, and his boys join him, and the rest of the valley plays stunned witness to the Ashlord messenger's death.

"Main entrance, hold!" Bastian shouts, leaning down for his other pistol. "Have the boys along the second passage retreat. Get them safely up on the ramparts. Let's teach the burners how we fight out here in the mountains."

I expect Ashlords to come pouring forward, but they don't. Instead, there's the distant beat of drums, the call of a general, and the steady march forward. They move as one toward the walls and Bastian's crew do their best to take advantage. Every patient step sees another Ashlord drop, but the ranks fill in and there's something terrible about their unsmiling faces.

A barked command finally sends Ashlords streaming forward. The units break into perfect formations. Groups of three or four stream toward the two gaping holes: the main entrance below us and the abandoned side entrance off to the right. I'm trying to figure out what Bastian was thinking pulling his men from such an accessible entryway when rifle shots sound and bullets snap angrily against the stone ramparts.

"Down," Bastian barks, shoving a pistol into my stomach. "Take this and wait."

Smoke fills the air. Below us, the first wave of Ashlords meets Bastian's men. I hear the scrape of metal and the cries of the dying. My heart is a riot in my chest, but one glance shows Bastian is clearly in his element. He's humming some bastardized version of the March of Ashes. I shout over the sound of gunshots.

"If they get in that second entrance, they'll surround us. What are we waiting for?"

He grins crookedly. "The explosions."

And the foundations shake. The sky screams, full of light and heat. I squint through the smoke. The entrance his crew abandoned—and lured the Ashlord troops toward—is a mess of shattered stones and fallen soldiers. The sight is so horrific that I cover my mouth. The luckier Ashlord soldiers work to remove the wounded, dragging them safely away.

The other Ashlords divert back to the main—and only remaining—entrance with their blades drawn. Bastian stands up and fires his pistol. He looks over and sees I haven't fired, so he snatches my pistol, finds another target, and fires again. Even with the explosion, there are still hundreds of them. All coming for us.

"Hold the main entrance," Bastian shouts. "All we have to do is hold them."

He pulls me back a step as the Ashlords return fire. People are streaming up to the higher sections of the wall. There's a fire in the stairwell that's connected to the entrance Bastian's rigged explosions caved in. Everything's hazy and chaotic. Bastian shouts orders. I barely hear him.

Some deep part of me is horrified. This is battle. This is war.
The Ashlords have ruled my people unfairly, but is this how
we win our freedom? In blood and smoke?

Everything that follows is a nightmare. Like most dreams,
I'm not completely in control of my body. The Ashlords finally break through the main entrance, forcing Bastian's
men to retreat up a set of flanking stairwells, working hard
to hold the higher ground. In the chaos, I search for Luca,
hoping he's survived the first part of the battle.

Below, Ashlords keep pushing through the smoke and
shoving ladders up against the sides of Gig's Wall. Every attempt is a threat to break our control of the upper ramparts.
Bastian's men call out the threats and we rush the climbing
soldiers, shoving them back as new Ashlord soldiers appear
to take their place.

Their troops are gaining ground on the stairwells, and
even as we make our stand, death's grasp feels closer than
ever. One of Bastian's men collapses by the nearest staircase, blood spurting out. An Ashlord rushes up through the
gap, body flexed in righteous anger, only to be shot in the
stomach. He takes a slack-armed swing at the nearest Dividian before collapsing.

Bastian's voice starts to sound like music compared to
the constant ring of gunfire. The mountains look beautiful against the smoking ruin being made around us. Bastian keeps shouting the same thing. "Hold them! Help is
coming!"

If help really is coming, it feels like it's too late. Someone
misses a ladder on the far side of the ramparts. Ashlords are
swarming up that side now. They're pressing up the two

staircases, too, lashing out with swords. Our group pinches tight, backs pressed together. Everyone is bleeding and every chest is heaving. This feels like the end.

Trumpets.

Every eye swings to the valley as a stream of mounted men thunder toward us. Bastian screams his triumph, tells his boys to take heart, as the world quakes. Every Ashlord rallies, trying to take up their formations, but in their desperation to scale the ramparts, they've become too scattered. A wind-whipped flag leads our liberators into battle.

The Reach. Longhand soldiers. Hundreds of them.

Up on the ramparts, Bastian tightens our circle. I stand behind them, knowing now that we can live, and craving it so much that my whole body rebels against the idea of dying at the last possible moment, catching a stray spear or bullet. I would feel like more of a coward if Bastian and the others weren't doing the same thing. My heart beats a little faster seeing Luca standing in our circle, blood running down one arm, but alive. We hold our ground as the fresh Longhand troops come pouring into the entrances of Gig's Wall.

Caught between both groups, every single Ashlord falls. When it's done, the Longhands whoop and holler. Bastian looks carved from blood-spattered stone. His crew shouts and whoops but his eyes lock on mine. We're both quiet and an understanding passes between us.

This was about more than my stolen powders. This was about more than rebels.

The Longhand presence means one thing: war.

45

ONE FACE

ADRIAN

They don't treat my wounds properly. That's the first sign that something's wrong.

Normally I wouldn't care, but with each minute that passes, I'm learning new definitions of pain. The Dread's protection has long faded. My fall at the finish line is going to be watched across the Empire for weeks, but none of them will feel what I felt, what I'm still feeling. My whole right side is fire. I've got a pair of gashes that can only ever become scars. Lights are too bright and noise is too loud.

My head's a dying storm, but I stay as focused as I can as they escort the riders to the waiting carriages. There are never any ceremonies on-site at the end of the Races. We'll be taken back to Furia to get cleaned up, dressed in designer clothes, presented to the masses. I'll stand below Pippa on the stone tiers and wonder what happens next.

Daddy wanted me to win so he could start a war, but I came in second. What now?

All of it sits uneasily in my stomach. Officials whisper nearby. There's a tension riding their shoulders as they escort a broken Thyma into the first carriage. Only nine racers remain. I count the number twice, just to make sure I'm not going mad. I know Capri's dead, but on my second count I realize the Dividian has gone missing, too. That has me worried. Now the only witnesses are Ashlords. What'd they do to her?

I wish I hadn't handed over my switch. Not that I could do much with it right now. They lead me into the final carriage. By some traditional mandate, I have to share a carriage with Pippa. She enters. The fire and fight have burned out of her. She looks half a ghost herself.

I want to stay alert, but my body rebels. The horses start and the bumps of the road draw out every ache and tired muscle. My eyes slip shut. I shake myself, but it happens again . . .

. . . and I wake to night. Pippa sits across from me, eyes tracing the stars. Lights glow in the corners of our carriage. Everything else waits in shadow. We're not moving anymore. The officials are gone. I reach for my face and groan as the motion tugs one of my wounds.

Pippa's eyes find me. She drinks me in and an unexpected emotion flashes over her face. I watch as she reaches down into her bag. I'm only half awake, but the movement has me on guard. It's not a knife, though. She pulls out bandages. The look she's giving me is the same look most people reserve for dying animals. In her eyes, I'm a broken thing.

"I was waiting until you woke up," she says, still picking through medical supplies. "It's dishonorable not to treat your wounds. I wanted to wait until I could ask for your permission."

I stare back at her. "How do I know you won't poison me?"

That drags a laugh from her lips. The smile on her face is not the one she flashes in her interviews. It's less forced somehow, more honest.

"The Races are over, Adrian. What would be the point of poisoning you now?"

The reality behind those words thunders through me. She thinks this is the end. This was only ever a race to her. It didn't stand for something bigger and brighter. It was not the collective dream of her people. No, it was a bright crown to add to her pile of gold. She has no idea that a war might be coming or that the two of us could be leading armies against one another.

It takes a few seconds to process everything. I nod permission.

"It does hurt like hell."

Her lips slip into another smile. "Sit back."

I watch as she wets a rag and dabs it with antiseptic. She gestures for my right arm, but raising it even slightly drags another groan out of me. Pippa slides across the carriage instead. The light dances across her features. I stare straight ahead and pretend I can't feel the heat of her knee pressed against mine. She gently takes my right arm and starts to scrub carefully at the wounds. Her dark brows knit together as she works.

"Stop flexing," she says.

"I'm not flexing."

She rolls her eyes and keeps working. When most of

the packed dirt and dust have been wiped clean, she twists around to grab a needle and thread. Her dark eyes lock on mine.

"Do you want me to stitch them?" When I nod, she lifts a questioning eyebrow. "I'm being serious. If you complain, I'm not going to do it."

I lean back, gritting my teeth, and nod again. She repositions my arm delicately before starting. I can feel the tempered needle diving in and out of my flesh, but the warmth of her hands keeps most of the pain at a distance. She finishes the first wound and moves on to a second.

"You're good at this," I note.

She makes a thoughtful noise. "Of course I am. No one else can fix your wounds on the course. My father taught me. You should be pleased to know I inherited his steady hands."

The daughter of champions. I've always thought of her father and mother as former winners of the Races, not as parents who taught their daughter useful skills. Of course they did.

"Knowledge that you're now using to help a sworn enemy. I thought this kind of work was beneath someone like you."

The next stab is just a touch sharper. It's quiet for long enough that I open my eyes, expecting her to be glaring at me. Instead, she's focused on her work. Steady hands and a focused expression. I watch as she draws the thread up into the air.

"You have misinterpreted this gesture."

I almost laugh. "Is that so?"

"This is an ancient tradition." She pulls the thread again.

"In the Old Games, victors would often tend the wounds of the person they defeated. It was an intimate moment shared between them. A reminder from the victor. These wounds? I gave them to you. I defeated you once, and every one of these scars will be a reminder that I can beat you again."

She finishes her final stitch before looking up at me, one hand still resting on my arm. Her expression isn't guarded. This is not the carefully groomed champion everyone sees on the Chats. There's fire in her eyes. Heat pulses in the air and this time I can't tell if it's something in her or something between us. My body feels like it's charged with the same heat and lightning.

And the moment ends. We both look away.

She hands me the extra bandages before returning to her side of the carriage. The retreating heat produces a chill, and I do my best not to shiver as she speaks.

"The other wounds require an actual doctor. I'm sorry I was the cause."

Back to neutral, guarded. We are competitors again.

I frown. "Are you really?"

She raises an eyebrow but doesn't answer.

"What was it?" I ask, remembering the ghostly face. I can't get that flash of blue out of my head. "Revel had one, too. I saw the thing jump from your horse. I saw its face."

"Quinn," she says. "Her name was Quinn."

That has me grinning, which hurts like hell. "You gave it a name?"

"She already had a name. But she's gone now. Back to the underworld."

There's no one present to hear that admission but me.

The Ashlord gods supposedly live in the underworld. Anything that comes into our world does so with their permission. That can mean only one thing: She cheated. "You know I had you. I'll definitely tip my hat to that bit of riding you did when Bravos slammed you. Never seen anything like that. Your whip strike? It was gorgeous. But at the end, I had you."

That brings a little of the fire back to the surface. Pippa raises her chin and her eyes look like a pair of burning coals. "I would have won either way."

"Hard to tell with the gods tipping the scales."

Annoyance flashes over her face. I'm surprised how quickly it bleeds into outright anger.

"You think it's unfair? That the gods favor us? You know nothing, Longhand. You forget that the Dividian came here to make us bow. You forget that we were loyal worshippers to the gods that your people abandoned. We bowed to them so we would never have to bow to either of you. There's a price in ruling this world. Always there has been a cost. We rule with iron and fire because it's the only thing someone like you will respect. So tell me. Is it our fault you're too afraid to dance with the gods?"

She doesn't look very satisfied with her own answer, but she turns her eyes back to the window. I can tell she wants the conversation to end. She's not wrong, but she's not right, either. Our past is complicated. Our history is bloody. This land was shaped as much by the dying as it is now by the living. I think about why Daddy sent me in the first place. His own son. He sent me into a den of snakes to start a war, one that might avenge his beloved wife.

And then there's the lesson I learned from Capri. The only way to beat them is to become them. We have to be as bloody, as cruel. We might even need some of their gods to pull it off.

"It never ends," I say quietly. "You'll hate me. And my children will hate your children. Your gods must be excited. Things are about to get bloody. Just the way they like it, right?"

I'm expecting her to bite back. Instead, Pippa turns to look at me. Her glare burns across the carriage and I can tell for the first time she has a sense of what is coming. This was more than just a race. Our world is about to burn.

And the two of us are the ones who will set it on fire.

The door of our carriage opens. Officials stand beneath the stars.

"Adrian. Come with us."

Pippa watches with curious suspicion. All my fears return. They've stopped on the road in the middle of the night. What will they do with me, out here in the desert?

An official sets a hand on my shoulder as I exit. He leads me forward without violence, but it waits like a promise in his open palm. If I resist or flee, he won't hesitate to punish me. A second flanks my opposite side. It's never a fair fight with the Ashlords.

Other officials wait in the distance. The riders watch from their carriage windows, some curious and others simply bored. A new carriage sits in the road ahead. I note the three men standing in front of the unwelcome carriage. Their uniforms mark them well.

The Quespo.

Ashlord society has employed the question-police ever since the war. They're the subtle threat that lurks in every tavern, a network of spies. As the officials lead me over, I note the insignias on each breast. Two of them are interrogators in the Ashlord army. One's a police general. None of them are good news.

My eyes search the night. I wonder how far I could get before they caught me. One of the Quespo steps forward and speaks. It's the only thing that stops me from breaking the hand on my back. It's a voice that I know, because Antonio made me memorize it. The man's uniform has changed, but he looks exactly as he did in the wine cellar. An Ashlord who styles his hair in a faux-hawk and looks far too old to wear it well. His dark eyes weigh me.

One of the ten faces I need.

His name is Atl. His favorite food is goose liver.

"Adrian Ford. You are to be arrested for the death of Capri. His family and the Empire Racing Board are invoking the third amendment of the contract you signed, which expressly forbids that you, under any circumstances, kill another contestant during the Races. Accused of this crime, we cannot allow you to appear in the ceremonies to come. You will come with us."

Atl gives no sign that he's ever seen me before. I realize that he's acting, the accusation is a trick, and he's clearly expecting me to play my part. I let my eyes narrow and my arms flex.

"That's not fair!" I shout. "He stole my horse. You *saw* him steal it!"

I turn, struggling against my officials, so that all the

other riders can hear me. I'm not sure exactly what Atl's plan is, but I'm guessing that whispers of my arrest are the first move. It won't be hard for people to believe that the Empire Racing Board attempted to imprison me on false charges. So I sell them my anger in the hopes that it'll buy me my freedom.

"He stole my horse! He knew what would happen! He stole my horse!"

The butt of a switch lands against my stomach. A second blow punishes the back of my head. All the echoing pain has me on hands and knees, with the world tilting around me.

"Get him up and get him inside," Atl commands.

Hands move me. Someone twists both arms behind my back and starts tying my hands together. I can hear Atl and an official bickering about paperwork. Atl quietly reminds the man of his rank and of his ability to use that *against* the man if needed. Someone calls out a taunting jeer from the other carriages, but I can't make out which rider it is. I'm shoved into the back of a carriage. The door slams shut.

I wait in the dark cabin, thinking. Atl has come for me. Antonio gave me ten faces to trust, and his is one of them. My fears quietly shift. Away from fear of an arrest and to the fear of being discovered. What if the officials question him? What if they don't believe he's really there to arrest me? There's a faint rattle as the other carriages start moving again. I hear their wheels and their horses grind past us, grow distant, and fade. There's silence outside of our carriage until the door opens again. A toss of black night and distant stars frame Atl's figure.

"Let's get you home," he says softly. "The Reach is marching."

I frown at him. "But I didn't win."

"You did the next best thing," he answers. "That vid of you coming down the homestretch is playing on *every* screen in the world right now. We all saw you nosing ahead at the end. And we all saw the flash of light that knocked you off your horse. We saw it the night before when you tried to go for Revel. Even some of the Ashlord analysts were questioning their methods. Everyone thinks Pippa cheated to beat you. A victory would have worked, but I think you handed your people something even better. You're a living and breathing example of the injustice they've faced their whole lives."

So war comes.

Every labor of the last five years has been to take that word from a whisper and make it into a shout. The Reach is rising. The revolution begins. But the expected adrenaline doesn't come. My mind doesn't start working through tactics or battle plans. Instead, I see the couple at the Crossing match. The father and his three sons. Capri's words echo.

You're just like us.

"We'll head to the eastern front," Atl is saying. "You've got a war to win."

46

THE BRIGHTNESS

PIPPA

You sit perfectly still as a crew does your makeup and hair. You watch in the mirror as magician's hands resurrect the beauty of your tired face. They powder and pull and press until you're a statue again, beautiful and cold and unfeeling. There's no thrill to any of it now. You do not take any pleasure from the way they've remade you.

Instead, you think about Quinn.

Where has the girl gone? You can still see that wicked smile on her face. It's the same one she gave you when she first arrived in this world. You secretly hope that she escaped. That she's causing chaos somewhere and freeing her loved ones. It sounds romanticized, but after spending a few days with the girl, you think she's capable of anything.

"Pippa?"

The name pulls you back to the present. All the stylists have stepped away. There's a perfection about you now. They've made each curl of your dark hair shine seductively.

The bruises you earned during the Races are well hidden. Someone's contoured your cheekbones until they look sharp enough to draw blood. Everything's dark. The eyeliner, the lipstick, the clothes. It's a surprising scheme. In former years, the winner was made to look delicate and graceful.

A jewel to be set in a crown.

But they've sharpened your soft edges.

They've made you into a blade.

"I don't understand."

"I asked them to do it." The Brightness stands at the entryway. You notice him in the mirror for the first time. With a brief signal, he empties the room of other ears. "The Races are over. The War begins."

You know you should turn, honor him by speaking face to face and not through a mirror, but his words cut through the very core of you. It's impossible to do more than repeat them.

"War begins?"

The Brightness nods. "We have reports out of the mountains. A company of Ashlords was attacked by Longhands. Other reports suggest the Reach's armies are moving. I would have you speak to our people. Not just as the winner of the Races, but as a leader in our army. I want our people to rally around your defeat of the Longhand."

"I am to be a symbol?"

"At first," he says. "But then you will do what every winner of the Races was trained to do. You will lead armies. You will win battles. You will drive the enemy back to the Reach. You already know the names of the generals who will serve you."

He steps aside. Three familiar figures have appeared in the doorway: Etzli, Revel, and Bravos. The sight of Bravos turns your stomach. He looks rightfully embarrassed. You stare him down and the anger you'll need to lead armies into battle rages in your chest. All three of the defeated riders step forward and perform standard bows of allegiance. It's a small victory to see the man who betrayed you bend the knee.

After a moment, the Brightness steps forward again. You know that he's waiting for your answer. As if you could have ever said no. You nod to him before rising from your seat and knocking on the door. The sound brings stylists flooding back from the hallway. You hand the first one your safeguarded switch.

"Bring me a real blade and make sure it's sharp."

You turn back to the Brightness. War knocks on the door of the Empire again, and he looks youthful because of it. You realize the threat is feeding him energy. He's not alone in that. You can feel the space Quinn left in your heart filling with hunger and lust. War is the natural state of your people. It is the calling of your kind. You are raised knowing it will come.

A voice in the back of your mind whispers doubt. It almost sounds like Quinn. You have not quite cleansed the taste of *wrongness* you felt as you left Etzli behind in the caves. It is what your parents would have done. It is what the Empire has always taught you. Win at all costs.

For now, you bury that voice.

"We reign," you say.

"In fire and blood," the others finish.

47

THE PRICE OF WAR

IMELDA

Bastian marches me through the halls. He lost four of his men. They took time to bury them, and mourn them, and drink in their honor. Bastian even helped dig the graves. When the job was done, he offered once more to escort me deeper into the mountains. But a summons came first. The Longhand general who saved us at the last minute wants to talk to me.

I'm thankful that Bastian is walking beside me.

The Longhand troops are as rowdy as their captain is quiet. He camped them for a few days, but now they're busy with movement. They're ready to march on to the next strategic location. Bastian assured me that the Longhands didn't come on my account. They came because the Reach is ready to rise up and rebel. They've been recruiting in the mountains for months. Pacts have already been purchased. Armies and supply chains are being prepared.

The Ashlords will strike back, and they'll do so with the

gauntleted fists of their gods, but for now the rebellion has ridden out to a quick lead. It'd be easy to think of it all as a race if I could ignore the smell of burning bodies. Bastian turns a corner. Two guards part to allow him into their general's office. The man stands over a map of the Empire. I can see some of the towns he has marked off. Pieces representing armies. Where will his troops move next? He sets his dusty hat over the etchings and takes a good long look at us.

"Thank you, Bastian. I'd speak to the girl alone."

A piston in Bastian's arm releases pressure with a hiss of steam.

"She's not as familiar with wartime arrangements as I am. I think I'll stay."

The general considers him, nods a concession.

"That's acceptable. Imelda, my name is Antonio Rowan. I am second in command of the Longhand Legions. First, I wanted to thank you for creating such a perfect opportunity. Your flight from the Races allowed us to strike clean and early against the Ashlord army."

He pauses long enough for me to answer.

"You're welcome."

"With that noted, I would see the belt that you stole."

The words are bold and direct, but not unexpected. Bastian warned me it would come to this. I've known all along that my way through the mountains would not be easy, not with that kind of price attached to my hip. Too bad for him I expected this from the beginning.

"Mountain rules," I reply. "What I steal from an Ashlord is mine."

"You're not from the mountains," Antonio points out.

"She is now."

Bastian speaks a new truth into existence. I take heart from his words. I set everything I've ever known on fire, but he's offering me a new home, a new family. It's mine if I want it.

Antonio waves a lazy hand. "All beside the point. Our contracts with the mountain rebels carry weight, even with lesser known insurgents like Bastian. You might have stolen the belt yourself, but there's a tax applied to all earnings during wartime. We won't take from the hands of those who fight, but we have to fund our efforts somehow. You will find this is true of *every* man and woman in my army. You will find this is true of *every* man and woman who fights with us. There's a tax taken from every spoil of war now. It is law."

"How much?" Bastian asks.

"Thirty percent."

Bastian makes a disbelieving noise. Antonio Rowan doesn't reply. He simply folds his hands and looks my way again. "We saw the components you chose. We know their values, especially during wartime. You keep seventy percent of the profits. That's more than enough."

I could draw this out into a negotiation, but the general is already two steps behind.

"I'll give you all of it. The whole belt."

I hear the rustle of boots behind us, the shifting of weight. Bastian's looking at me like I've lost my mind.

Antonio Rowan leans forward hungrily. "At what cost?"

"No cost. Free of charge."

"Imelda—" Bastian starts to interrupt, but a look from me cuts him off.

I unclip the cubes from my belt and slide the whole thing across the general's desk. He carefully opens the first latch. His eyes narrow, though, as he opens the second, and third. . . .

"These are not the components you stole."

I raise both eyebrows in surprise. "No?"

"I do not have time for games."

"I think I just proved to the entire world that I don't play games."

His lip quivers with checked fury. There's a flash of danger in his eyes, and I brace myself, thinking he'll reach for the pistol at his hip. Instead, he calls the guards back into the room. "Search her," he says to the first. "And you search her things. Find the other belt."

I smile as they obey his command. Bastian looks a little lost. I smile, because I know they won't find them. I made sure of it. I left the belt where only one person would know to look. The guard searches me roughly, finds nothing. Antonio Rowan looks up skeptically when he's finished. The other returns to report the same. The Longhand general doesn't hide his anger now.

"Where are they?" he asks.

"The belt on your desk is the only one in my possession."

He snaps each container shut, opens the nearest drawer, and dumps the belt inside.

"Leave. Go now before I have you arrested."

Bastian offers a quick bow to the Longhand before shoving me back into the hall. He doesn't talk until we're beyond the Longhand patrols. The second we're out of earshot, he breaks into laughter. "What'd you do with them?" he asks giddily.

"They're in good hands," I reply. "They'll get back to the right people."

He smirks. "The Alchemist. I'm starting to see it now."

And to my surprise, he throws a friendly arm around me. Heat rushes up my neck and into my cheeks. My heart pounds in my chest. Mostly because I almost got thrown in prison, but some of it has to do with how comfortable Bastian's arm feels around my shoulder.

It feels like home.

Outside the Longhand camp, his crew are packing saddles and preparing ashes. Like proper rebels, they look ready to move on to the next place on the map. We're walking that way when Bastian pulls me to a stop. His face looks surprisingly serious for once.

"Look, I know you want to go to your uncle's," he says. "Live a quiet life and all that. I just want to square up with you. War is coming. The mountain folks aren't exactly neutral. We don't do quiet. We're the sons and daughters of revolutionaries. Our parents delivered secret messages; they defied the gods. That's who we are. . . ." He locks eyes with me. "I think that's who you are, too. We'll take you to Dig's place. If all you want is the quiet life? No worries. I wish you well, but someone like you will make a difference in what's coming. Think about it."

He winks once before turning and barking orders at his men.

I watch the crew rally to him, excited for new marching orders. The wildness of his invitation thrums in my chest. It takes effort to bury that rebellious voice. I know that a quiet life is the right choice. Some pasture up in the mountains with a couple of horses. My family visiting when they can. That wouldn't be the worst life in the world.

But my mind is drawn back to the map on Antonio Rowan's desk. The next few months will transform those figurines into *real* armies. The towns he marked will become battle locations. I've known the names of some of those towns my whole life. There are Dividian people—my people—who call those places *home.* Who's going to fight for them?

The sun is rising over the mountains.

I spread out my phoenix's ashes. As I kneel over them, Luca approaches with the belt of components I requested. He stands there at my shoulder like he's about to witness a miracle.

"Finally get to see the Alchemist in action."

I smile. "I fell in love with alchemy when I was a little girl. It wasn't the rebirths. Or the riding, really. It was the components. I loved that a pinch of onyx could summon a horse with shock-resistant hooves. But if you take a whole handful of the stuff?" Carefully, I start spreading the necessary powders, mixing them in perfect circles. "A whole handful will get you a horse with an armored hide. Just a few ounces. That's the only difference between a proper country riding horse and one that's ready to ride into battle. I love that even the smallest details count."

Luca asks the one question that matters.

"Which one are you going to summon?"

I rise, dusting my hands off, eyes to the distant mountains. We watch the sun cut through the valley and stir my ashes. I stare into that blinding light and smile.

"Let's ride."

48

HOME

MARTIAL

On the first holy day after the Races, he returns.

I knew I'd never have to seek him out. Instead, he walks around the ranch like he's in mourning. Twice around the empty pastures, circling and circling before the sun's even up. I warm some old coffee and watch, knowing how hard it must be, how lost he must feel without Imelda. My eyes roam the dark, checking for others, but he's alone. The Empire's too busy to have much interest in a kid like him. All the better.

I throw on a coat and head out to meet him. He's pulled himself up onto a fence by then. He sits, thumbing a hole in his jeans, acting like he's seven again. Poor kid.

"Farian," I say. "This is unexpected."

He barely looks up. "I didn't know where else to go."

"She'll be back. You know that, don't you?"

For a while, he doesn't say anything. Which is fair. I'm

not sure I believe it, either. Every whisper carries war with it. There's talk of conscriptions. Imelda's name might get forgotten in all the mess, but there's also talk that she's the one who started what's coming. One newspaper claimed she actually fought in the first battle. Sounded like a load of wash until I saw the location of the fight: Gig's Wall. Just a few miles north of where she was planning on heading. It didn't sound so impossible then.

"Why'd she do it?" Farian asks. "Why not just try to win the *right* way?"

"She wanted to break the rules. That was the whole point."

Farian shakes his head. "So now we look like cheaters. Ashlords can point at her and say, 'Look what the Dividian do with what we give them.'"

"Oh, wake up, Farian."

He looks a little shocked by the exhaustion in my voice.

"Did you ever wonder at our people's name?" I ask him, pressing. "The Dividian. It originates in Ashlord documents. It's the history they gave us. A simple meaning: *the divided ones.* We arrived at their shores divided. We live in their land *divided.* It's become second nature to us, almost like breathing. And I have no doubt it is how the Ashlords like us."

My eyes trace the distant land, hills that were never really ours.

"Imelda took something back from them, Farian. We don't live high and mighty. We live in their world, by their rules. One of those rules is that we're never allowed to rise too high. They've been stealing who we are from us for centuries. Imelda defied that. For at least a few minutes, she united all of us. On their biggest stage, with the entire Empire watching, a Dividian outdanced the Ashlords. Don't look down on her for changing their rules."

Farian breaks beneath the weight of that, shaking his head, on the verge of tears.

"We don't know if she outdanced them. She got over the fence, but then what? I think—I think I'm trying to be mad because it's easier than being afraid. What if they killed her, Martial? What if they tracked her into the mountains and captured her?"

I reach out and set a hand on his shoulder. "She made it."

"You know that?" Farian asks desperately. "You can't possibly know that."

"I feel it. Down in my bones. Don't you?"

It takes a second, but he nods. "I'm just worried. Until I see her and know she's all right, I'll always be worried. Those components she stole are worth a lot, Martial. Even if she escapes the Ashlords, someone else might kill her for them. I'm worried I'll never see her again."

I let out a sigh. "Well, I can help a little with that fear."

Reaching back, I remove the bills from my pocket. I've had them hidden in the floorboards for days. Farian's cut of the winnings. I thought I'd have to scatter the sales, but with war coming on, vendors are positioning themselves for the long run and buying up what components they can. It's been easy to sell off everything, except the Ivory of Earl. That one's rare enough to get someone's attention. I'll sell it off when the time comes, but for now I'll have to wait. I take the banded wad of money and stuff it into his hand.

"Twenty-five thousand legions."

He stares at it. "What?"

"That's your cut. Twenty-five thousand legions."

"Martial . . ."

"It's not from me." I smile at him. "It's from Imelda. She said go to school. She better be invited to all your premieres."

He fans a thumb through the bills, stunned. "But . . . her family . . ."

"Will get plenty of money. Don't worry about that."

He shakes his head in disbelief. "I don't get it. I mean . . . How could she possibly . . ."

I smile again. "Might never know. But I have to say, you were spot on with your nickname for her, Farian. All Imelda did was snap her fingers. And here we are, enjoying all the something she made out of nothing. If I were you, I'd give up on trying to figure out *how* she did it and just be thankful she did it at all. Be thankful the Alchemist thought your pockets were worth filling."

He nods, keeps quiet, and pockets all of it. We sit and talk a little while longer, but he's too excited to stay for long. He heads on home, talking about some video he's already got in the works. I nod him off as the sun starts to rise. It's quiet now. Later today, the Ashlords who board their horses here will start to arrive. They'll come to collect their phoenixes so that they can ride them into the kind of bloody battles this world hasn't seen in decades.

There's more than enough work to keep me busy, but I sit up on the nearest fence and watch the sunrise instead. I don't know if Imelda's alive. I really don't. But today it's enough to stand here watching the sunrise and hope that somewhere she's setting out her ashes, adding all the right components, and resurrecting a beautiful new phoenix.

I like to think that someday she'll ride it back to us.

ACKNOWLEDGMENTS

I have to start by thanking the Reintgen boys. I'm the middle child in a set of three boys. My dad was an ACC championship wrestler at UNC. It should come as no surprise that the four of us competed at *everything*. My earliest memories are of racing my brothers through grocery store parking lots, knowing the first one to touch the car could claim shotgun. We were each other's test subjects for every soccer move, every fadeaway jumper, every new video game discovery. The fire and competition that this book is built around was learned through a lifetime with each of them. Which reminds me, any of you have a sheep for trade?

The second group that deserves thanks for this story is my writing group and beta readers. This particular story needed as much of their help as it could get. Back in 2013, I had an idea for a story about a young girl (you know her as Quinn) who has to race through four different dimensions to earn her freedom. It was a really fun story. When I finished, I sent it to my trusted writing group. Every early reader adored the phoenix horses. I'd always ask about the other races, and they'd shrug before continuing to praise the phoenixes. Eventually, I took the hint. With their advice guiding me, I cut the other races to focus on this world. This story would not be what it is without that brilliant group.

As always, I have to thank the team at Random House, specifically the folks at Crown BFYR. I am always indebted to my brilliant editor, Emily Easton. Thank you for trusting me so much on this story, and as always, thank you for taking it beyond where I could have taken it on my own. A huge thanks to Samantha Gentry for being the reason the ball keeps rolling no matter how many times I almost drop it. Thanks to Josh Redlich for working to get this out into the world, and to the countless folks at Random House who have pitched this book to librarians and booksellers around the country. I'm always honored to call you my team.

My other team at the Nelson Literary Agency deserves all the credit imaginable. Thank you so much to Kristin Nelson, James Persichetti, and all the folks who pull the strings to get these books to my editors, not to mention out to the rest of the world.

I also want to thank the teachers and librarians out there who are working to match students with the right books. I've been to hundreds of schools in the past few years, and I can always tell when you've carved out that crucial role in their lives. I'm proud to know you and proud to work with you, and I hope this is one more book in your arsenal. Thank you for what you do.

Finally, I married way out of my league and have a loving family that supports me every step of the way. Thank you, Katie, for your constant support. Thank you, H-man, for always smiling and giving me good reasons to take writing breaks. I love you both.

PART ONE

MORTALS

No stars winked over my birth. No crown
was set on my head. I was born into a
world of possible gods. My name whispers
through the caverns of time because I
whispered it first.

—The Dread,
Cautions and Concerns

1

CHANGING SKIES

IMELDA

A single flame shines in the ghostly fog like a jewel.

I stand there, neck craned, waiting for Bastian to complain about the plan. Wind howls over a sprawl of dunes. The dark sea reaches for us with iron fingers and sand hisses against exposed ankles. I knew the cliffs would be high, but it's actually nauseating to stand in their shadow and dream of scaling them.

Locklin Tower—a supposedly impenetrable Ashlord fortress—hides in the clouds. Only the weathered map in Bastian's back pocket and the glinting flame above us confirm that the castle is actually there. After a long second, Bastian turns back to face me and the rest of the crew.

"You're sure this will work?"

I can hear the way he pitches his voice. Loud enough that the wind will carry his question back to the others. He knows the plan is sound. He just wants them to hear the promise in my voice. Their crew saved me after I escaped the Races—they rode out to my rescue when Martial whispered my plan to the mountain rebels. They are also the crew who gave me my first taste of blood and war at the Battle of Gig's Wall. After riding with them for a month, most of the riders are still learning to trust me, but Bastian knows my words carry a different kind of currency. He's their leader. I am their expert, especially in alchemy.

"It'll be the smoothest ride we've had in weeks."

A few laughs at that. Bastian nods once. "Show them."

The crew circles to stand in front of their ashes. Only twelve volunteered for our task. More than expected, honestly. Bastian didn't spare the cowards on the other crew. I almost smile, imagining them piled in the cargo hold of our stolen carriage, wedged against each other and cursing under their breath. While they approach the castle as luggage, our group will ride in more glorious fashion. I glance around the circle, unsurprised to find my favorites of Bastian's crew.

"So this one's called Changing Skies. . . ."

And it's like I'm back on the ranch with Farian, shooting our next video. Walking out to Martial's barn early on a holy day to make one of our films and hope enough people will watch to pay the bills. That's how I got looped into the Races in the first place. It all feels like it happened to someone else, in some other lifetime.

It takes less than fifteen clockturns to get the group's powders properly settled. Every gust of wind complicates the task. It whips cloaks into faces, snatches powders from palms. Only when the group is finished do I circle, triple-checking their work. The last thing I need is someone dying today because they mixed the wrong ratios into their ashes.

Everything checks out.

Now we wait for the sun to rise.

The Rowe siblings—Harlow and Cora—adjust their belts and weapons, their motions a perfect mirror of one another. Layne tightens her hood and comments on what fine weather we're having. The girl is shaped like a knife and twice as sharp as one. Our eldest member—a man named Briar—laughs at Layne and says it's nothing compared to mountain cold. I thought he was a little boring until someone told me he was a member of the original Running Rabbits. Any man who marched with Gold Man Jones is a legend in his own right. My cousin Luca is with us, too. He hums some mountain song I've never heard. Bastian picks up the notes, tapping a rhythm with the fingers of his metallic arm. I know it's the more dangerous of the two limbs. When I first met him, he was winning a duel with an Ashlord sentry. His prosthetic arm is a deadly weapon, even if right now he's using it more as a glorified musical instrument.

I smile at their talk and pretend I'm one of them.

It hasn't been easy to carve a place in this family. Especially when half of my heart is somewhere else. I miss the way my mother clucked her tongue when I came home too late. The way my father's chair groaned like a ghost in the kitchen whenever he sat down to read the morning paper. Prosper's constant smile and Farian's pursuit of the world. I spent so long trying to leave that town that I never thought I would actually miss the place.

Sunlight finally claws over the western cliffs.

My skin drinks in those first rays, and in the same breath, our phoenixes rise. Out of death and into life. Great bursts of fractured light. I glance up at the tower and am thankful for the fog. A curious soldier might see a speck of light if he looked down, but it wouldn't be enough to raise suspicion. Besides, most soldiers wouldn't look down on this side of the castle. Locklin's never been approached from below. Which is half the point. I learned this strategy from the Races.

Change the game. Make them play by your rules.

"Mount up," Bastian orders. "Low in your saddles. Complete silence until we're inside."

There's the crashing waves, the crunch of sand, our beating hearts. I have to tighten my grip on the reins just to keep my hands from shaking. I try to remind myself that the plan will work. The phoenix magic will not fail us. My nervousness has more to do with how my decisions echo now. Back when Farian and I were filming stunts on Martial's ranch, the only neck I could break was mine. Now there are other lives depending on my choices.

Bastian studies his stolen map one more time before directing us over the dunes. The horses lower their heads, forelegs flexing, hooves flicking sand. We break into two distinct rows. Six riders up front and seven behind. Bastian takes point. Against his wishes, I claim the right corner of the front line. We have argued more lately. But this decision was simple. How could I ever ask the others to put their lives on the line if I'm unwilling to do the same?

We reach the end of the beach. Here, the ocean and cliffs embrace. There's a great smash of water on stone. Spray hisses into the air and scatters into mist. Above, the fog continues to thin. We have a few more minutes to make this a surprise. Bastian aims us at a specific section of stone. There are no handholds. No winding and forgotten stairways.

There is only waiting magic.

"Ride hard," Bastian calls. "Let's make something from nothing."

His eyes lock briefly on mine. There's a fire in them that only surfaces before a fight. I always wonder if I have that same fury buried in my bones. Is it a Dividian thing? Or something burned into the mountain-born? He grew up with a pistol in one hand and a shovel in the other. If he wasn't working the land, he was busy defending it. His whole crew is the same way.

I watch him urge his horse into motion.

My body answers. Great snorts echo. My horse's hooves dig down into the sand. Breath smokes into the air. Less than a few seconds and we're sprinting. Our entire row holds the pace. I smile, imagining some witness farther down the beach. What a sight this must be.

Thirteen horses galloping right at the stone cliffs.

A string of curses sound. Faith always slips through our fingers in such moments. My faith is in the horses, though. I know the magic will work right before we make impact. I know because none of the horses hesitate. Not so much as a flinch from them. There's no fear because they were born for this moment. It's the same summoning I used on the first day of the Races. The one that had me sprinting sideways up a wall, in defiance of gravity, to avoid Thyma's swing at me.

We hit the wall at a full sprint.

Normal horses would die. And we would probably die with them. Instead, gravity snatches us like playthings. The sky trades places with the ground. Our horses sprint straight up the stone rises. I've got a death grip on the reins. Bastian lets out a low whoop as we ascend like gods.

It was one thing to taste the impossible on my own. It's an entirely new feeling to perform this magic alongside brothers and sisters. A glance shows all thirteen horses sprinting to heaven. We are breathless with joy and fear and everything in between.

The only sound is thundering hooves on stone.

Ahead, the fog scatters. Our sprint is no longer hidden. I can see where the cliff ends and the castle walls begin. The blocks of stone are massive, dotted by moss, carved smooth over the centuries. Two guard towers loom on either side of the ramparts. From our angle, they look like dull spears being thrust into the sky by invisible hands.

Both towers are empty. I can't help smiling. The timing is perfect. Our other crew must have arrived. Devlin was assigned the role of the bloody priest. He'll have crashed his carriage just short of the gate. I can imagine him running forward in his stolen monk's robes. The crew covered his hands with sheep's blood. He's supposed to approach them and pretend he's been attacked by enemy soldiers. Locklin's guards won't be foolish enough to open the gates, but every one of them will be drawn forward by the spectacle.

And we'll ride up the undefended back ramparts.

Bastian shifts our formation, urging his horse ahead. His movement draws the Rowe siblings forward as well. Squinting, I can see Harlow grinning briefly at his sister. Another hand signal has them both swinging over in front of me.

My eyes dart to Bastian. He sees the scowl on my face and shrugs once. Fury thunders in my chest. He's been doing this for weeks. Ever since Gig's Wall. That first battle was chaos. My first real taste of war. I was so shocked that I could barely reload his pistols.

Which means he thinks I need his constant protection now.

There's no time to wrestle with anger. We reach the bottom of the castle wall. Our horses gallop through a final curl of fog and burst out into sunshine. The ramparts are empty. Bastian tugs on his reins just as he reaches the top of the wall.

The rest of us follow suit. Momentum carries us over the lip and then gravity slams down on our shoulders again. I almost let out a shout. This is an ancient castle. The waiting ramparts are narrower than we expected. Bastian's horse digs its hooves in and still slams into the opposite wall. My horse skids and the second row of riders almost sends us toppling into the courtyard below.

There's a chaotic press of bodies as we get a look at Locklin. Our view of the castle is elevated. Looking down, there's a courtyard that's been converted into a training ground. Stone staircases lead up the opposite end of the ramparts, and that's where most of the movement is. A pair of Ashlord soldiers stand above the castle's barbed gates. One calls down in an annoyed voice.

More soldiers wait below, listening in on the conversation. Our group takes in the scene, awaiting Bastian's command, when a *tinkle* of broken glass sounds.

Everyone turns.

A guard stands five paces away. His eyes are shocked wide. At his feet, a shattered teacup. Dark liquid carves rivers through the cobblestones. Cora Rowe smiles as she raises her pistol and points it at the interloper. "Well, good morning, sunshine!"

The boom echoes. Gunpowder and death fill the air. Bastian curses once before barking out new orders. Our crew divides into three groups. Two groups circle the upper ramparts, tasked with holding the upper ground at all costs. Bastian dismounts, leading me and four others down the only access ramp in sight. Ashlord soldiers shout their own orders. More gunshots.

Luca is pressed in beside me. My uncle's bulky frame follows. I catch a brief glimpse of someone falling from the ramparts as we whip around the corner. An older Ashlord guard barrels right into us. The impact sends him stumbling back. Bastian shoots before the guard can even ask where the hell we came from. Blood slicks the floor. My stomach tightens at the sight, but we keep on moving and searching and aiming. Our path takes us inside the castle proper.

This is war.

We turn down a long hallway. It's bright with morning light. So bright that we almost miss the Dividian standing at the end of the corridor, his rifle raised. Bastian shouts a clipped warning that has our whole crew darting behind random pieces of furniture. We're barely hidden when the first blast punches a hole in the artwork behind us.

"Ho, friend!" Bastian calls into the echo. "We're here for them, not for you."

A moment of silence. "For who?"

Bastian lifts his head a little. "The Ashlords! We don't kill our own!"

Another blast forces Bastian back down, cursing.

"The Longhands don't take prisoners," the Dividian calls back. "Look at what happened in Vivinia! Your lot burned a sanctuary town to the ground!"

"Do we *look* like Longhands to you?"

There's another shot, followed by a groan. I peek around the corner as Harlow Rowe comes strolling toward us, stepping gracefully around the fallen Dividian.

"If you're done hiding," he says, "we can finish securing the castle, dearies."

It doesn't take long to reach a surrender. Locklin is known for hosting very few troops. The Ashlords have held this castle for nearly two centuries, against any number of attacks. Always they have boasted that the elevated fort could be held with just ten good soldiers.

I guess they should have hired twenty.

One Ashlord soldier makes his final stand in the kitchens until a Dividian cook knocks him out with a skillet. Bastian claps the man on the shoulder as we tie the soldier's wrists. When it's all over, our crew rallies back to the courtyard.

Devlin oversees the proceedings, handing out blasphemous blessings in his robes. Layne is picking the pockets of the dead and taking meticulous notes of our earnings. I see that one is a priest to the gods. He's facedown, but I spy silver mechanics grafted into the back of his neck. One of the Striving's creatures.

Eight Ashlord soldiers are bound in one corner. Dividian servants wait opposite them. Some of us watch the proceedings with drowning eyes. We've freed them, but I know by now it doesn't always feel that way at first. We've upturned their quiet lives here.

Bastian looks ready for his usual speech when Cora crows her way out of the basement living quarters. She's marching men at gunpoint: three startled Ashlords. Two are shirtless.

"Gods below," Bastian whispers.

It takes a second to recognize them. These are not everyday soldiers, nor everyday citizens. Their mouths are shaped perfectly to beckon servants with. Even now—marching as prisoners—they look as if they're on the verge of waving a hand to dismiss the lot of us.

All three are kin. Their father has marked them with a sharp chin and narrow lips. Their mothers, however, have left each of them with eyes of different colors, singular shapes.

Cora offers a mocking bow.

"Might I present the sons of the Brightness . . . some of the lesser ones, anyway."

It's impossible to recall their names, but I've known their faces all my life. Always wearing their regalia on the Empire-wide broadcasts. I can tell Cora is right, too. These are three of the younger children. Not directly in line for the throne, but still, princes all the same.

My eyes find Bastian. I can see the gears turning. He cannot believe our good fortune. Our plan for the war has been simple. We fight for bargaining chips. Sometimes that means stealing Ashlord supply carriages. Other times it's sacking a strategic castle. Everything we win gets sold off to the Longhands. We use everything to increase our resources and free Dividian prisoners.

We came here thinking that Locklin would fetch us a pretty penny, but we never thought we'd stumble on royalty. Bastian's eyes shine like a pair of gold coins. The entire crew are exchanging looks now. He smiles like a man who knows his way around a scandal.

"I've forgotten, Cora. What's the going rate for princes these days?"

DON'T MISS SCOTT REINTGEN'S NYXIA TRIAD!

THE ULTIMATE WEAPON
THE ULTIMATE PRIZE
WINNER TAKES ALL

 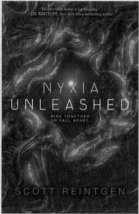 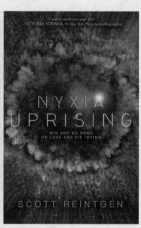